Rockin' Around the Chickadee

ALSO BY DONNA ANDREWS

Rockin' Around the Chickadee

A Meg Langslow Mystery

Donna Andrews

MINOTAUR BOOKS

NEW YORK

First published in the United States by Minotaur Books, an imprint of St. Martin's Publishing Group.

ROCKIN' AROUND THE CHICKADEE. Copyright © 2024 by Donna Andrews. All rights reserved. Printed in the United States of America. For information, address St. Martin's Publishing Group, 120 Broadway, New York, NY 10271.

www.minotaurbooks.com

Title page illustration by Gabriel Guma

Library of Congress Cataloging-in-Publication Data

Names: Andrews, Donna, author.
Title: Rockin' around the chickadee / Donna Andrews.
Description: First edition. | New York : Minotaur Books, 2024. | Series:
    Meg Langslow mysteries ; 36
Identifiers: LCCN 2024022376 | ISBN 9781250894359 (hardcover) |
    ISBN 9781250894366 (ebook)
Subjects: LCGFT: Detective and mystery fiction. | Christmas fiction. |
    Novels.
Classification: LCC PS3551.N4165 R63 2024 | DDC 813/.54—dc23/
    eng/20240517
LC record available at https://lccn.loc.gov/2024022376

Our books may be purchased in bulk for promotional, educational, or business use. Please contact your local bookseller or the Macmillan Corporate and Premium Sales Department at 1-800-221-7945, extension 5442, or by email at MacmillanSpecialMarkets@macmillan.com.

First Edition: 2024

1 3 5 7 9 10 8 6 4 2

Rockin' Around the Chickadee

Chapter 1

"This stupid peace and quiet is killing me!"

Delaney, my sister-in-law, waved her arms wildly, like a windmill in a tornado—a familiar gesture. I'd seen her do it while pacing up and down like a red-maned tigress, celebrating a victory or venting her frustration over a project gone awry. Or while seated at a conference table, having a lively discussion with her fellow programmers and techies. But the seated windmill almost always gave way to the pacing version, as if only by covering ground could she cope with overwhelming emotion.

Pacing wasn't an option right now, and the windmill looked a little silly when she was lying on the chaise longue in our sunroom, tucked up under a fluffy lavender-and-pale-green afghan, with the soothing strains of an instrumental version of "O Little Town of Bethlehem" filling the air so softly it was almost subliminal.

"Now, now," my cousin Rose Noire said. "You need to stay calm."

Delaney rolled her eyes and looked at me as if for support. I smiled and nodded. I knew how she felt. How annoying those words were. After five months of bed rest—made necessary when her obstetrician had declared her pregnancy "high risk"—Delaney was thoroughly sick of being told to stay calm and not overexert herself. I'd gone through the same thing for the last month or so of my pregnancy. Not that there had been anything high risk with me—just the fact that twins often came early, and bed rest had been the best way of giving Josh and Jamie as much time as possible to grow and mature before they entered the world. Delaney wasn't having twins—just one very large and healthy single baby of as-yet unrevealed gender.

"The last few days do seem like years," I said. I didn't add my view that maybe it was time to stop torturing her with bed rest. Let her do whatever she felt like doing—it probably wouldn't be much. And let nature take its course. If she gave birth today, at eight and a half months, the baby would be in good shape—even Dad admitted that.

But saying it aloud would be heresy, particularly to Rose Noire, who had dedicated the lion's share of her waking moments over the last five months to waiting hand and foot on Delaney. And providing just about every known herbal, Wiccan, or New Age remedy for the minor indignities or major perils of pregnancy—at least those that passed muster with Dad and Dr. Waldron.

At the moment, Rose Noire had her phone out, and appeared to be using it to dial up the volume of the music coming from the little speakers hidden around the room. "O Little Town of Bethlehem" went from almost subliminal to merely soft.

"I don't know why we had to chase everyone away," Delaney said. "We always have a houseful of family and friends for Christmas. This just feels weird and depressing. And there's never anyone to talk to."

"Dad's orders," I said. "He didn't think the usual holiday chaos would be good for you."

Delaney sighed loudly.

I almost reached for my notebook-that-tells-me-when-to-breathe, as I called my combined calendar and to-do list. But that would probably remind her of her own organizational system, which lived in an app on her phone. Dad hadn't been joking when he ordered her not to open that app for the duration. I decided to wait until I was out of Delaney's sight, so I wouldn't remind her of all those lovely, neglected tasks—and wouldn't have to tell her the task I wanted to jot down: find someone to talk to Delaney. Someone interesting but calm.

"At least I've got the chickadees to keep me company," Delaney declared, in a tone that suggested she'd have been completely abandoned if not for her tiny feathered friends. "There's no suet out. Don't they like suet? And don't they need it when the weather is this cold?"

"They're very fond of suet," I said. "And we ran out this morning, but we're getting another delivery later today."

"Delivery?" Delaney frowned. "Caerphilly has a suet delivery service now?"

"One of Randall Shiffley's farmer cousins sells very nice organic suet," Rose Noire said. "And he's happy to deliver it."

"Which isn't surprising," I murmured. "Given the amount of the stuff we go through."

"In the meantime, do you want me to bring in your laptop?" Rose Noire asked. "I could set up a Zoom call with your mother."

"It isn't even eight a.m. here," Delaney said. "Which means not even five in California. Mom loves me to pieces, but she doesn't want to hear from me in the middle of the night."

"And if you forgot and did call her this early, she'd probably assume something was wrong and panic," I said. "Besides, isn't this the day she's flying out to the East Coast? To visit your aunt and then spend the holidays with us and be here for the birth?"

"Yes." Delaney sighed heavily. "She doesn't have time to talk to me today."

"I'll bring your laptop in anyway," Rose Noire said. "You can listen to the birds again."

"Oh, yes." Delaney's face brightened. "And I can try that Merlin app to learn more bird calls. I do have one down: chick-a-dee-dee-dee! Chick-a-dee-dee-dee-dee-dee-dee!"

Just then my grandmother, Cordelia, appeared in the doorway.

"Very nice," she said. "But don't go crazy with the extra dees at the end. They only tend to add those in when they're alarmed." She glanced at her wrist, and I deduced this was her subtle way of telling me it was time for us to leave.

"I'd stay and talk to you," I said to Delaney. "But at the moment I have to take Cordelia over to the Caerphilly Inn for the conference."

"Just what is this conference anyway?" Delaney's tone was fretful, so I didn't think it was a good time to mention that I'd already explained it to her. Several times. She kept falling asleep in the middle of my explanations.

Which meant maybe it would be worth giving another sleep-inducing explanation. Although it would have to be a brief one—Cordelia needed to be at the Inn well before nine.

My grandmother must have had the same idea.

"It was Kevin's idea, actually," she said.

"So another true-crime thing?" Delaney asked. A good guess—my nephew Kevin was an up-and-coming true-crime podcaster.

"Not exactly," I said. "It's designed to provide practical help for people who are working to exonerate someone they believe has been wrongly convicted."

"Kind of a niche market, isn't it?" Delaney frowned at the idea.

"Not really," I said. "Cordelia could rattle off the statistics better than I can—"

"I'm not really that keen on statistics." Delaney shuddered slightly.

"And I'm not awake enough to recite any right now," Cordelia replied.

"Just as well," I said. "So I assume that means you won't care if this next bit is approximate. We have something like two million people in jail or prison across the country, and experts estimate between one and ten percent of them are innocent. That's between twenty thousand and two hundred thousand people serving time for something they didn't do."

"Oh, that's so sad!" Delaney clutched her baby bump—actually, more like a baby mountain these days—as if already trying to protect her unborn child against the perils of unjust incarceration.

"But good people are busy working to exonerate them," I said—quickly, before the tears started. "People like our cousin Festus Hollingsworth—his law practice includes a lot of exoneration work."

"That's so wonderful of him," Rose Noire exclaimed. Delaney nodded and shed a few tears after all, but they looked like happy, sentimental ones.

"But he can't possibly represent everyone in need of exoneration," Cordelia said. "So I suggested we organize a conference to help train other people to do the same thing. And Festus and Kevin thought it was a good idea. Especially since we've got so many experts right here in Caerphilly."

"And most of them in the family," I added. In addition to Festus and Kevin, Dad was the local medical examiner, my cousin Horace Hollingsworth was a well-respected CSI, and Grandfather was always happy to talk about the cutting-edge forensic work the J. Montgomery Blake Foundation's DNA lab was doing.

"We've also got Chief Burke giving pointers on working productively with law enforcement," Cordelia went on. "And a couple of actual exonerees who are going to tell their stories."

"It sounds so interesting," Delaney said. "Wish I could go."

It occurred to me that we might be able to set up a Zoom connection to let her watch a few of the presentations. I made a mental note to ask Kevin. No, maybe I should clear the idea with Dad first to see if he thought true crime would be too stimulating. And I wasn't optimistic. These days, Dad considered Parcheesi and backgammon too stimulating for Delaney.

"If we pull this first one off, we might start doing others," Cordelia said. "And we could rope you in to talk about tech issues. But for now we should run." She glanced at her watch again. "Festus is giving the keynote speech at nine, and I should be there to introduce him. Have a good day."

She nodded to Rose Noire and Delaney and strode out of the room.

"I'll see if there's anyone interesting that I could bring home to have dinner with you," I said before following Cordelia down the hallway to the rest of the house.

When I reached the hall, I glanced through the door of our once-and-future dining room—now serving temporarily as a bedroom, so Delaney wouldn't have to go up and down the stairs. I saw Rob, sitting on the foot of the bed, looking glum.

"Not bad news, I hope," I said as I stepped into the room.

"What?" He started slightly and looked up. "No, not bad news. Not yet, anyway."

"And what bad news are you expecting later, then?"

"I just put in a bid on that house," he said. "The one in Westlake."

"And are you more worried that you won't get it or that you will?" I asked.

Rob laughed at that, and the tension on his face eased.

"I haven't decided yet," he said. "It's certainly not where we saw ourselves living."

I nodded. Westlake was a relatively new neighborhood on the outskirts of Caerphilly, an enclave of large, imposing houses in meticulously manicured yards. Rob and I had a running debate on whether the houses there qualified as McMansions. I argued that you couldn't insult a house that way just because it was ostentatiously large, unimaginatively designed, and not that well built—you also needed the obligatory postage-stamp yard, and some of the Westlake houses had half an acre. To Rob, they were McMansions, period. The fact that he'd actually put in a bid on a Westlake house showed how desperate he was getting in his search to find a suitable house for him and Delaney and the impending new arrival.

"I was really hoping to find something out in the country," Rob said. "Big house, big yard, but nothing too fancy or fussy. No traffic. Good neighbors. Something a lot like what you and Michael have here."

"We have no plans to move, if that's what you're hoping," I said. "Sorry about that." I didn't add that we had more than enough spare bedrooms so that he and Delaney—and eventually the new arrival—could stay as long as they liked. He already knew that. As I knew that the impending birth of his son or daughter had fired up some atavistic urge to make a home for his family. A home of their own.

"Even if you were moving, it wouldn't be the same," Rob said. "Because we'd want you guys as neighbors—you and Seth and the Washingtons and the Rafferties, with Mother and Dad close enough that we can see them as often as we want but they can still go home at the end of the day when the grandkids wear them out. And Westlake won't be so bad. Shorter commute to the office. And . . . um . . ."

He'd run out of good things to say about Westlake rather quickly.

"That's true," I said. "And you've heard me say that the best thing for Westlake would be if we could insinuate a few sane and sensible people into the neighborhood. I just didn't expect you and Delaney to have to be among the ones making the sacrifice."

"Yeah." He chuckled, and stood up, pocketing his phone. "Well, keep your fingers crossed."

"That the sellers accept your bid?"

"That whatever would be best in the long run is what actually happens." Rob sounded uncharacteristically thoughtful. "That we get what we need, not what we think we want. Damn—I sound like Rose Noire, don't I?"

"Sometimes she's pretty wise," I said.

"Is this the day Michael's going up to Washington to collect Delaney's mom?" Rob asked. "Because doesn't he have classes to teach today? I feel guilty letting him do that if—"

"The trip to D.C.'s not till tomorrow," I said. "And he has to go up there anyway, to pick up his mother at Dulles and take her to the pier in Baltimore for her Christmas cruise. So it's more efficient to let him do it."

And also, as Michael and I had discussed, less nerve-racking for Delaney's mother, given how distracted Rob was these days.

"Oh, that's right," he said. "It's all good then?"

"Absolutely," I said. "Laters."

Out in the front hall I found Josh and Jamie, my just-barely-teenage twins. Jamie was helping their great-grandmother with her coat while Josh was carrying two copier paper boxes, presumably full of stuff Cordelia was taking to the conference.

"No, it doesn't look as if you'll need your snow boots today," she was saying.

"But tomorrow for sure!" Jamie exclaimed.

"It's only a fifty-percent chance." Josh's tone made it very clear that Mother Nature needed to shape up and produce the longed-for white Christmas.

"Now remember what I told you," Cordelia said as she opened the front door. "And you should keep out of any trouble."

"Of course." Josh rolled his eyes as he said it.

Jamie just nodded solemnly.

"Quick," I said, as I led the way toward where the Twinmobile was parked. "Tell me. Because I want to stay out of trouble, too."

Chapter 2

"I'm sure you'll be fine," Cordelia said as we settled into the Twinmobile, our elderly but well-maintained van.

"We're not supposed to argue with anybody about a case," Jamie said. "Even if we know for sure they're absolutely wrong. Because they're our guests."

"And because Gran-gran doesn't want fights breaking out in the hallways at her conference," Josh added. "Also, it's rude to ask the exonerees if they really are innocent."

"And stay away from the Gadfly," Jamie added. "Because he's just plain nuts."

"The Gadfly?" I echoed.

"Godfrey Norton," Cordelia said. "You'll probably want to avoid him, too."

"That name sounds familiar," I said.

"Probably because you know your Sherlock Holmes," Cordelia said. "It was originally the name of the lawyer who married Irene Adler in 'A Scandal in Bohemia.' It's also the name of one of the conference attendees, although I seem to recall that it isn't his real, legal name."

"It's an alias?" I asked.

"More like a stage name or a pen name," Cordelia said, "or whatever you call the name someone uses for his podcasting career."

"Nom de pod?" Josh suggested.

"Podcasting," I echoed. "A friend of Kevin's then?"

Jamie and Josh both burst into raucous laughter.

"Alas, no," Cordelia said. "If you asked Kevin to give you a list of people he really, truly hoped wouldn't show up at the conference, the Gadfly would be number one on it."

"And he's mad 'cause Gran-gran and Uncle Kev wouldn't put him on a panel," Jamie said.

"The Gadfly's a contrarian," Cordelia explained. "And very invested in the idea that genuine wrongful convictions are quite rare."

"So you figure he's only showing up at your conference to cause trouble," I said.

"Yes." Cordelia frowned slightly. "Remind me to point him out to you, so you can help deal with him if necessary."

"Are you going to suppress him?" Jamie asked. "Like the guinea pigs in *Alice in Wonderland*?"

"We're not going to put him in a bag and sit on him, if that's what you mean," Cordelia said. "But we'll intervene if he tries to hog the microphone during a question-and-answer session. And do our best to keep him from harassing the rest of the attendees, the way he did last night at the opening reception."

"Oh, dear," I said. "I didn't hear that you had problems."

"Not big problems," she said. "I shut him down pretty quickly. But I suspect it was a clue to what he has planned, and I can't be everywhere at the same time. So keep your eyes open for him."

I nodded.

"And we'll help," Josh said.

"I don't want you confronting anyone," I said. "Especially not anyone your great-grandmother thinks is nuts."

"I didn't say he was nuts," Cordelia protested.

"You didn't argue when Kevin said it," Josh pointed out.

"We won't confront anyone." Jamie's tone was reassuring. "We're just supposed to come and get you or Gran-gran and let one of *you* confront him."

Josh's sigh was not reassuring, since it suggested that he rather liked the idea of confronting the Gadfly.

"But we can watch," Jamie reminded him.

"Sorry we weren't there to help last night," I said to Cordelia. "But the boys had a rehearsal for the Trinity Episcopal Christmas pageant, and I'd already promised Robyn to help wrangle the younger cast members. I'd much rather have been at the reception. I think next year Robyn should have a rule—no sheep in diapers. If your kid hasn't graduated to training pants, they don't get to join the flock until next year."

"Sounds sensible to me," Cordelia said. "Glad to hear we'll be having the pageant again this year—I look forward to seeing it. And we managed without you—as I assumed we would. I didn't expect we'd have too many problems at the opening reception—everyone would be pretty much all in the same room, and most of them would all still be on their best behavior, and if they weren't we had plenty of peacekeepers available, what with Festus, Kevin, your parents, Chief Burke, and me all there."

I noticed that she hadn't mentioned Grandfather. I knew he'd been there, too. But even if he was trying to be on his best behavior, his natural fondness for argument and drama wouldn't make him very useful as a peacekeeper.

"But today people are going to be a lot more spread out," she said. "We have two tracks going on during some parts of the day, plus we set up a small side room as a lounge where people could get together informally to pick the experts' brains or discuss the cases they're interested in. A lot more scope for people like the Gadfly to stir up trouble."

"Just point him out to me when we get there," I said.

"Here," Josh said, pulling out his phone and fiddling with it. "I've got pictures."

"So do I." Not to be outdone, Jamie also pulled out his phone.

I frowned, wondering how they happened to have photos of the Gadfly, since they'd both been at the Christmas pageant rehearsal all evening.

"They checked him out online," Cordelia said, correctly interpreting my expression.

"Here's a picture of him from CrimeCon," Jamie said, leaning over my shoulder to stick his phone within my field of vision.

"Hang on till I hit a stop sign," I said.

"I've got video," Josh said. "From his YouTube channel."

I came to a full stop at the next stop sign, and put on my flashers, just in case some impatient tourist pulled up behind me. I glanced at Jamie's phone first. Godfrey Norton was a stocky thirtyish man, with a full black beard. The photo showed him talking to two young women and shaking his forefinger in their faces.

"You can put that one in the dictionary," I said. "Under mansplaining."

Cordelia chuckled. I glanced at the phone Josh was waving at me. He pressed a button to start a video of the same young man, looking straight into the camera and talking. Make that lecturing. Josh hadn't turned the volume up high enough for me to make out more than half of the Gadfly's words, but I could gauge his tone. Pugnacious. Bombastic. Self-important. And he was still shaking that stubby forefinger or stabbing the air with it to make his points.

"Thanks." I turned the flashers off and set the car in motion again. "I'll know him if I see him."

"And to know him is to . . . well, never mind." Cordelia left the end of her thought unspoken, but I got the point.

"What's for lunch, Gran-gran?" Josh asked.

"Didn't anyone feed you this morning?" Cordelia glanced at me with a slight frown.

"They had their usual enormous breakfast," I said. "But they're growing boys. They can always eat."

"We're basically tall hobbits," Jamie said, echoing something Michael and I had said more than once.

"And I like to let my stomach know what to expect," Josh added.

So, for the rest of the way to the Inn we discussed not only to-day's lunch but also Saturday's lunch, Saturday night's banquet, Sunday's continental breakfast buffet, and where they wanted to eat tonight, which was marked in the conference schedule as "dinner on your own."

"I'll pass along your suggestions to your dad," Cordelia said. "He already volunteered to pick up something delicious, so we don't have to worry about it."

We arrived right behind—and parked next to—Chief Burke. Was his presentation on working harmoniously with law en-forcement today? Accompanying him was Adam, the youngest of the three orphaned grandchildren he and Minerva were rais-ing, who happened to be the boys' best friend.

"Anything special you want me to do?" I asked Cordelia.

"For now, just wander around, get to know the attendees, and use your common sense if you see Norton up to anything," she said. "Or anyone else. And take lots of pictures. Only pictures—I've imposed a no video or audio rule, so everyone can speak freely about cases."

She strode off toward the Inn's front door. Adam, Jamie, and Josh grabbed her boxes and hurried after her into the hotel. The chief and I followed at a more leisurely pace.

"Do they have you giving some kind of presentation?" the chief asked. "I don't remember seeing it on the schedule."

"Just helping Cordelia out," I said. "Looking forward to hearing your talk."

"I hope it goes off well," the chief said. "Cordelia seemed to think this was a group that would be open to hearing the perspective of a law enforcement officer."

"I think most of them are," I said. "And as for those who aren't—that's one of the reasons Cordelia recruited me."

"Not to shut them down, I hope," the chief said. "Because I'd be the first to admit that not all law enforcement officers are perfect. And that bad police work could definitely be a factor in some of the cases people will be discussing this weekend. Shutting down discussion of that issue would only lead to a hardening of attitudes."

"And shutting down isn't the plan," I said. "Just keeping things civil."

He nodded with approval and we both greeted Enrique, the bell captain, as he opened the Inn's front door and bowed us in.

Inside, I stopped to appreciate the lobby. It was always a stunning sight, with a soaring glass wall several stories high and an oversized stone fireplace, complete with the most realistic fake gas fire I'd ever seen. People regularly tried to poke it when it was on low. Or add logs to it, which was a little peculiar, since the only logs in the lobby were a small stack of fragrant cedar logs, frosted with a dusting of fake snow, that formed part of the winter decor.

And this time of year the lobby was breathtaking. If whoever evaluated hotels took their holiday decorations into account, the Inn's hold on its five-star rating was secure. Enormous ever-green garlands were draped everywhere and festooned with rib-bons and tinsel in the purple-and-gold color scheme Mother and Ekaterina, the Inn's manager, had chosen, on the grounds that it was festive but not quite the ordinary Christmas look. Neither of them was a fan of ordinary. Or of minimalism. Flocks of glass balls in purple and gold hung from the ceiling on mono-filaments so thin you couldn't really see them, making the orna-ments seem to be floating in the air. More purple and gold glass balls decked the enormous tree by the fireplace, along with gold-colored bells, snowflakes, birds, and musical instruments.

"Eight forty-five," the chief said, glancing at his watch. "Plenty of time to get some coffee before the first session."

"You go on." I pointed to where I could see Cordelia and the boys disappearing through a door at the other side of the lobby—the door that led to the hotel's various meeting rooms. "I have a few things to do out here first."

"It's Festus, you know," he said. "Giving his keynote speech."

"I know," I said. "And I plan to be there." I really did. I was vastly proud of my cousin Festus. When not representing the un-justly convicted, he regularly did legal combat against people or corporations that despoiled the environment, abused animals, enabled discrimination, or just plain exploited the weaker and more vulnerable members of society. But—

"As it happens, I've already heard his keynote speech," I ex-plained. "Festus tried it out on me yesterday. Not that I won't try to catch it, but I want to look around a little first. See if any of the people not listening to Festus are getting up to anything."

"Good idea," he said. "Not wanting to hear Festus might be a clue that they're here for some reason other than learning from us so-called experts."

"Or it could just mean that, like me, they are not morning people," I said.

"Also very true." He laughed and headed for the door to the conference area.

Actually, while I did want to scope out anyone not attending Festus's speech, my first priority was to find some caffeine—preferably cold bubbly caffeine rather than coffee, which I disliked, even if it was the premium gourmet stuff the Inn served. And as I had realized during the drive to the Inn, the can of Diet Coke I'd gotten out of the fridge to bring with me was still sitting on the kitchen counter.

I was heading for the corridor that led to the elevators so I could pop up to one of the guest floors that had a soda machine. But Becky, the desk clerk, gestured dramatically for my attention.

"I'm just going upstairs to—" I began as I drew near.

"Ekaterina said to give you this when you arrived." Becky was holding out a cold can of Diet Coke, beaded with moisture, and a napkin with a purple-and-metallic-gold border.

"You're a lifesaver." I popped the top and took a swallow. "Everything going well so far?"

"So far," she said. "You see that gentleman over there? He's part of your conference, isn't he?"

I followed her discreet nod and saw an elderly Black man seated in one of the comfortable easy chairs at the far side of the lobby. At his feet sat a medium-sized tan-and-white dog of indeterminate breed, wearing a harness that resembled a service dog's vest, although it lacked the usual writing to announce the dog's mission. As I watched, the dog lifted up its floppy-eared head and looked at the man, as if hoping to be given an order or task. Then it sighed softly and laid its head back on the rug.

"He's wearing a badge, so he must be." Was something about him bothering Becky? Was she turning up her nose at his appearance? His clothes were a little on the shabby side, but perfectly neat. Did she think he looked out of place in the Inn's elegant lobby? Granted, he didn't look like the Inn's typical affluent guests, but . . . "What's the problem?"

"Could you ask him if he needs anything?" Becky said. "Some coffee, perhaps? He seems a little . . . unsettled. And we like to see our guests looking happy. I'd go over and ask him myself but every time I begin to step away from the desk—"

Just then the desk phone rang, and she pointed at it while answering.

With a silent apology to Becky for doubting her motives, I strolled over to the man.

"Good morning," I said. "You're with the Presumed Innocent conference aren't you?"

Chapter 3

The man looked up, and I had the sudden feeling of being courteously but efficiently assessed by the deep-set brown eyes behind his thick spectacles.

"I am indeed," he said, with a trace of a southwest Virginia accent. "And unless my eyes deceive me, you must be related to Ms. Cordelia Mason. I can definitely see a family likeness."

"She's my grandmother," I said. "I'm here helping her with the conference."

"And that means Mr. Festus Hollingsworth, Esquire, would be your cousin."

"He would indeed," I said. "He'll be starting to speak any time now if you're interested."

"I know," he said. "Interested, but not sure I'm quite ready to deal with the crowd. I kind of have to work my way up to that. But if I don't make this speech, I'll get to see him later today. And appear on a panel with him when he talks about how he managed to exonerate me."

"You must be Ezekiel Blaine, then." I held out my hand. "I've heard Festus mention your case. Meg Langslow."

We shook hands.

"And this is Ruth," Mr. Blaine said, gesturing to the dog at his feet. Ruth sat up at the sound of her name, wagged her tail, and leaned against the outside of his leg. "Named after the one in the Bible."

"Whither thou goest, she goes?" I asked.

"At least till she's fully trained," he said. "I'm raising her up to be a PTSD support dog. Help some poor veteran who brought home more sorrow than he can handle. Maybe get him back to something like a normal life."

He smiled down at the dog and scratched her behind the ears.

I studied his face and tried to recall what Festus had told us about Ezekiel Blaine's case. He'd been tried and convicted of a particularly vicious murder at only eighteen or nineteen. Festus had managed to get his conviction overturned, largely due to trace DNA evidence that Grandfather's lab had recovered—evidence that proved another man had committed the crime—but not until Mr. Blaine had spent almost fifty years in prison.

He was nearly seventy now and looked even older. His weathered brown face was seamed with wrinkles. His hands were so contorted with arthritis that I wondered how much his firm handshake with me had hurt him. And something lurked behind the warmth and friendliness—something tentative, cautious, and wary. Here was a man who didn't trust easily. Festus had earned his trust, and my connection to Festus made him a little more ready to accept me—but nothing would ever be a given with him.

"May I pet her?" I asked, looking down at his dog.

"You certainly may," he said. "And thank you for asking first."

I scratched Ruth behind the ears, and she wagged her tail happily and snuffled at my jeans.

"She likes you," he said.

"She probably just likes that I smell like other dogs," I said.

"You have dogs, then?"

"Our household includes two Pomeranians, an Irish wolf-hound, and a small furball of unknown ancestry," I said. "We think maybe a cross between a T. rex and a wolverine. And most days we have two or three other visiting dogs that belong to friends who are deputies and don't want to leave their fur babies alone when they're on shift."

"Mercy," he said. "You do indeed have dogs. And—"

He stiffened and frowned, as if he'd seen something behind me that unsettled him. I glanced over my shoulder. A man was standing in front of the front desk, haranguing Becky about something. I couldn't hear what they were saying, but I could tell Becky wasn't enjoying the conversation.

The man snapped off a few more words to Becky. Then turned around, as if dismissing her not just from the conversation but from the planet, and I recognized him from the images the boys had shown me: Godfrey Norton. He scowled as he scanned the lobby, as if looking for something new to fuel his foul mood. I noticed he was wearing a black t-shirt printed with the slogan I SEE GUILTY PEOPLE.

"Then again, maybe I should run along and catch the end of Festus's presentation," Mr. Blaine murmured.

"Mr. Blaine," I began.

"Just Ezekiel," he said. "Being called Mr. Blaine makes me think I might be back in court."

"Yikes," I said. "Ezekiel, then. If your main reason for relocating is to avoid the jerk standing by the front desk, let me know. I can probably chase him away. Even get him thrown out of the conference if he doesn't behave."

"You've met Mr. Norton, then?" He seemed amused rather than worried.

"No," I said. "But my grandmother already warned me about the Gadfly."

He chuckled at that.

"And I could see how he was treating Becky. Maybe it's harsh, but I judge people by how they treat the service staff. And yeah, I know judging's bad. I can't help it."

"'Judge not, that ye be not judged,'" Ezekiel quoted. "'For with what judgment ye judge, ye shall be judged.' Not a hard-and-fast commandment against judging if you ask me. More a warning about what's gonna happen if you don't show others the mercy and kindness you hope to receive yourself."

I remembered Festus mentioning that Ezekiel had found religion while in prison and become something of a lay preacher.

"That's reassuring," I said. "And is it just me, or is it pretty tone deaf of him, wearing that t-shirt at a conference whose whole reason for being is helping exonerate the innocent?"

"Well, Mr. Norton seems to think there aren't all that many innocents in prison," Ezekiel said. "And he's never shy about expressing his opinions. He's told me to my face that he thinks I got away with murder. And that if he ever sees me so much as littering or jaywalking, he'll report me."

"Sorry you have to put up with him," I said. "Especially when you're here trying to help other people instead of spending time celebrating the holidays with your family and friends."

"Oh, don't feel too sorry for me," he said. "I'm actually having a better Christmas than I expected, thanks to this conference. If I wasn't here, I'd be spending the time pretty solitary. I don't really have that many friends and family on the outside. Not yet, anyway. 'Specially family. The respectable ones long since washed their hands of me, and the wild ones have mostly managed to do themselves in by now. When Festus invited me and apologized for how close it was to Christmas, I had to laugh. And confess to him that the only thing I had planned for the holiday season was church services. At a couple of different churches—I still haven't settled on one. Hard to find one that's a good fit for me. Lot of them aren't all that welcoming to ex-cons."

"That would be a deal-breaker for me, even though I'm not one myself," I said. "I'd have thought ex-cons might be among the very people they'd most want to reach."

He nodded. Then, seeming to spot something, he frowned and clenched his jaw.

"Well, if it isn't our own axe-murderer," said a nasal voice behind me. I turned to find that the Gadfly had sneaked up behind me on us.

"Morning, Mr. Norton." Ezekiel's tone was neutral, a little cool, but courteous.

"You know who you're talking to, don't you?" Norton said, turning to me. "He's the guy who—"

"Who spent nearly half a century in prison until my grandfather's DNA lab came up with the evidence that enabled my cousin Festus to prove his innocence." I couldn't see any reason not to let Norton know up front where my sentiments—and alliances—lay. "I'm looking forward to hearing him talk about his experiences."

Norton jerked back as if I'd slapped him. But he recovered quickly.

"You might feel differently if you knew what kind of man he is," he said. "He—"

"I'll be covering all that when Mr. Hollingsworth and I do our panel," Ezekiel said. "And I think Ms. Langslow already knows most of it. I'd be the first to admit that I was no angel as a young man. I took drugs. I sold drugs. I beat people up—including the young lady who had the good sense to break up with me and get on with her life."

"You see," Norton said. "Even he admits—"

"But I'm not a killer." Ezekiel was speaking louder now—not angrily, just projecting more, the way Michael taught his acting students to do. He had a lovely voice, deep and musical. "I didn't kill that man in the filling station. I never killed anyone. And I'm not the person I was fifty years ago."

"No," Norton said. "You've gone from street-smart punk to hardened criminal. And—"

"Mr. Norton, you need to stop harassing Mr. Blaine." I stepped between the two, just in case. "By registering for the conference, you agreed to our code of conduct. Which includes being civil to your fellow attendees. If you keep this up, we'll have to ask security to remove you from the premises."

"Oh, great," he said. "You threaten to remove me when—"

"Give it a rest, you miserable troll." A tall, slender thirtyish blond woman stepped in beside me—and between Norton and Ezekiel. She stood glaring at Norton, fists clenched, feet planted solidly on the plush carpet as if to brace herself for a blow. "Why did you even bother to come if all you're going to do is parrot your usual garbage and insult people?"

"The Black Widow speaks," Norton said.

Chapter 4

"And she's finished speaking to you," the woman said. "Now leave us alone, or I'll call hotel security and complain that you're harassing us."

Norton took a step backward, as if the combined force of our frowning faces repelled him. He pulled his phone out of his pocket, glanced at it, and pretended to start.

"Got to run if I'm going to get a good seat for the next panel." He turned to go, then stopped and looked back at us. "Just you wait." With that vague threat—and a final scowl—Norton turned and walked away with the nonchalant air of someone who was leaving of his own volition.

"The next panel?" I echoed, softly enough that only Ezekiel and our blond ally could hear. "Festus has already started by now, and the good seats are probably still occupied by people who are aren't all that keen on giving them up."

Ezekiel chuckled softly.

"Yeah. What a jerk," the blonde said. She turned to me and stuck out her hand. "I'm Amber Smith. The other exoneree. At this conference, I mean."

"Meg Langslow," I said as we shook hands. "Festus Hollings-worth's cousin. Are you another of his flock?"

"No, he turned me down." She grinned. "Don't worry—I don't hold a grudge. And it wasn't for any dire reason, like he agreed with that jerk Godfrey I was guilty of bumping off my husband or anything like that. But his plate was full and then some. Plus, he said he didn't really see any solid openings in my case. No footholds or toeholds to start the long climb, as he put it. Still, I owe him one. He allowed that another appellate attorney might see it differently, and he gave me the names of a couple of possibilities, and one of the ones he recommended took me on. William Morgan of Mason, Morgan and Friedman."

"Nice," I said. I'd heard of Mason, Morgan, and Friedman before—heard of them, and figured out that Festus wasn't their biggest fan, although he would never diss them in public. But I gathered he didn't so much doubt their competence as think they were a little too hungry for power and publicity, a little too unscrupulous. "Not destined to be a shining ornament to our profession," as he'd once said.

But they were sharp and aggressive, and it sounded as if they'd been able to help her.

"So far we've been doing great," Amber said, as if replying to my thoughts.

"So far?" I probably sounded puzzled.

"Mr. Morgan got my conviction overturned," she said. "But the prosecution's appealing. And they did their best to have me thrown in jail until they either win their appeal or can get up a new trial, but Mr. Morgan managed to convince the court that I wasn't a danger to society. So for the time being, I'm only partially exonerated, but at least I'm out on bail."

"Congratulations," I said.

"Thanks," she said. "Here's hoping it lasts." She glanced around the lobby, as if seeking some kind of reassurance. "Bill—Mr. Morgan—thinks it would help if I could get some positive social media buzz. That's why I'm here, really. I mean, obviously I'm very big on the whole idea of exoneration, but I wasn't sure how I felt about doing the conference. I predicted this would happen, you know—that someone like Norton would show up."

"Yeah," I said. "We don't need that kind of negative energy to discourage people who are already facing a long, uphill battle."

"It's not just negative energy," Amber said. "The man's a bald-faced liar."

"Ms. Smith is correct," Ezekiel said. "If Mr. Norton cannot find incriminating evidence about a convicted person whose case is being discussed, he invents it."

"Exactly," Amber said. "And once a juicy bit of dirt gets out there on the internet, good luck trying to shut it down or disprove it, no matter how bogus and ridiculous it is. Especially if someone like Norton gets you in his sights. Between him and *The Real Scooparino,* it's a wonder anyone ever gets exonerated."

"*The Real Scooparino?*" I echoed.

"Another of the self-proclaimed online true-crime experts," she said. "Look him and Norton up if you want to see why some of us have such an uphill battle. Just don't believe a word they say. It could be worse—we could have had both of them here. Anyway, I need to run off and make some phone calls. Nice meeting you."

With a nod to each of us, she strode across the lobby toward the elevators. I could see several people turn to watch her. Not surprising. She wasn't conventionally pretty, but quite attractive—arguably even beautiful—with high cheekbones, large blue eyes, and an elegant, slightly aquiline nose. She was probably an inch or two shorter than me in flat feet, but her boots added a couple of inches, and she looked even taller thanks to long legs clad in well-fitting jeans. I tried not to resent that she'd drawn her long, blond hair back into a perfect French braid. I coveted that skill. And the boots, too, which looked as if they might be as practical as they were stylish. Next time I saw her I'd ask the brand.

And I realized I'd heard about her case. Kevin had told me about it, more than once. The facts hadn't sounded all that fascinating. After meeting Amber, maybe I could understand his interest. In Amber, even if her case wasn't particularly memorable.

I looked back at Ezekiel and was about to suggest that we catch what was left of Festus's speech when someone spoke behind me.

"Mr. Blaine?"

I turned to see two pleasant-faced older women whose expressions suggested they weren't sure of their welcome.

"If we're interrupting something, just shoo us away," one of them said.

"But we'd really like to talk to you, Mr. Blaine," the other said. "If now isn't a very good time—"

"Just Ezekiel, please," he said. "I do want to catch the next panel, at ten thirty, but I should be free till then. Or we could make time later if that's better. What can I do for you?"

"I'm Ginny Maynard," the first one said. She stuck out her hand and Ezekiel shook it gravely. She was a short, plump woman whose disheveled mouse-brown hair was liberally threaded with gray, and the smile lines on her face suggested that anxious wasn't her usual expression.

"Janet Pollard," the other said, offering her hand in turn. She was taller, more angular, with iron-gray hair pulled into a sleek updo. And I had the feeling her fierce, alert expression was customary.

"We won't hold you up right now," Ginny said. "But is there

any chance we could buy you a coffee later? We want to pick your brains about your whole experience. You see, we really want to help a friend of ours."

"For years, we sort of wondered what had happened to a fellow student from our high-school graduating class," Janet continued. "Jim never showed up at reunions. Never called or wrote to any of us. Ginny finally got one of her grandkids to help her do some research on the internet and we found out he'd been in prison for murder since a few years after we all graduated."

"I see," Ezekiel said. "Who'd they think he murdered?"

"His ex-girlfriend's new boyfriend," Janet replied.

"He dropped out of college and fell in with a rough crowd," Ginny added. "But he was turning his life around when it happened. Cutting ties with the rough crowd, including the ex-girlfriend. And we think she resented being dumped and fingered him for the murder."

"Which we also think she committed," Janet said. "Don't forget that part."

"This would have happened a few decades ago, right?" Ezekiel asked.

Ginny and Janet both nodded.

"Time could be your ally," he said. "You could start by locating the ex-girlfriend. Maybe a friend gave her an alibi, and then they fell out and the friend no longer wants to lie for her. Maybe she found her way to the Lord and needs to confess. Maybe by now she has a son or even a grandson about the age the boyfriend was when he was killed, and she can't live with her deeds any longer. People change over time."

"We thought of that," Ginny said. "Unfortunately, she won't change."

"Can't change," Janet clarified. "She died of an overdose not long after the murder. So that road's closed."

Ezekiel closed his eyes briefly and nodded.

"So we're having a little trouble figuring out how to help him," Ginny said.

"Frankly, we're having a little trouble getting him to work with us," Janet added.

"He blows hot and cold," Ginny said. "One visit he's all for it, the next we can hardly get a word out of him."

"If he's reluctant to work with you," Ezekiel began. "I wonder if you've considered that perhaps—"

"That he might actually be guilty?" Janet finished his sentence. "Of course we've considered it."

"He doesn't ever waver on saying he's innocent," Ginny said. "Not one bit."

"More important, his case looks solid to us," Janet said. "We've been through all the documents—the trial transcripts, all the briefs and appeals documents. But we're not lawyers, and I think we're at the point where we need to get him one."

"And all of a sudden he's wavering," Ginny said. "We're not sure why."

"We don't agree on why," Janet said.

The two of them exchanged a grin, and I felt I'd been given a glimpse of their friendship. Two friends who knew each other so well that they could finish each other's sentences, and could disagree, even on something very important to them, without any damage to the friendship.

"Gin thinks we've offended him," Janet said.

"Like maybe I come on too strong," Ginny admitted. "It's possible."

"Or that something we said or did rubbed him the wrong way and he's backing away from us."

"We knew each other in high school, remember?" Ginny said. "Which you can probably figure out from looking at us wasn't all that recently."

"And we couldn't possibly have been living more different lives, us on the outside and him on the inside." Janet shook her head as if she despaired of ever understanding their old friend.

"But Janet thinks it's something else," Ginny said. "She thinks it's all the social media that's got him spooked."

"From what I've seen, it used to be that publicity could help an exoneration effort," Janet said. "But getting it was an uphill battle. Now, getting publicity isn't as hard. There are so many people fascinated by true crime. So many websites and podcasts and YouTube channels and who knows what else. And they're all looking for information."

"For content," Ginny put in. "It's just content to them. Entertainment."

"And that means, now you have a different problem," Janet explained. "It's not nearly as hard as it used to be to get someone's story out—but what if it's the wrong story? A negative story or a false story. If that happens, getting the truth out can be like trying to stop a wildfire."

"We were hoping maybe if we could talk to you we might figure out what we're doing wrong," Ginny said. "Get back on track."

"Could be you're both right," Ezekiel said, with a curiously melancholy smile. "Perhaps something about the way you're trying to help him doesn't set right. No offense meant, but if he's been in prison since shortly after y'all were in high school together, he's had lots of time to become knowledgeable about the system. It's like being on another planet, really. And it can be hard work, helping people who haven't been there to understand how it works. And while you're absolutely right about the whole true-crime thing these days, I'm not sure I have any wisdom to offer on that score. But if you think picking my brain about life inside or my own exoneration journey would help you help your friend, I'd be happy to do what I can."

"I'll leave you folks to it," I said. "See you later."

They had all pulled out their convention programs and were comparing schedules. I dropped by the front desk to snag another of the stash of Diet Cokes Ekaterina had left for me, then headed for the door to the meeting rooms.

Just inside the door—actually, an elegant set of double doors, decked with purple-ribboned spruce wreaths—was a sort of junior version of the lobby that the Inn called the Gathering Area. It also featured a glass wall, although it was only double height and contained less acreage than the one in the main lobby. But while the Gathering Area lacked the soaring, glass-walled grandeur of the lobby, and the holiday decorations were a little less over-the-top, it was still a beautiful, elegant space. And when you walked in from the lobby, you actually got the impression that it was downright cozy.

A few people were sitting in the chairs that were scattered in little groups, both along the walls and in the center of the space. In the far wall two sets of double doors led into the Hamilton Room, the bigger conference room. Someone had propped one of the doors open and was standing just outside, peering in. I could hear Festus's voice, although I couldn't make out more than one word in ten.

Between the two doors was the coffee-and-tea service. Which would turn into a coffee, tea, and soft drink service after noon, but Cordelia seemed to think I was the only person who went for soda in the morning.

Above the doors was a banner that said WELCOME TO PRE-SUMED INNOCENT! Actually, at the moment all you could make out was WELCOME TO PRESUMED INN—the top right corner of the fabric had come loose and flopped down. Two hotel staffers were dealing with it, one atop the ladder with tools, the other standing at the foot of the ladder to steady it.

The door to the Lafayette Room, the smaller conference

room, was in the right wall of the Gathering Area, along with the opening to a wide hallway that led to the Dolley Madison Ballroom. Between them was the registration table, staffed by a young Asian woman with spiky purple hair and an elegant black silk pantsuit. One of Festus's interns or paralegals. I smiled and waved at her while I searched my insufficiently caffeinated memory for her name. She'd probably be wearing a name tag, but it was a point of pride for me to remember it, rather than being caught staring at someone's chest. And I was pretty sure it was something distinctive enough that I should remember it. Something Shakespearean. Emilia? Rosalind? Desdemona?

Ophelia. Yeah, that was it.

Thus armed, I strolled over to the table.

"Morning, Ophelia," I said. "How's it going?"

"Who is that jerk in the I SEE GUILTY PEOPLE t-shirt?" she asked. "And how nasty does he have to get before someone kicks him out?"

"Godfrey Norton," I said. "Has he been bothering you?"

"He tried," she said. "Fussed about why we even let in some of the people who were attending. I just batted my eyes and said I was sorry, I didn't have anything to do with policy, I was just helping out, and if he had any questions or complaints, he should talk to Ms. Cordelia Mason, the organizer. I felt bad about steering him your grandmother's way, but those were her orders. Send any complainers her way before they disrupt the conference."

"And he's one of the main reasons for those orders." I glanced around the Gathering Area and was relieved to see that the Gadfly wasn't in sight. Of course, that meant he was probably in Festus's talk, plotting ways to disrupt it. "And don't worry—Cordelia can handle him," I added, as much to reassure myself as anything.

"Definitely." She nodded emphatically. "I think she might

even enjoy it. The only reason he stopped bothering me was that he saw two people he knew, only it turned out they weren't friends of his, and he was giving them a hard time about something, and I had to sic your grandmother on him after all."

"Who was he bothering?" I asked.

"I don't know them." She swept her eyes around the Gathering Area. "And I didn't check them in, or I'd have remembered their names. I think they went in to hear Festus speak after your grandmother rescued them. Woman in her forties or fifties, young woman in her twenties. Both tall redheads—I wondered if they were mother and daughter. And I bet they're here with a case. They had that look."

Chapter 5

"That look?" I echoed.

"The true-crime fans mostly look happy and excited," she said. "Like they figure maybe they're getting the inside track on the next big case. But people who are here in the hope that they can learn something that will help them with a case they care about, or maybe even enlist the help of someone like Festus—they all look serious. Maybe even stressed, as if this was their one chance to do something for whoever they're trying to help."

"Do we have a lot of true-crime fans attending?" I asked. I knew Cordelia and Festus had spent a lot of mental energy strategizing how to promote the conference so it would attract mainly people with a serious interest in getting someone exonerated.

"I expect about half of the attendees," she said. "But Festus says that's no problem. He says it's a win if even one of them who came for the fun of it gets fired up to take on a worthwhile case. He says he's seen it happen more than once at events where he's given talks."

Yes, if anyone could convince other people to take on the injustices of the world, it would be Festus. I'd done my part a time or two, helping him. Tilting at windmills, as he called it—though his results were usually a lot more on target than Don Quixote's.

"I do have one question." Ophelia frowned slightly, as if reconsidering the wisdom of asking. Then she shook her head and forged ahead. "Mr. Norton complained that the after-dinner entertainment was going to be the local police chief's wife singing Christmas carols. Is that, um . . ."

Was the Gadfly that clueless or was he deliberately trying to stir up trouble?

"Well, it's true that Minerva Burke will be on the program," I said. "But I have no idea if she'll be doing any singing herself. She's the director of the New Life Baptist Choir. They're nationally famous—and deservedly so. But if you hear any complaints about the fact that they'll be doing Christmas carols—"

"So far no one's complained," Ophelia said. "I mean, Ms. Cordelia made it clear that it's entertainment, not an official part of the program."

"And they're joining forces with the Temple Beth-El choir for the occasion," I said. "So I expect there will be a few Christmas carols, a few Hanukkah songs, and a whole lot of winter seasonal songs. 'Winter Wonderland,' 'Jingle Bells,' 'Let It Snow, Let It Snow, Let It Snow'—you get the idea."

"That sounds nice," she said. "And I wasn't complaining about the Christmas part of it. I'm sure someone will, but not me. And after all, Ms. Cordelia's trying to do everything she can to make sure anyone who wants to attend any kind of religious or spiritual service can get there. And Temple Beth-El—is that the synagogue that invited anyone and everyone at the conference to join them for their Sabbath dinner?"

"It is," I said. "And you should seriously consider going. The food will be awesome."

Just then I saw Ginny and Janet, the two women who were hoping to exonerate their high-school buddy, come bustling in from the lobby. From their cheerful expressions, I gathered that the prospect of talking to Ezekiel Blaine had encouraged them. They waved at us before disappearing into the Hamilton Room.

"Have you met those two?" Ophelia asked. "The Keepers, as Kevin calls them."

"Ginny and Janet? Yes," I said. "Why does he call them the Keepers? Keepers of what?"

"You'll have to ask him," she said. "I haven't had time yet to find out. I assume I will eventually. They're going to present their friend's case in a roundtable session—I think they're hoping Festus will take it on."

I nodded and made a note to look for their session—and ask Kevin the reason for the nickname.

Ezekiel followed a minute or so later, with a coffee cup in his hand and Ruth trotting obediently at his side. He waved cheerfully at us before strolling over to the door of the Hamilton Room.

"I should go in and catch the end of Festus's talk," I said. "And isn't my grandfather on after that?"

"After the fifteen-minute break," she said.

I nodded and strolled over to join Ezekiel. We listened as Festus fielded questions from the audience. The Gadfly was waving his arm frantically, but with luck the session would end before he was called on.

"Festus should wrap up in five minutes or so," Ezekiel said in an undertone, while another audience member asked a rather long-winded question. "You going to stay around for your grandfather's talk on DNA?"

"Or whatever else he's talking about," I said. "He'd never forgive me if I didn't."

"Of course not." He chuckled. "I definitely want to hear it. Partly because I probably owe my freedom to that DNA lab of his. And partly because when Dr. Blake is talking, he almost convinces you that you understand all that science."

I nodded.

"And truth be told," Ezekiel went on, "I also wouldn't miss it because I bet Mr. Norton is planning to cause trouble, and if he does, I surely would enjoy seeing your granddaddy take him down a peg."

I smiled and nodded. Actually, I hoped the Gadfly wouldn't prove too annoying—Grandfather was always more pleasant to be around when he was in a good mood. But yes, if necessary he could deal with Norton. And Cordelia would probably intervene if Norton was too obnoxious. Although in their youth she and Grandfather had once been close enough to produce Dad, they no longer got along all that well. Lately they'd been working hard on maintaining the truce that allowed them both to enjoy spending time with the family. If anything could bring them into a temporary alliance, it would be someone like the Gadfly. Neither of them suffered fools gladly.

Festus was wrapping up, reminding the audience that he'd be back after lunch for the panel on Ezekiel Blaine's case, and around generally if people wanted to ask him questions.

"And are you actually going to answer people's questions this afternoon," the Gadfly shouted out. "Or are you going to keep stonewalling anyone who doesn't agree with you?"

Festus's smile was catlike.

"If you've got a question that's even remotely relevant to anything I've said over the last hour and fifteen minutes, I'd be glad to hear it," he said. "But if all you want to do is make another speech about how you disapprove of the whole idea of this get-together . . . well, you're welcome to go start your own conference to promote your point of view."

The audience greeted this with light applause and scattered laughter.

"Fifteen-minute break, folks," Festus said. "Coffee and tea in the Gathering Area."

"Well, maybe you don't care if you're turning dangerous criminals loose on a society that's unprepared to deal with them," Norton said, in a voice designed to carry over the conversations that were starting up and the rest of the crowd noise. "Maybe you don't care about the trauma you're causing to victims who thought the people who slaughtered their family and friends were getting the punishment they deserve. Maybe—hmph!"

Norton had caught sight of both Cordelia and Ekaterina, converging on him from opposite sides of the meeting room. I had to hand it to him—he did a pretty good job of managing to look as if he'd decided to leave on his own. You could almost believe the way he was barging through the crowd like a steam engine was due to his own natural rudeness. Or maybe a dire need for caffeine.

Ezekiel and I both stepped well aside until he'd stormed out of the door and headed for the coffee-and-tea service. Then we began working to buck the main tide of people leaving the room, so we could find good seats for Grandfather's session.

"Did you hear what Mr. Norton tried to pull last night at the cocktail party?" Ezekiel asked.

"No," I said. "Nothing horrible, I hope."

"Milder than most of his nonsense," he said. "Your grandmother made an announcement about tomorrow night's concert, and he tried to make a big fuss about it being a Christmas concert, and what about people who weren't Christians."

"I do hope Cordelia explained that it was a Christmas, Hanukkah, and winter concert."

"She did better than that." He was grinning with pleasure at the memory. "She told him she'd be happy to try to connect him with any locals who shared his religious affiliation, if he cared to enlighten her on what it was. So he shouted out that he was a pagan. And she actually reached into her handbag, pulled out a list, and started reading off options. That the local Unitarian Universalist church had a pagan group, and did he want her to introduce him to them? Or would he prefer a Wiccan coven? She knew of several, including a Gardnerian one, whatever that is. And she knew some local Druids and Discordians, and while she wasn't entirely sure they counted as pagans, she could introduce him to some Voodooists and some Rastafarians. And that was the point when he got annoyed enough to storm out of the room. Does Caerphilly really have that many . . . unusual religious groups?"

"I have no idea," I said. "I know we have the Unitarian pagans and the Wiccans. The rest? No idea. But if we don't have them, I bet my husband, Michael, could find some people to put on a good show of pretending, either to placate the Gadfly or play a prank on him. Michael's on the faculty of the Caerphilly College drama department, so he knows a lot of aspiring actors who'd have fun doing it."

"In any case, I'm looking forward to the concert," Ezekiel said. "And is your grandmother serious about having fireworks afterward?"

"Absolutely," I said. "She's hired the same firm that does our town's Fourth of July fireworks."

Actually, Things That Go Boom, the firm in question, consisted of three youthful Shiffley cousins who'd turned their love of setting things on fire and blowing things up into a lucrative part-time business. But they were good at it—and very safety-conscious, as Cordelia had taken the trouble to learn.

We arrived at the front row and grabbed seats at the far-left side.

"Just so you know, these really aren't safe seats," I said. "Grandfather likes to pick on people in the front row—ask them questions or make them volunteer to be guinea pigs."

"I doubt if I'll know any of the answers, but I'm happy to volunteer if he needs me," Ezekiel said. "I owe him more than I can ever repay. Him and all his laboratory scientists."

And why wasn't Grandfather already at the podium, reassuring the audience—and Cordelia—that he'd be here to start his session on time? I turned and began peering toward the entrance doors. I was going to give it five minutes before I went to hunt him down.

Chapter 6

While keeping my eye open for Grandfather, I noticed that several audience members had waylaid Festus on his way out—a tall, gangly, but attractive young woman with flaming copper-red hair and a tallish, plump middle-aged woman whose hair was more of a faded version of the young woman's, possibly because it was shot through with more than a few strands of silver.

The older woman was speaking, with an air of nervous intensity. I stood up again, stretched, and eased a little closer so I could eavesdrop.

"It's just that . . . well, she isn't innocent," the woman was saying. "She did kill him. Mr. Norton's right about that. But it wasn't murder. It should have been voluntary manslaughter."

"Or self-defense," the young woman put in.

"If the jury had been able to hear about why she did it." The older woman was wringing her hands.

"Relax," Festus said. "Mr. Norton doesn't have a say in what cases we discuss in the roundtable sessions. And if he tries to give you a hard time when you're presenting your case, we'll kick him out of the room."

"Assuming he's even still around tomorrow," Cordelia said as she arrived and handed Festus a cup of coffee. "Because I wouldn't bet on it. Don't you fret, Madelaine," she added, looking at the young woman. "I'm sure most of the attendees will be very interested in hearing about your mother's case." She turned to the older woman. "And I bet your sister is proud of all you're doing to help her."

The two redheads smiled at her.

"Come on, Aunt Ellen," Madelaine said. "Let's get you some hot tea. And let Mr. Hollingsworth relax a little after his speech."

She took her aunt's arm and began to steer her gently toward the door.

"And don't worry about tomorrow," Festus called after them. "It'll be fine."

They looked back and nodded—Madelaine solemnly, her aunt with a tremulous smile.

"It'll be a lot finer if I kick out that rascal Norton," Cordelia said, though not loud enough for the redheads to hear.

"Not until and unless he does something that's both truly awful and completely public," Festus replied. "We don't want to seem as if we're stifling free expression."

"We also don't want him ruining the whole weekend for the very people we're trying to help," Cordelia said.

"I hear you," Festus said. "And I've got something in the works that should take care of Mr. Norton. But how'd he manage to get in, anyway? I thought you were planning to lose his registration until the event was sold out."

"That was the plan." Cordelia frowned. "I just talked to our registrar to find out what went wrong. It seems he registered under his real name—Gustave Niedernstatter, or something like that."

"So you were right that Godfrey Norton was a pseudonym," Festus said.

"Yes," Cordelia said. "And we didn't realize it was him until he showed up and requested that we print him a name tag with his pseudonym on it."

"I figured it was something like that," Festus said. "Don't worry. It will take more than the Gadfly to derail the conference."

"Here he comes again," I said. "I guess he's planning on hearing Grandfather's DNA talk."

"Oh, I do hope he tries to annoy your grandfather," Cordelia said. "Normally I feel sorry for people unlucky enough to get on Monty's bad side, but in this case . . . I want a ringside seat."

"Do you want mine?" I asked, gesturing to my chair. Ezekiel also rose as if to offer his seat.

"Thanks," she said. "But I'm going to find one at the back of the room. That'll be ringside enough and will let me keep an eye on what the audience is up to while Monty's speaking. Plus I want to duck out for a few minutes at some point to check on the roundtable that's going on in the Lafayette Room."

"You scheduled a roundtable opposite Grandfather?"

"Not everyone gets as excited about DNA as your grandfather does," she said. "And this is a last-minute addition to the program—a paralegal from Richmond who's offered to meet with anyone who's working on a case and needs help deciphering legal documents. It's not going to draw a lot of people away from Monty, but if she's as sharp as she sounds, it will be a really useful session for the small number of people who attend."

"Excellent," I said. "We just won't tell Grandfather about it."

She rolled her eyes, nodded, and strode toward the back of the room.

Behind me, the microphone emitted several ear-piercing squeals—followed by several salty words from Grandfather. A hotel staffer rushed over, grabbed the microphone away from him, did something to it, and then handed it back—very ceremoniously, as if to atone for the abruptness with which he'd snatched it away.

"Thank you," Grandfather said, nodding at the staffer. "Darn fool machines have it in for me. So," he went on, turning to the audience and speaking a little too loudly into the microphone, "let's get started here."

Conversation rapidly died down as Grandfather strutted toward the podium. He was dressed, as usual, as if about to take a long hike in the woods. His shirt and pants were in two shades of khaki, as was his many-pocketed utility vest. Like the magic carpetbag Mary Poppins carried or The Luggage in Terry Pratchett's Discworld, Grandfather's vest seemed to have nearly infinite capacity to hold any or all objects he wanted or needed. As we watched, he fished a small bottle of throat spray out of one pocket and used it before starting his talk.

"They wanted to call this session of mine DNA for Dummies," he began. "But I talked them out of that. There are a lot of dummies out in the world, no question. But I figure anyone willing to show up for an event like this can't be too much of a dummy."

Scattered laughter rippled through the crowd.

"So that's why I called it DNA for Non-Scientists," Grandfather went on. "Or, if you prefer, the ABCs of DNA."

"Why don't you call it how to use junk science to get killers out of prison?" the Gadfly called from the back of the room.

Grandfather didn't visibly react, but if the Gadfly thought that meant he hadn't heard the comment, or didn't have an answer for it, he was mistaken.

But luckily, instead of retaliating, Grandfather launched into his talk. I'd heard him cover much the same ground before, but he wasn't one of those speakers who went on autopilot and gave the same content in the same words every time. And he had a gift for explaining a complicated subject in simple terms, and using examples that made the subjects relatable to his audience. Here, with an audience who had at least an inkling of the importance of DNA in crime solving, he was in his element.

And the audience loved it, especially when he opened the floor for the audience to lob questions at him—and if they were hoping to stump him, they were disappointed. Yes, law enforcement did sometimes use the DNA of animals, as early as 1994, when the Royal Canadian Mounted Police had used hairs from a cat named Snowball to help convict a killer. No, the police aren't going to be using DNA to solve crimes like burglary or car theft anytime soon, since the cost of processing the DNA could easily equal or exceed the value of the stolen merchandise. Yes, there is DNA in a human hair, but unless you have the hair root, all you've got is highly degraded DNA, and scientists haven't figured out how to use it for forensic purposes. At least not yet.

"Although my guys are working on it," he said. "Guys and gals," he added, since we'd drummed into him the fact that not everyone considered "guys" a unisex collective noun.

At this point, the Gadfly yawned ostentatiously and made an exit that was somewhat noisier than seemed quite necessary. He might be feigning boredom, but I suspected the real reason for his departure was that he'd tried to disrupt Grandfather a few months ago at a true-crime conference and it had ended badly for him. I'd give him one thing, though. He'd figured out what a bad idea it was to challenge Grandfather to a battle of wits.

"So is it true that identical twins have identical DNA?" This question came from Adam Burke, who was envious of Josh and Jamie for being twins. By contrast, Josh and Jamie were mildly annoyed with Michael and me for producing them as fraternal rather than identical twins. They seemed to think that being able to impersonate each other at will would have given them much wider scope for pranks, practical jokes, and other exploits. And they were probably right, which was why I was grateful they'd turned out fraternal.

"Absolutely not!" Grandfather exclaimed, delighted at being given one of his all-time favorite questions. "For starters, you can have mutations that happen after the zygote splits. One study found that on average, identical twins have five point two mutations in their DNA. Which is not a lot, considering how many thousands or millions of mutations are possible, but it's something you can detect if you do a full enough analysis."

The session was drawing to a close, but the questioners were still going strong. Then, right in the middle of Grandfather's explanation of why DNA wasn't particularly useful in a murder case in which the victim and all of the suspects lived together and probably shed DNA on each other on a daily basis, I heard some kind of noise coming from the adjacent Lafayette Room. What was going on there? It was supposed to be the Richmond paralegal helping would-be exonerators decipher legal documents. While I'd often felt daunted when confronted with a complicated legal document—at least until I could reach Festus to explain it to me—I couldn't recall any documents that had inspired me to shrieks or bellows.

Cordelia quickly rose and exited. I stayed where I was, but I kept an eye on the back of the room. If she didn't come back soon . . .

"I'm going to go see if my grandmother needs any help," I whispered to Ezekiel. He nodded and spread his arm over the back of my seat, as if to hold it for me.

I slipped out into the hall as quietly as possible and met Cordelia, about to reenter.

"What was going on?" I asked.

"That stupid man," she muttered. "Norton, that is. He got

hold of one of those pens of Kevin's and was annoying the people at the roundtable with it."

"Pens of Kevin's?" I echoed.

"The ones he's giving away to promote the podcast."

"I know," I said. "I helped him pick them out. They're a combination pen and LED flashlight. But I didn't realize he had any of them here—he was complaining last night about the fact that they hadn't yet arrived from the manufacturer."

"Evidently they did arrive, and the Gadfly was doing this with them."

She held up a shiny silver pen, pressed something on it, and suddenly a painful brightness hit my eyes.

"Yikes," I said. "Not cool."

"I took this one away from him," she said, handing me the pen. "But he'll probably get hold of another. There's a box or two on the giveaway table."

"He's welcome to a pen or two," I said. "As long as he doesn't try to blind people with them."

She nodded, and we went back into the Hamilton Room together. Grandfather was closing his speech with a pitch for people to upload their DNA profiles to the databases that were available for law enforcement to access.

"Unless, of course, you're part of a crime family," he said. "If you're one of the Gambinos or the Luccheses, maybe you don't want to do it. You don't want to get your godfather mad at you."

Laughter from the crowd.

"But for the rest of us, it's a good thing. You might help solve a crime or identify one of the more than ten thousand John and Jane Does here in the US alone. This time of year—the Christmas and Hanukkah season—is particularly hard for the family of someone who has gone missing. You can't bring them home for the holidays, but maybe you can help give closure to a family

that's been worrying and wondering for years—even decades.
And thank you for considering it."

He stepped back from the microphone and basked in the
enthusiastic applause that followed. Cordelia snorted, but her
expression was one of grudging approval.

When the applause died down, a few of the audience began
drifting toward the exits—including Ezekiel, with Ruth in tow.
A few also rushed up to talk to Grandfather, including Janet and
Ginny, the high-school friends. And most of the audience was
still sitting or standing around, talking energetically. Not surprising, since there were no other sessions taking place at the
moment and lunch would be served fairly soon.

I worked on getting some interesting pictures.

"After lunch, are we—" I began, turning to Cordelia.

Suddenly I heard a commotion out in the Gathering Area.
Cordelia noticed it in the same instant, and the two of us raced
out of the room.

"Call the cops!" the Gadfly was bellowing. "That vicious cur
bit me!"

Chapter 7

Norton stood in the middle of the Gathering Area, glaring at Ezekiel. And at Ruth, who had climbed into Ezekiel's lap and was doing her best to burrow into his chest. She didn't look like a vicious cur. More like an animal that had been abused.

"I've been attacked!" Norton bellowed. "I want the cops! I want to report—"

"No need to shout." Chief Burke appeared at the Gadfly's side. "Meg, could you text Horace and your dad and tell them I could use their help?"

I nodded and pulled out my phone. The chief turned back to Norton.

"Now what seems to be the trouble?" he asked.

"That vicious dog bit me!" Norton pointed at Ezekiel and Ruth, taking a step toward them as he did. Ruth flinched away from him and buried her head deeper in Ezekiel's chest.

"I see." The chief had pulled out his notebook and pen. "Let me get some details on this. When did it happen?"

"Just a few minutes ago," the Gadfly said. "I was passing through the lobby, minding my own business—"

"No he wasn't!"

It was Josh speaking. We turned to see him, along with Jamie and Adam Burke, standing in a cluster at the other end of the Gathering Area.

"Let me finish taking Mr. Norton's statement first," the chief said, holding up an admonitory finger. Josh nodded and visibly tightened his mouth, as if keeping quiet was an effort. The Gadfly smirked as if he'd won some skirmish. Maybe he had, but I suspected the chief's gesture to Josh didn't say "wait your turn," much less "shut up, kid." More like "let's give him the chance to hang himself first."

"I was minding my own business, and when I happened to be passing by that savage dog, it lunged out and bit me!" Norton said. He had wrapped the bottom of his t-shirt around his right hand and was cradling it with the left. "I could get rabies."

"Not from Ruth he can't," Ezekiel said, pointedly looking at the chief rather than Norton. "She's up to date on all her shots, Chief—you're welcome to look at her tags. And you don't have to take my word for it. She had her checkup and booster shots a few weeks ago right here in Caerphilly, with Dr. Clarence Rutledge."

"Well, at least I don't have to worry about rabies," the Gadfly said. "But you're still not allowed to have a vicious dog running around loose in a hotel. I'm filing charges."

"Mr. Blaine," the chief said. "Can you shed any light on what happened?"

"No, sir," Ezekiel said. "Except to say that I've never known Ruth to bite anyone. Ever."

"Maybe if you kept her under control instead of running off and leaving her, you'd know what she gets up to behind your back," the Gadfly said.

"I had to go to the restroom." Ezekiel's eyes were on the chief. "So I asked that young lady if I could leave Ruth with her, since she was sitting there at the registration table." He pointed at Amber.

"And I said I was fine with it." Amber swept a few loose tendrils of her long blond hair back as if preparing to leap into action. "She's a perfectly sweet little thing. And he told her to stay, and she did just that, even though I could see she really wanted to follow Mr. Blaine. She was just lying quietly by my feet, watching the men's room door, and the next thing I knew, she was cowering against me and that man was shouting that she'd bitten him, and I didn't see what happened but I can't imagine she'd do anything of the kind."

"Well, she did," the Gadfly said. "And my hand's starting to swell up."

"Josh," the chief said. "I think you had something to contribute?"

"He was poking her with something," Josh said. "And you could tell she was scared, and he kept poking her and poking her, and we were going to go over and stop him, but then Ruth snapped at him and cowered away."

"But she only snapped *at* him," Adam added. "She didn't actually get anywhere near him."

"And I think he was hurting her," Jamie said.

"Are you going to take the word of a bunch of lying teenagers against mine?" the Gadfly snarled. "They're just trying to—"

"I've known all three of those boys for their whole lives." The chief's tone was cold enough to freeze boiling water in an instant. "I've generally found them to be pretty truthful and reliable. You, on the other hand, I've only just met. I think—"

"Chief Burke!" Ekaterina rushed over to his side. "I have heard the distressing news. Do you wish me to retrieve the video footage of the incident from our security cameras?"

The Gadfly started at that.

"If you would be so kind," the chief said. His lip quirked slightly, as if he was amused by the Gadfly's reaction. And no one piped up to ask an inconvenient question, like since when did the Inn have security cameras in the Gathering Area.

"He was hurting Ruth," Jamie repeated. "We should call Clarence and have him check her out."

"Check who out?" Dad came trotting in from the main lobby, with his medical bag in hand and Horace trailing after him.

"Ruth," Josh and Adam chorused. Jamie settled for pointing at the terrified dog.

"Thank you for coming so quickly, Dr. Langslow." The chief pointed at the Gadfly. "Could you start by checking Mr. Norton's hand? He's reporting a dog bite."

"Oh, dear," Dad said. "Let me take a look at it."

He took a few steps toward the Gadfly, who backed away.

"Thanks, but I'm fine now." Norton was still cradling his right hand. Or maybe more like trying to hide it.

"Dog bites can be serious," Dad said. "There's quite a high risk of infection—almost as high as with a human bite. Were you able to identify the dog who bit you? We need to—"

"We have secured the dog," the chief said. "And will be checking with Dr. Clarence Rutledge, our local veterinarian, to verify that she's up to date with her rabies vaccinations." This was obviously aimed at the Gadfly, since Dad knew perfectly well who his friend Clarence was. "But since Mr. Norton wants to file a complaint, I'd like you to examine his injury so we'll know how serious it is."

"It's not that bad, actually." Norton was looking more and more like a cornered rat. "I was just kind of shook up at first. I don't need to file a complaint after all if—"

"You need to show Dr. Langslow your alleged dog bite." The chief was using what I thought of as his inexorable tone—the boys called it the Morgan Freeman voice. "I need to know if you were really bitten."

"But I just told you—" the Gadfly sputtered.

"And if you don't show Dr. Langslow your hand, I'll be putting you under arrest and taking you down to the station to see how many interesting things we can charge you with." The chief smiled blandly at Norton.

"Falsely summoning or giving false reports to a law enforcement officer," Horace suggested, in a bright, helpful tone.

"Pretty sure he's already earned that," the chief said. "But if he keeps refusing to show us this alleged dog bite of his we can probably think of a few other charges."

"Interfering with a police investigation?" Horace sounded hopeful.

The chief gave a thoughtful, judicious sort of nod.

"A pity Vern isn't here," Horace said. "I bet he could think of others." Yes, Vern—the chief's senior deputy—had all but memorized the Code of Virginia, and often demoralized wrongdoers by quoting excerpts from it.

The Gadfly surrendered, pulling his right hand out and shoving it in Dad's face—almost bopping him on the nose. Unruffled, Dad took the hand and examined it minutely. We all watched in tense silence.

"You're sure this is the hand that was bitten?" Dad asked, after a minute or two. "It doesn't seem to have broken the skin."

"I was pretty shook up," the Gadfly said. "I guess I overreacted."

"He was poking her with something," Amber said. "Look—it's right down there."

"Don't touch it!" Horace exclaimed. He raced over to the registration table, stopped in front of it for a moment, looking as if he was considering the idea of leaping over it in a dramatic gesture. Then he steadied himself and walked around the end of the table, pulling a pair of gloves out of his pocket as he went. He squatted and peered down at the spot on the rug where Amber was pointing.

"It's a fork," he said. "A really tiny fork with only two tines."

"An oyster fork, maybe?" Amber said.

"It is a *fourchette à escargot*," Ekaterina said. "A snail fork."

Dad had moved over to where Ruth was still cowering in Ezekiel's lap and was kneeling beside them, examining her.

"Horace, you might want to bag that fork as evidence." He was too focused on Ruth to see that Horace was already doing just that. "You know how she got these little wounds on her head and neck?" he asked, looking up at Ezekiel.

"Wounds?" Ezekiel repeated. "She didn't have any wounds this morning."

He and Dad both turned to stare at the Gadfly.

We all stared at him for a few moments—well, except for Horace, who had knelt down to take swabs from Ruth's fur. Then Cordelia took a few steps forward until she was directly facing Norton.

"Mr. Niedernstatter," she said. "You are no longer welcome at this conference."

"Or in this hotel." Ekaterina appeared at Cordelia's side. "I must ask you to vacate your room immediately."

"But—" the Gadfly began.

"I will be refunding your conference registration fee," Cordelia said. "You can pick up the check at the front desk when you drop off your room key. Chief," she added, turning to him. "Might we ask to have one of your officers escort Mr. Niedernstatter until he vacates the premises?"

"Of course," the chief said. "Horace, why don't you accompany the gentleman to his room and see that he starts packing.

I'll get another deputy out here to take over as soon as possible, so you can get back to the conference."

"Right, Chief," Horace said. He had deposited a last swab in a brown paper evidence bag and was writing something on the label. He held out a small handful of bags to the chief. "I'll let you take charge of these."

The chief nodded and took custody of the evidence bags.

Horace turned to the Gadfly. "Ready when you are, Mr. . . . Norton."

Everyone watched in silence as Norton trudged to the door that led to the lobby, with Horace following a few paces behind him. I wasn't the only one who let out a relieved breath when the door closed behind them. I wondered if anyone else felt a fleeting urge to applaud. The boys had gathered around Ezekiel and Ruth and were petting the still-trembling dog while Amber looked on approvingly.

I was starting to like Amber. Anyone who sticks up for animals was okay in my book.

I spotted Grandfather threading his way through the crowd, patting the many pockets of his khaki utility vest as he went.

"Can she have chicken jerky?" he asked when he reached Ezekiel and Ruth. "All natural—same thing I feed my wolves."

"Thank you for asking," Ezekiel said. "And I think she'd find a bit of chicken jerky mighty comforting at the moment."

Grandfather produced the treat from one of his vest pockets, and while Ruth was enthusiastically chewing it up, he scratched her head while performing what I suspected was a quick but expert visual inspection of her little wounds.

"Chief," he said. "If you want to check out that snail fork to confirm that it has Ruth's blood on the tines and that jerk's DNA on the handle, the Blake Foundation Laboratory will do the testing pro bono. Could support an animal cruelty charge."

"I'll take it over to the lab myself," the chief said. "Soon as I've written up the blasted paperwork."

Grandfather and the chief had long ago bonded over their fierce, shared conviction that Virginia needed to enact stiffer penalties for animal cruelty.

Meanwhile, the crowd that had gathered began drifting away—a process that was hastened when Cordelia made an announcement.

"Lunch in the Madison Ballroom in five minutes," she called out.

Chapter 8

Luckily the announcement of lunch distracted everyone from the departing Gadfly. Some people hurried toward the lobby door—presumably to drop by their rooms before the meal started. Others, no doubt hopeful of being near the beginning of the buffet line, headed for the hallway that led to the ballroom. The boys, reassured that Ruth was being well protected, joined that crowd—although before scampering off, Adam gave his grandfather a fierce, wordless hug. Cordelia came over to where I was standing, watching as Dad, Grandfather, and Ezekiel hovered over Ruth.

"It doesn't happen often," she said, in her normal tone of voice. "But every once in a long while, the old coot does something that reminds me of what I once saw in him."

"A good thing Rose Noire didn't hear you say that," I said. "Or she'd jump to the conclusion that you and Grandfather were an item again."

Cordelia's snort told me just what she thought of that idea.

"Next time she gets that idea into her head, let's figure out a way to let her down easy," she said. "Because that's one Christmas miracle I don't see happening. Getting back to Norton—Ekaterina's giving a heads-up to all her staff. If he tries to regain entry, he will be rebuffed."

"I'll keep my eyes open," I said. "And do you think maybe we should make a diplomatically worded announcement at lunch? Let everyone know that he's persona non grata, and they shouldn't open any of the hotel's side doors to him."

"An excellent idea." She pulled out the tiny notebook that was her equivalent of my notebook-that-tells-me-when-to-breathe and jotted in a quick entry.

Then she made a familiar gesture—a glance at the pocket of her slacks, followed by pulling out her phone and looking at it.

"Blast the man," she said. "If he actually thinks I want to talk to him on the phone—"

"The Gadfly?"

She nodded and touched her phone's screen to decline the call. She was about to stick the phone back in her pocket when it vibrated again—visibly this time. She stabbed at the screen with obvious annoyance.

"One of the few things that's better on a landline," she said. "Hanging up on someone is so much more satisfactory."

The phone vibrated again.

"Three strikes and he's out," I said. "Block him."

"I am," she said. "Wretched man. Let's go get something to eat."

Lunch was a soup, salad, and sandwich buffet. Of course, since it was the Inn providing it, the dozen different steaming-hot soups were the chef's finest creations, the half-dozen salads were fresh and organic, and the spread of sandwich ingredients featured a bewildering variety of artisanal breads, meats, and cheeses. Ekaterina had even solved one of the perennial problems with hotel buffets—the difficulty of juggling multiple plates or bowls—by providing a supply of sleek, elegant bent-wood trays.

Cordelia's announcement about the Gadfly earned a spontaneous outbreak of cheers and applause.

"Well, that went over well," she said when she rejoined me in the buffet line.

"Obviously we're not the only ones delighted by the idea of never, ever setting eyes on him again," I replied.

We took our trays to a table in a corner of the ballroom—a table that was both dangerously close to the buffet and conveniently located for observing everything that went on at every other table. We sat with our backs to the wall, so focused on keeping an eye on the attendees that we conversed only sporadically and paid far less attention to the food than it deserved.

Josh, Jamie, and Adam waved at us on their way to sit with Dad and Grandfather. Kevin and Casey, his podcasting partner, were ensconced a few tables away from us, with half a dozen attendees who I suspected were among the true-crime aficionados, rather than committed exoneration volunteers. I'd have made a bet, though, that before the conference was over, at least a few of them would sign up to help with one of the unjust cases *Virginia Crime Time* was promoting. Festus was having a serious and rather intense conversation with the two redheads, aunt and niece.

"Mind if I join you?"

I glanced up to see Minerva Burke, the chief's wife, holding a tray.

"Of course," Cordelia said. "I didn't know you were coming today. Were you planning to see Henry's presentation?"

"I wasn't." Minerva set down her tray and settled her well-padded frame into one of the Inn's comfortable dining chairs with a sigh of appreciation. "Though now that I'm here, I might take it in, if that's okay."

"Of course," Cordelia said.

"I only stopped by to check on a couple of details about tomorrow's concert, but you know Ekaterina." Minerva was inhaling the fragrance of her two small bowls of soup, as if trying to decide which to start with. "If you walk through her doors anywhere near mealtime, she won't rest till she's fed you. That's not a complaint, of course."

"Is this seat taken?"

Ezekiel Blaine was standing by the fourth chair at our table, holding his tray. Ruth was standing by his right leg, tail wagging.

"It is now," Cordelia said, with a smile.

"Set your food down and get comfortable," Minerva said.

Ezekiel seemed to be waiting for permission from all three of us. I hurried to swallow the bit of Gorgonzola I was nibbling.

"Please, take it," I said. "Before Godfrey Norton sneaks back in to grab it."

They all three chuckled at that, and Ezekiel took the open seat. Ruth turned around a couple of times before settling down at his feet.

"Have you two met?" Cordelia asked. "Ezekiel Blaine, Minerva Burke."

"Ezekiel is one of Festus's exonerees," I said to Minerva. "And in addition to being Chief Burke's wife, Minerva is the director of the New Life Baptist Choir," I added to Ezekiel.

"Oh, my," Ezekiel said. "I'm impressed. Festus played me a recording of one of your concerts. Mighty fine."

"Thank you," Minerva said.

"They'll be part of tomorrow night's after-dinner program," Cordelia added.

"Yes," Minerva said. "We're the opening act for the fireworks show."

"I particularly liked the range your group has," Ezekiel said.

"Hopping straight from a gospel hymn to a Bach cantata and nailing them both. And doing a darn fine job on some pretty difficult pieces."

"Do you sing yourself?" Minerva asked.

"Used to," he said. "Used to lead the choir sometimes, if there was a choir at whatever prison I was in. Hope to get into it again, when I find the right church."

"Well, you come on down to New Life Baptist this Sunday," Minerva said. "We'd love to have you, and just because we've got a choir doesn't mean the congregation is allowed to slack off. We're in favor of everyone making a joyful noise unto the Lord."

"I just might do that," Ezekiel said. He glanced over his shoulder. "If I'm still out free by Sunday."

"I thought you were fully exonerated," Minerva said.

"I am," he said. "But if that Norton fellow comes back and says one word to me, I just might give way to temptation and punch him in the nose, and your husband's going to have to lock me up again."

"No worries about that," Minerva said. "If he sets foot back on the Inn grounds, he'll be the one getting locked up. I heard about what he did to your poor puppy."

Just then my phone emitted the faint ding that signaled an arriving text. It was from Kevin.

"Why does the Gadfly keep calling and texting me to ask me to let him back in?" it said. "Back into what?"

"Cordelia kicked him out of the conference," I texted back. "Just block him."

He didn't respond for a minute or so. Then another text came through.

"Give her my thanks."

"Anything urgent?" Cordelia asked.

"Kevin's turn to block the Gadfly," I said. "And he said to give you his thanks for kicking the jerk out."

Cordelia nodded, then turned and waved at someone. At Kevin, I realized. He was still at the table with the true-crime crew. And Amber Smith, who was sitting right beside him. The Black Widow, as Norton had called her. Why the rather ominous nickname? I thought of it as something you'd call a female serial killer, one with a track record of bumping off multiple husbands or lovers. As far as I knew, Amber had only been convicted of the one murder, and was in the process of being exonerated for that. The fact that Norton was the one giving her the nickname made me want to take her side, but I made a mental note to find out more about her case. And as the conversation at my table flowed on, I kept what I hoped was an unobtrusive eye on them.

A good thing Rose Noire wasn't here, I decided. She was perceptive enough—and knew Kevin well enough—to have noticed what I noticed: that while he was doing his best to appear to be paying attention to the general conversation at his table, his focus was on Amber. And unlike me—or Cordelia, who had probably also noticed it—Rose Noire wouldn't just smile and silently wish him well. She'd have begun teasing Kevin and encouraging him to invite Amber back to Caerphilly for family events and generally focusing way too much attention on their budding relationship. If it even was a relationship, rather than just the faint early days of one. Or maybe just a passing flirtation.

I'd have a word with Cordelia. And with Mother. Between the three of us, we could probably figure out ways to divert Rose Noire. Unless, of course, either of them thought Amber was "not precisely whom we would have chosen." Long ago, in a rare, candid moment, Mother had uttered those very words about Samantha, my brother's first fiancée. Not that she—or any of us—had done anything to undermine their relationship, but her departure from Rob's life had been the cause for general rejoicing. But I'd been dubious about Samantha from the first time I'd met her. Amber, I liked.

"I'm going to save the rude voicemail Norton just left me," Cordelia said, looking up from her phone. "Just in case he tries to claim that he reacted calmly and professionally to his expulsion. Does he really think dropping the F-bomb half a dozen times will intimidate me?"

The afternoon passed enjoyably. No doubt a few of the attendees weren't thrilled at the Gadfly's involuntary departure—either because they agreed with him or because they enjoyed the kind of drama he liked to provoke. But I think if we'd taken a survey, "good riddance to bad rubbish" would have been the overwhelming reaction.

In fact, only one person expressed any concern in my hearing.

Shortly after lunch, as most of the attendees were milling around, deciding which session to attend, I got a call from an unfamiliar number. The caller ID only said NAME UNAVAILABLE. I almost let it go to voicemail, but then I remembered how very many visiting relatives and out-of-town conference attendees just might have been given my number as someone they could turn to if they needed help.

So I excused myself from the conversation I'd been having with Amber and Ophelia at the registration table—which, now that registrations were over, had turned into a sort of general help desk and information table—and answered the call.

"You need to tell your grandmother to stop trying to silence me!"

Chapter 9

For some reason Norton's words—and his aggrieved tone of voice—struck me as funny. He ranted on, while I took a few seconds to control the urge to giggle. Then I hung up on him.

He called back again immediately. I stared at the screen, waiting for his call to go to voicemail, after which I could block him. Though not before screenshotting his phone number so I could warn anyone else who might be hearing from him.

Ophelia and Amber noticed what I was doing.

"Junk call?" Ophelia asked.

"You could say that." I held up my phone so they could see it.

"What have you got against poor Mr. Name Unavailable?" Amber asked.

"It's Godfrey Norton, calling to inform me that I need to tell Cordelia to stop trying to silence him." I gave way to the temptation to echo the Gadfly's outraged tone.

"'Help! Help! I'm being repressed!'" Ophelia exclaimed, in what I recognized as a quote from *Monty Python and the Holy Grail.*

"'Come and see the violence inherent in the system!'" I quoted back, and we both burst into laughter.

Amber looked thoughtful.

"I know he's annoying," she said. "But I worry that kicking him out could backfire. I mean, if word gets around that he was kicked out for trying to express unpopular opinions—"

"But he wasn't kicked out for expressing unpopular opinions," I pointed out. "He was kicked out for abusing an animal and harassing his fellow attendees."

"Not to mention trying to keep anyone else from expressing any opinion he disagrees with," Ophelia added.

"I know," Amber said. "And believe me, I'd have been really glad if he hadn't come to begin with. But you know how good he is at warping the truth. Before you know it, he'll have the rest of the world thinking we kicked him out because we didn't want him to present his convincing evidence against me, and Ezekiel and what's-her-name—that redheaded girl. Whatever her name is."

"Madelaine," I said.

"Right." Amber frowned slightly. "She didn't actually bump off anyone, did she?"

"No," I said. "She's working to help her mother, who's in prison for killing her husband. Madelaine's stepfather."

"Lucky lady," Amber said. "With four people showing up to plead her case."

"Four people?" Ophelia sounded puzzled.

"Madelaine and the older redhead and the two little old ladies," Amber explained. "They're always hanging around together."

"Oh, right," Ophelia said. "They seem to have hit it off together, but they're not here about the same case. Two different cases—Festus is trying to decide which one to tackle next. Madelaine and her aunt—the redheads—are here about Madelaine's mother's case. The two older ladies—Ginny and Janet—are working to help an old high-school friend of theirs."

"What's the old friend supposed to have done?" Amber asked.

"You'd have to ask them," Ophelia said.

I wondered if she really didn't know or if she was just being discreet. After all, she worked for Festus, and if Ginny and Janet were talking to Festus about their friend's case, she might have heard information that fell under attorney-client privilege.

"Probably a murder case," Amber said. "That's mostly the kind of case people consider it worth working for exoneration. And it could be worse—at least Virginia's not a death-penalty state."

"They're going to present the case in a roundtable session while they're here," Ophelia added. "You could try to catch that."

"I'll look for it," Amber said. "Maybe a good thing Norton won't be here for that. He'd try to twist everything they say. Probably will anyway."

"And Kevin and Casey will do what they can to get the real story around," I said.

"Yeah, but the more people see Norton, the more they realize what a jerk he is." Amber made a face, as if suddenly noticing a bad smell. "And what a liar. I'm wondering if Cordelia should have let him stay, if only to make sure everyone at the whole conference knows it."

"If anyone here hasn't figured it out by now, they're not paying attention," Ophelia said.

"But now he'll have something he can make look like a legitimate grievance," Amber said.

"He can try." I held up my phone to show that the Gadfly was calling again. "Might not work, though. Especially if he leaves a few more salty, self-entitled voicemails."

"I think even online people eventually figure him out," Ophelia said.

"I hope so, but I just don't know." Amber shook her head. "He's not the only miserable troll in the true-crime community, but he's one of the worst. Have you checked out his YouTube channel? Or his Facebook group?"

"No," I said. "But please tell me what they're called, so I can shun them."

"I hear you." Amber laughed. "His YouTube channel and his main Facebook group are both called *Godfrey for Justice.* Trust me, you're better off not seeing them. And you should also avoid *The Real Scooparino,* on Facebook or Reddit or Discord."

"You mentioned *The Real Scooparino* before," I said. "Another of Norton's aliases?"

"No, the leader of another group of nutcases who need to get a life instead of spending most of their waking hours spreading misinformation about the cases they're obsessed with."

"So allies of Godfrey's."

"Good heavens, no!" She gave the kind of laugh that makes you smile and want to join in, even if you have no idea what's funny. "They hate each other, Godfrey and the Scooparino. When they get tired of harassing and doxxing people like me and Ezekiel Blaine, they go to town on each other. It can be a pretty toxic place, the internet. I am not looking forward to reading what Norton posts about his brief time here."

"Same here," I said. "And I only just met him. I can't imagine how you feel."

"Oh, yes." She closed her eyes for a moment. Then she opened them, straightened her shoulders, and put a cheerful expression on her face. "Well, as my mother would have said, never borrow trouble. Let's just enjoy the peace and quiet his absence will bring and hope for the best."

Ophelia and I nodded.

"Ooh," I said. "Look what he just texted me: 'How can you do this to me? Don't be such a grinch.'"

"He's one to talk," Amber said.

"I wish he'd lay off long enough for me to block him," I muttered.

"Where's your Christmas spirit?" she countered.

"Cancel the kitchen scraps for lepers and orphans, no more merciful beheadings, and call off Christmas," I quoted.

"Something from *Monty Python*?" Amber asked.

"Alan Rickman as the Sheriff of Nottingham," Ophelia exclaimed. "He was the best part of *Robin Hood: Prince of Thieves*."

"The only part worth watching," I said. "There. I've blocked Norton. Time for the chief's session on working harmoniously with law enforcement," I added, seeing the time on my phone's screen.

"Ooh, yes," Amber said. "I definitely want to hear that. Not that there's much hope of me going back and building a harmonious relationship with the cops who investigated my case. But maybe I didn't handle it well when they first started interrogating me. The idea that I would even think of doing anything to my poor husband just seemed like such a farce that I laughed out loud at it. And I don't think cops like being laughed at."

Her words stirred my curiosity, so while the crowd was settling down to hear the chief, I took a seat in the back of the room, then pulled out my phone and did a search to find the details of Amber's case.

And it was an interesting one. At the tender age of twenty-two, she had married a man thirty years her senior—a prominent and affluent Virginia Beach attorney. They moved into a million-dollar house with a view of the Lynnhaven Bay and began taking their place in the local social scene. Then one cold winter night, Amber stayed home with a migraine while her husband went to dinner at his country club. The next day, a little before noon, a friend who had come by to collect the husband for their regular Sunday morning tee time found the front door open a crack and the husband lying on the living-room floor, dead from a gunshot wound. The house had visibly been ransacked, and a lot of small valuables had been taken—silverware, small electronics, and Amber's jewelry chest, full of the sort of pricey baubles a doting husband would give to a trophy wife. Which is what the prosecutor had called Amber, in spite of testimony from a number of their friends that she and the husband had appeared to have had a mutually loving relationship. Amber herself was so deeply asleep that the husband's friend thought, at first, that she had also been killed. But it turned out that she'd taken a sleeping pill on top of her migraine medicine and hadn't even awakened when the intruder rifled the master bedroom.

The cops didn't believe her story from the get-go. The evidence they produced was largely circumstantial—witnesses who had overheard the couple arguing, a friend who claimed the husband had confided that he'd made a mistake and was going to retain a divorce attorney, and the fact that the house's state-of-the-art security had been turned off after the husband left for the country club. The prosecutor was particularly scornful at Amber's assertion that before taking her sleeping pill and crawling into bed she had nervously checked to make sure the system was on and must have accidentally disarmed it.

Not exactly a slam-dunk case, but Amber was convicted. And then had her conviction overturned on a Brady violation.

I'd been listening to Kevin's podcast long enough to know that a Brady violation was when the prosecution failed to turn over to the defense attorney evidence that might help prove the defendant's innocence. In this case, the fact that a few months after the husband's murder, the police had recovered some of the stolen jewelry from the squalid apartment where a known fence had been found dead of a drug overdose.

So Amber was out on bail until the Virginia Beach authorities either scheduled a new trial or issued a nolle prosequi notice—which the article I was reading helpfully translated as meaning "we shall no longer prosecute." I felt a pang of sympathy for Amber. If she was innocent—and the evidence did appear thin—she was in limbo, not knowing if she'd be going on trial again. Was there some kind of deadline by which the prosecution had to notify her and her attorney if they wanted to retry her? I made a mental note to ask Festus.

I thought of looking up the Gadfly's online presence, to see what he had to say about the case. But even if I was forewarned—by others in addition to Amber—that he was prone to spreading unfounded rumors and even making things up out of whole cloth, I wasn't sure I wanted to read what he had to say. Maybe later.

So I focused back on the chief, who was now answering questions.

"No," he was saying. "I don't assume someone who asked for an attorney is guilty. I assume they've read the Constitution. Or at least watched a few episodes of *Law & Order.*"

This was greeted with laughter.

Overall, his session went well, as did the following presentation by the University of Virginia Law School's Innocence Project. And the surprise hit of the day was Horace's hands-on crime-scene demonstration. Kevin and Casey set up a fictitious crime scene in the Lafayette Room, complete with a wide range of clues and red herrings. They'd used a five-foot-tall plush flamingo as the corpse, and I thought the way they handled the blood evidence was a particularly nice touch—instead of trying to make the blood a realistic reddish brown, Kevin and Casey used washable paint in a vivid hot pink, with blood pools cut out of matching construction paper.

"You couldn't find any blood-red paint and paper?" Amber asked. She was leaning against the wall of the room right beside Kevin. In fact, that had become her default mode, hanging around near Kevin. Or, perhaps more accurately, hanging around wherever she was had become his default mode. Kevin didn't wear his emotions on his sleeve—in fact, he usually kept them buried deep under several layers of sarcasm and cynicism—but anyone who knew him could tell he wasn't indifferent to Amber's charms.

"The pink was a deliberate choice," Kevin said.

"To match the flamingo?"

"To avoid triggering anyone," Kevin said. "I mean, what if someone here has actually had to witness a bloody crime scene?"

"If someone would be triggered by a bunch of red paint and construction paper, maybe they need to work on getting over it," she said. "Toughen up so they can handle the next curveball life throws them."

Kevin frowned slightly, as if he didn't quite like this attitude. I didn't like it myself.

And Amber noticed his expression.

"Don't mind me," she said, smiling and patting his arm. "With everything that's happened over the last few years, I've had to grow a pretty tough shell."

That seemed to satisfy Kevin, but I wasn't sure how I felt about it. I made a mental note to see what else I could find out about Amber.

And almost immediately found myself feeling slightly guilty. It was the season of peace on Earth and goodwill to all—was I suddenly turning into a grinch?

No, just being a protective aunt. My sister, Pam, Kevin's mother, had married an Australian architect and lived in Sydney—on the other side of the world. She'd never come right out and said it, but I knew she expected me and Mother to be there for her kids who'd settled in the US, even though they were all adults now.

And I well remembered how stressful it had been when I'd had to introduce Michael to the sprawling hordes of the Hollingsworth clan, Mother's family. If it turned out that Kevin was serious about Amber, he might be grateful to have a trusted ally who could say, "Don't worry—I've checked her out and it's all fine."

Kevin and Casey had obviously enjoyed creating their crime scene, throwing in a lot of silly props like a rubber chicken, a whoopie cushion, and a toy gun that, when you pulled the trigger, emitted a large bright red flag with Bang! printed on it. I had fun with it, too. I was trying to follow Cordelia's instructions and take lots of pictures, but I had long since run out of interesting ways to take photos of the speakers, the audience, and the groups of conference attendees chatting between sessions. And my photos of Horace working the crime scene were all the more amusing since he maintained an utterly serious demeanor. He photographed the bits of evidence just as he would at a real scene. He explained about securing evidence in the proper container—usually brown paper bags. He demonstrated dusting for fingerprints, swabbing for DNA, and using various chemicals to determine the presence of blood. And along the way, he explained a lot of the ways less savvy and methodical criminalists could mess up a case.

It was great fun. But it had been a long day, and I wasn't disappointed when he eventually wrapped up his presentation and I could head for home. When I walked out of the meeting room, I was momentarily surprised to see how dark it was outside the big glass wall in the Gathering Area. It was only a little past five. But, of course, tomorrow was the winter solstice. That made today the second shortest day of the year, didn't it? I'd long ago decided it was a good thing we celebrated the Christmas season with light and song, to brighten what could otherwise be a rather dark and depressing time of year. Even so, I was glad to be heading home. Cordelia had been wise, declaring that Friday night's dinner was on your own.

Of course, I suspected the boys would want to hang around the hotel. If I couldn't talk them into leaving now—

"Mom?"

Josh, Jamie, and Adam appeared, all three struggling into their coats, hats, gloves, and scarves.

"You're impatient to leave?" I tried not to sound surprised.

"We volunteered you to take Gran-gran to see the Christmas lights," Jamie said. "And then drop Adam off at his house before we go home."

"Sounds like fun," I said.

"Ready when you are." Cordelia appeared, holding not only her own wraps but also mine. "The boys are going to make sure you take me to see all the best decorations."

"And Dad's fetching dinner," Josh said. "He won't say what, but he promises we'll all like it. Probably pizza again."

"But that's okay," Jamie said quickly, no doubt worried that I'd interpret Josh's comment as a criticism. "We really like pizza."

"I never say no to pizza," I replied.

So we all piled into the Twinmobile and set out to see the Christmas decorations.

Chapter 10

We started by heading away from town, toward the zoo, where Grandfather had gone all out with the decorations. In addition to an immense quantity of evergreens, red ribbons, and twinkly white lights, he'd set up a series of moving light displays atop the fence that surrounded the zoo and its parking lot. One set of lights outlined an elephant lifting and lowering a wrapped present atop his trunk. Another featured a seal balancing a spinning red ornament on his nose. A bear in a Santa costume emerged from a fireplace, held his belly and shook it, as if shouting "ho, ho, ho!" and then vanished into the fireplace again. And at the far end of the parking lot, in pride of place, a larger-than-life-sized Santa rode in a sleigh pulled by the eight rank-and-file reindeer, with Rudolph at the front, his large red nose blinking on and off.

On the way back to town we passed by the New Life Baptist Church, where every single architectural feature of the building was outlined in multicolored lights that matched those on the soaring Christmas tree gracing the front lawn. And then by Trinity Episcopal, which didn't have quite so many lights, but made up for it with a display of three life-sized papier-mâché camels decked with elaborate bejeweled bridles and saddles, tethered to a wooden rail just outside the front door. Josh and Jamie, who had contributed significantly to the production of the camels, were justly proud of the display. So was I, as one of the parents who'd figured out how to waterproof them so we didn't have to haul them inside the sanctuary every time our weather apps predicted precipitation.

And then on to the town. By this far in the holiday season, I'd worked out my optimal route for showing visiting friends and family the sights. I knew which blocks were entirely decorated with over-the-top Christmas, Hanukkah, and nonpartisan winter decorations. I knew where to find quiet streets with mostly evergreens and a few window candles that added up to a look of old-fashioned charm. Instead of competing with each other, more and more townspeople joined forces with their neighbors to produce an increasing number of theme blocks, like the Christmas with Dinosaurs block and the *Charlie Brown Christmas* block.

We circled around to take a second look at one of my favorite houses, whose owners spent the first of November transforming their over-the-top house-and-yard Halloween decorations into the world's spookiest Christmas display. Skeleton Santa appeared to be grinning wildly as he climbed out of his black-and-silver sleigh, pulled by eight lively skeleton reindeer, and his spiderweb present sack was filled with grinning skulls and assorted toy bats. The skeleton nativity scene had been expanded with several skeleton sheep. But the new pièce de résistance was the skeleton Santa's workshop, with half a dozen skeleton elves—would they be skelves?—using bone hammers and saws to craft an amazing variety of creepy toys.

After that it was on to the town square—although not until

I'd reminded everyone that this close to the holiday, the tourist traffic would be incredible, so it would probably take at least half an hour to make the slow, one-way circuit around the square. But my passengers all thought it was worth it—after all, we'd get to see all the shops around the square, decorated to the nines . . . the several bands of singers and musicians in Dickensian costume, serenading the passersby . . . the giant Santa sitting on the edge of the town hall's roof, appearing to throw trails of light down at the onlookers . . . the life-sized nativity scene on the front lawn of the Methodist church . . . and of course the town Christmas tree, which either was or wasn't a smidgen taller than the National Christmas Tree, depending on whether the speaker thought exceeding that mark was a good thing or a bad thing.

It made a fine ending to our tour. We dropped Adam off at his house and headed home, eager to find out what Michael was bringing for dinner.

"We should have Christmas more often," Josh said.

"No, then it wouldn't be as special," Jamie countered. "I like it just the way it is."

We passed a few more Christmas decorations on the way home. The Washingtons, whose farm was only a little down the road from our house, had a giant star on top of their enormous barn, shedding light around the entire countryside. It certainly added a note of authenticity to the display Seth Early set up across the street from us—he dressed half a dozen secondhand store dummies as shepherds, and had them abiding in his field, surrounded by his sheep. Last year, he'd made the shepherds' robes out of something that was apparently irresistibly delicious to the sheep, who had nibbled repeatedly and succeeded in denuding their keepers long before the holiday season was over. I was relieved that this time around he'd reclothed the dummies in something the sheep had, so far, turned up their noses at.

Although something about the way he'd posed the shepherds this year made them seem a surly, feckless lot, lounging lazily against the fence, for all the world like a pack of aspiring juvenile delinquents taking a cigarette break between misdemeanors. But then, maybe this was true to life—nothing I'd ever heard about the first noel had ever suggested the shepherds were also angels. Only that after getting over being terrified by the angel's appearance they had been curious enough to hike into Bethlehem to check out the new arrival. Since that was exactly what most of my friends and neighbors would have done if the Nativity had been happening nearby—and, for that matter, exactly what I would have done—it made the shepherds all the more relatable.

"I'm going to freshen up before dinner," Cordelia said when we reached the house. "Boys, can you bring in those boxes I put in the back?"

She strode toward the house. I waited until I was sure the boys had heard her request, then followed, more slowly.

"There's no place like home." I didn't tap my heels together, like Dorothy in Oz. I didn't even say it out loud when I walked through the front door. But I think my sigh of contentment and relief was audible.

"Yes, it is rather spectacular, isn't it?" Rose Noire beamed happily up at the hall's elaborate Christmas decorations. "I'll let your mother know you like the new additions."

New additions? I glanced around. Probably a good thing to let Rose Noire relay my appreciation, since I had no idea what new additions I was supposed to be impressed by.

Mother, who was in charge of all our holiday decorations, believed in doing the hallway up as elaborately as possible, on the theory that a dramatic initial impression improved the whole tone of the house. This year she had gone in heavily for prisms and mirrors in addition to the usual evergreen, ribbons, and blown-glass balls. Prisms and mirrors turned our hall light fixture into a good impersonation of the kind of chandelier you'd find in an ornate turn-of-the-century opera house. Prisms and mirrors shared branch space with lights, glass balls, and garlands on the tall, narrow Christmas tree Mother had found to fit into a corner of the hall. Prisms and mirrors were scattered all along the evergreen and ribbon garlands that festooned the upper third of the hallway walls. And all of them reflected light and colored glass and red velvet and evergreen needles so the whole thing looked even more extravagant than usual.

But while the prisms and mirrors were new for this year, they'd been up for weeks, and if Mother had added more things for them to reflect, I had no idea what was new.

Maybe the boys would figure out what the difference was. They'd lingered by the Twinmobile, their heads bent together over Josh's phone. Probably conspiring with someone about presents. But now they entered with a burst of cold air and holiday spirits.

"This was a good day," Josh announced, as he hung up his coat.

"Yes," Jamie said. "It's always a good day when you get to go someplace you really want to go, and then get to leave exactly when you're ready to come home."

"So dinner on our own was a good choice for tonight?" I asked.

"Definitely," Jamie said.

"That depends on what we're having for dinner," Josh said, in his usual contrarian fashion.

"And that depends on your dad," I said, glancing at Michael, who had just appeared in the hallway.

"Food's in the library," he said. "I did a run to the Shack."

"Awesome." The Shack was a local favorite, a no-frills barbecue restaurant run by a branch of the Shiffley family. Josh knocked a couple of coats off the hall coat tree in his eagerness to get to the food.

"Thanks, Dad," Jamie said, as he helped me pick up the fallen coats.

"How'd it go?" Michael asked, as he greeted me with a quick kiss.

"Pretty well." I fell into step beside him as we headed for the library. "I was kind of worried—I've heard stories about true-crime fans being a little obsessive about the cases they're interested in and getting into flame wars and spats. But I didn't see any of that. Almost everyone there was sane and well-behaved."

"Almost everyone?"

"Only one real pain in the neck," I said. "And we managed to kick him out."

"Permanently? Or just for the day?"

"Cordelia didn't actually come right out and say so, but yeah, he's definitely out for the rest of this conference, and I expect he's banned for life."

"Good—oh, by the way, Iris Rafferty's having dinner with us," he added.

"Oh, good." I enjoyed Iris's company. She was a lovely woman and a good neighbor—technically one of our next-door neighbors, but out of sight, thanks to the several fields and stretches of woodlands between us. Lately, though, we hadn't seen as much of her. She'd become increasingly absent-minded—Dad was worried that at ninety she might be in the early stages of dementia—and her three children and one adult granddaughter had been taking turns staying with her. "Only Iris? She doesn't have any visitors?"

"Her granddaughter brought her by to drop off some

Christmas cookies," Michael said. "I invited them both to stay, but the granddaughter—her name's Mary-something, isn't it?"

"Merrilee," I said, and spelled it.

"Merrilee said she couldn't stay, but Iris can let her know when she wants to be picked up."

"Or we can drop Iris off," I said. "It's not far, and I think Merrilee's got a lot on her plate these days. She might enjoy having the night off."

"I guessed as much."

When we entered the library, the boys were already seated on the floor at Delaney's feet, inhaling enormous helpings of food while telling her, Rose Noire, and Iris Rafferty all about the conference. Well, mostly all about the Gadfly's cruel treatment of Ruth and the important part they'd played in revealing his crimes. I didn't begrudge them the spotlight, and their listeners appeared to be enjoying their tale.

"Ought to put that despicable wretch under the jail," Iris said. She was a tall, angular woman—she'd probably have been eye to eye with me at five ten before losing a few inches to aging and a mild case of what the old-timers would call dowager's hump and Dad would refer to as kyphosis. And she was still remarkably fit and active. Which probably didn't make Merrilee's job any easier. Iris's snow-white hair was pulled back in an old-fashioned bun, but anyone who mistook her for a sweet, old-fashioned little old lady would be in for a rude shock. She was wearing a red-and-white *Die Hard*–themed Christmas sweater over black yoga pants and sipping what I suspected was a very dry martini. Michael had learned to make them to her exacting specifications.

Michael and I filled our plates from the buffet he'd set up on one of the sturdy Mission-style oak tables in the library. I forced myself to take only small helpings of everything, but when the spread included ribs, pulled pork, barbecued chicken, brisket, steak fries, corn bread, hush puppies, corn on the cob, green beans, tossed salad, and several other sides, even the small helpings filled up my plate.

"Where's everyone else?" Delaney asked. "Michael brought enough to feed an army."

"We'll have good leftovers," Josh said, through a mouthful of corn bread.

"Planned-overs," Michael said. "I had no idea how many people would show, but I figured all of this will heat up just fine if we don't finish it all."

"Dad and Grandfather and Festus are all dining out with various people from the conference," I said. "Cordelia should be here—she rode home with me."

"She went up to take a nap," Rose Noire said. "I wouldn't be surprised if the nap turns into going to bed early. Today tired her out. I'm going to see if she wants me to bring up a tray. And your mother will be here later. She recruited Rob to take her shopping. They didn't say where, so they're probably doing presents for some of us. We can warm plates for them if they come home hungry."

"I told Horace to drop by when he got his dinner break," Michael said. "And to let the rest of the deputies know they were welcome, too. Everything here will heat up beautifully for the latecomers. But for now, let's savor the rare peace and quiet—and dig in."

And we did.

Chapter 11

Much as I enjoyed the lively crowds we normally had this time of year, I could also appreciate tonight's smaller gathering. When we finished eating, we packed up all the planned-over food and put it in the refrigerator, the freezer, or the pantry. We could easily nuke a plate for any late arrivals, but in the meantime we settled in on the deep, comfortable sofas in the living room, got a fire going, adjusted the volume on the little speakers that were pumping out carols, and enjoyed the evening.

Michael and the boys got out Settlers of Catan, one of their favorite board games, and were soon absorbed in their competition. Rose Noire began brushing the various dogs, who all seemed to have gone for a romp in the woods and come home with hundreds of sticky seeds tangled in their fur. I focused on trading neighborhood news with Iris.

"It's nice that you'll have Merrilee with you for the holidays," I said at one point.

"It is." Iris sipped her second martini. "She's a little bossy, but she means well. Seems to think I'm a helpless old lady and can't do anything for myself. Whole family seems to think I need more help than I really do."

"Better to have more help than you need than less," I said.

"Maybe," she said. "But I expect they'll be after me again to go into the nursing home. And you know how I feel about that. I've always said that the only way they're going to get me out of that house is feet first."

I nodded, but I didn't say anything. Caerphilly Assisted Living had an excellent reputation—and a very well-run independent living wing. But I understood how she felt, and no way I was going to get in the middle of that kind of family discussion.

"That's why Joe and I added that mother-in-law suite onto the ground floor," she said. "It was a good idea—I'd have had to move before now if I didn't have it. But we always thought we'd move into it together when one of the kids took over running the farm. Only none of them ever wanted to, and I don't think any of the grandkids are going to be interested, either."

I nodded. Iris had raised a lawyer, a CPA, and a nun with a doctorate in nursing, and was very proud of their accomplishments. But none of them had wanted to assume the management of the family farm when they were younger. And I didn't think any of them were likely to take it on as a second career after they retired.

"And I worry about what happens to the land when I go," she said.

"Can't your kids keep doing what you're doing now?" I asked. "You're renting out the land, aren't you?"

"To that young Shiffley boy," Iris said.

I smothered a laugh. Ben Shiffley was well into his thirties. He might even have hit the big four-O.

"And that's a fine arrangement for now," she said. "But I'm not sure my kids would want to keep it up after I go. The farm's pretty much their whole inheritance, you know—what if they don't want their money tied up in land they're not living on?

What if they decided to sell the land, and it fell into the hands of a developer? Someone who would bulldoze everything and put up a whole mess of ticky-tacky houses? Would you want something like that next door?"

I shook my head. I wasn't sure anyone would want to put up a subdivision this far out of town. But the town and the county had already fought off developers who'd wanted to convert farmland into golf courses or executive retreat centers. And I didn't want those next door, either.

"Or what if they sell it to one of those big agricultural corporations that pays more attention to profit than caring for the land and raising good, healthy food." Iris scowled at the thought. "That would be just as bad. Joe and I worked hard to get the land certified organic, and I took on Ben because he wanted to keep that up. But what happens when I'm gone?"

"Talk to my cousin Festus," I said. "I think he knows something about conservation easements."

Iris tilted her head, rather like a bird, and I deduced she was about to ask what the dickens I was talking about.

"It's a way of permanently protecting the land from development," I said.

"Even if it's sold to someone who wants to develop it?"

"Even then," I said. "Lets the owner farm or harvest timber, but no subdivisions and no Big Agriculture."

"I'd be interested in hearing about that," she said. "You tell Festus to come and see me when he's finished with this big conference your grandmother's running."

"I'll do that."

"Aren't you going to write it down in that notebook of yours?" she asked with a puckish smile.

"I'll do better than that," I said, as I pulled out my phone. "Efficiency rule I picked up somewhere. If doing something would take less than five minutes, don't write it down. Just do it. Saves time in the long run."

So I fired off a quick text to Festus, asking if he could plan to talk to Iris about conservation easements as soon as possible after the conference.

I hadn't even put my phone back in my pocket when he fired back a reply: "How's Monday, ten a.m.?"

"Perfect," Iris said.

Rose Noire seemed to have finished brushing Tinkerbell, Rob and Delaney's Irish wolfhound. As she started on Watson, Horace's visiting Pomeranian, Tink strolled over and put her enormous head in Iris's lap.

"Just push her away if you don't want to be doggified," I said.

"We're fine, Tink and I," she said. "I might get another pup myself. What do you take me for—a dog hater like that creep the boys were telling me about? You think Chief Burke's going to do anything about him?"

"Probably," I said. "You know how the chief feels about animals."

"Hmph." She didn't sound encouraged. Of course, her relationship with the chief and his officers was a little fraught these days. He and his deputies had been incredibly patient with her increasingly frequent strange calls to 911. They'd gotten used to her insisting that they arrest the aliens disguised as deer that were eating all the blossoms in her garden, or trying to file a missing persons report on Joe, the husband she'd buried several years ago. But then last summer she'd called Father Donnelly, the rector of St. Byblig's, and asked him to come out to her farm to perform an exorcism on someone who had been possessed by a demon. Father Donnelly had arrived to find Danny Shiffley, our local FedEx driver, sitting in one of Iris's kitchen chairs— bound, gagged, and more than a little damp, since Iris had been spritzing him repeatedly with a plant mister containing her homemade holy water. Danny thought the whole thing was a hoot, and had played along, not only letting Iris tie him up but writhing in mock agony every time she squirted him, but her family had been mortified. It was after that incident that her three children and Merrilee, her only adult grandchild, had taken turns staying with her—and trying, without success, to convince her to move into Caerphilly Assisted Living.

It was hard to accept that the Iris of the 911 calls was the same calm and articulate woman sitting beside me on the sofa, gently stroking Tink's head. And thinking clearly and logically about the land she loved so deeply.

It occurred to me to wonder whether Iris really believed in aliens and demonic possession or if this was some peculiar way of entertaining herself. And getting a little human attention to while away what had become an overly solitary life.

We should be inviting Iris over more, I decided. How much of her mental confusion came from isolation? Since the death of her husband and her own decision to give up her driver's license before the county took it away, she was probably a lot more isolated than she ever had been. If we made a point of inviting her over for dinner, once or twice a week . . . Well, it wouldn't be a magic cure. But maybe it would help her. And take away a little of the burden her children and granddaughter were carrying. And would she enjoy going with Mother to the Garden Club meetings? Or sharing her knowledge of local plants and traditional remedies at Rose Noire's monthly gathering with her fellow herbalists?

I'd sic Mother and Rose Noire on the case the next time I got the chance.

"I like your mother's decorating style," Iris said. "Merrilee thinks we should just stick a wreath on the front door and call it quits. I call that lazy."

"Maybe she's a big fan of minimalism," I suggested.

"I'm not," Iris grumbled. "Especially not at Christmas. Christmas decorations shouldn't be minimalist. They should look as if joy threw up all over your house."

I burst out laughing at that.

"Just don't tell Mother that's what her decorating style looks like," I said. "But I like your description."

"Not mine," she said. "Stole it from a meme on Facebook. Tell me something—how come your gran decided to have her conference so close to Christmas?"

"Well, if you want the boring, pragmatic answer, that was when she could get the hotel conference space," I said. "But even if that weren't the case, she thinks it's a good fit with the season."

"Talking about murder and mayhem?"

"Talking about justice and doing unto others," I said. "And I think Dickens would agree. Remember what he had the two portly gentlemen say to Scrooge: 'At this festive season of the year, it is more than usually desirable that we should make some slight provision for the Poor and destitute, who suffer greatly at the present time.' Because the people who get unjustly convicted do tend to be poor people rather than rich ones."

"No argument with that," she said. "I just thought she might get a better turnout if she held it some other time of year."

"It sold out at this time of year," I said. "Heaven knows how many people we'd have to turn away if we had it at a more convenient time."

Delaney had begun yawning shortly after we finished dinner and went to bed early. As did Rob, when he arrived home after taking Mother shopping. He seemed to be sharing most of her late-pregnancy symptoms.

"Boy, am I tired of having to sleep so much," he remarked.

Michael waited until Rob was out of the room to comment.

"Famous last words," he said.

"Yeah," Iris said, with a chuckle. "That'll change when the kid arrives. And the kid lucked out in the parent department, if you ask me. It should get good looks, no matter what side of the family it takes after, and they're neither of them stupid."

"Let's just hope common sense is a dominant gene," I said, which made her guffaw.

And she was right about the looks. Growing up, I'd been envious that Rob had inherited Mother's slender, elegant, blond appearance. In fact, I'd stayed envious, up until my uncanny resemblance to Cordelia had helped reunite Dad with the mother who had had to give him up at his birth. By the time Jamie and Josh had come along, I was content with the fact that they looked more like Cordelia and Dad than Mother—and more like Michael than either.

About the time the game of Settlers was over, I caught Iris yawning, so I recruited Michael and the boys to take her home.

I put on my most festive red flannel reindeer pajamas, turned on the electric mattress warmer Michael had given us last Christmas, and drifted off to sleep, after muttering, to anyone who might be poking their head in to see if I was still awake, "Merry Christmas to all, and to all a good night."

Chapter 12

Mother was opening her Christmas present from me. For some strange reason I couldn't remember what I'd gotten for her, so I was looking forward to finding out. And she was taking forever at the whole unwrapping part—carefully untying the wide red ribbon and smoothing out all the wrinkles, slowly teasing every bit of tape off, to avoid damaging the elegant gold-embossed paisley wrapping paper. She finally finished flattening the paper and began easing the lid off the box within. She lifted up the lid—

And began screaming! Her face distorted by terror, she leaped out of her chair and—

I woke up. Mother and the elaborately wrapped present were all part of a dream.

The screaming wasn't. It was real.

"What's wrong?" Michael mumbled, sitting up and scrubbing at his eyes.

"It's coming from the backyard." I was already out of bed and running to look out the window. Dawn had begun, but only just. In the room it was barely bright enough for me to keep from tripping—but outside there was enough light to see the figure running toward the back door from the direction of the barn. And to recognize the voluminous lavender wool cape that swirled around her.

"It's Rose Noire." I grabbed my bathrobe from where I'd tossed it, at the foot of the bed, and struggled into it as I headed downstairs with Michael on my heels.

When I reached the bottom of the stairs the door to the dining room opened and Rob peered out owlishly.

"What's happening?" he asked.

"No idea yet," I said. I raced through the hall and into the kitchen, where the screaming was now coming from. Michael and Rob followed me.

In the kitchen, Rose Noire had collapsed in the middle of the floor, holding her cell phone in a hand shaking so badly she was in danger of dropping it. If she was trying to make a call—

"Are you all right?" I asked. "What's wrong?"

"It was terrible!" She launched herself at me, dropping her phone and almost knocking me over. "I found a dead body behind the barn. A dead body in a pool of blood."

"A dead body?" I echoed, putting my arms around her and patting her back. "Who?"

"I don't know," she wailed. "No one I've ever seen before. And he was all bloody and horrible."

"Someone call nine-one-one," I said, glancing around. Rose Noire's phone had disappeared. She was probably sitting on it. "My phone's upstairs."

"I'll go get mine," Rob said, after patting where his right pants pocket would have been if his red flannel Grinch pajamas actually had pockets. "I could use Rose Noire's if—"

"Use the landline," Michael said, gesturing to where our wall phone hung. "Let me get my coat and I'll check out what she found."

He ran out of the kitchen. Rob nodded and strode across to the landline.

"What's wrong?" Delaney appeared in the doorway.

"There's a dead body behind the barn," Rose Noire said. "I went out to scatter some grain and let the chickens out, and I saw him."

"We don't know yet," Rob was saying into the phone. "I think Michael's going to go out and see."

"Michael and I," I corrected. I was already putting on the boots I kept by the back door.

"Honey, you should be in bed," Rob said. "Sorry. Debbie Ann, I was talking to Delaney," he added, talking into the phone again. "She's—wait, Delaney, you should—"

"I'm sitting, I'm sitting." Delaney sat down heavily in a kitchen chair, close enough that she could pat Rose Noire on the shoulder. "Let me stay here and help take care of Rose Noire."

"Oh, no," Rose Noire moaned. "I should be taking care of you! Are you—"

Michael ran back in.

"Coat and phone," he said, handing both to me.

"Rob, you stay here and take care of Rose Noire and Delaney," I said, as I struggled into my coat. "Fix them some tea."

I stood, lifting up Rose Noire with me, and steered her into another kitchen chair, shoving it against Delaney's chair as I did. Delaney reached out and caught Rose Noire in a bear hug. Rob, still talking on the phone to Debbie Ann, the dispatcher, stretched the cord to its limit so he could turn the burner on under the teakettle Rose Noire always kept filled and ready to go.

"Debbie Ann says if you're going out to check on what Rose Noire saw—" Rob began.

"It *was* a body," Rose Noire muttered, as if she thought we were doubting her. "It *was*."

"Of course," Delaney said. "You should know. Who was it?"

"I don't know," Rose Noire said. "Not anyone I've ever seen."

"Debbie Ann thinks maybe I should hang up and you should call her on your cell phone," Rob went on. "So you can give her firsthand information. She has deputies and an ambulance on the way."

"Good idea," I said, as I followed Michael out the back door.

We both stopped on the back stoop, just for a few seconds, absorbing the shock of how cold it was. I had my cell phone in my hand, and I took a moment to check the temperature—nineteen degrees Fahrenheit—before calling 911.

"Meg, what's going on?" Debbie Ann asked.

"No idea yet," I said, as I followed Michael down the steps. "We're going to check out where Rose Noire reported finding the body."

"Be careful," she said. "Vern will be there in ten minutes."

I noticed that she didn't warn me not to go out to see the body. I had an answer ready if she did—we didn't yet know that the bloody body Rose Noire had seen was actually dead. What if it was an injured person who needed first aid?

She had probably already thought of that. Or maybe she just knew me well enough to know nothing she said would keep me from going out to see what was happening.

"The ambulance is on the way," she said. "In case whoever Rose Noire found isn't actually dead. Of course, if it really is a dead body, the chief will want to know. And your dad."

"We're almost at the barn," I said. "Rose Noire said it was behind the barn. I'll let you know what we—"

I rounded the corner of the barn, almost running into Michael, who had stopped stock still. I stepped sideways so I could see what he saw, and couldn't help gasping.

"Meg? What's wrong?"

"There's definitely a dead body. Call Dad and the chief."

The Gadfly was lying on the ground in a pool of blood. I didn't see any wounds, but his eyes were open and staring, and I wasn't sure how anyone could survive after losing that much blood. But he'd probably lost all he was going to lose—the pool wasn't spreading. In fact, were the edges of it starting to freeze? I took one more long, horrified look and then turned slightly so I could stop looking.

"Meg? Who is it?" I could hear keys rattling in the background, indicating she was sending out messages over the computer system. "Are you sure they're dead? Can you check for a pulse?"

"I can check his pulse if you like," I said. "But—"

"Let me do it," Michael said, moving toward the body.

"Michael's checking," I said. "But I'm pretty sure he's dead."

Michael circled around the body until he found a place where he could reach Norton's outflung left arm without stepping into the blood. He reached down, applied his fingers to the wrist, and grimaced slightly.

"No pulse," Michael reported. "And he's pretty cold."

"No pulse, and he's already cold," I relayed to Debbie Ann. "And it's the Gadfly. A guy who was attending Cordelia's conference out at the Inn. He blogs under the name of Godfrey Norton, but that's not his real name."

"That explains why Rose Noire didn't recognize him," Michael murmured.

"An alias?" Debbie Ann asked.

"More like a pseudonym," I said. "His real name's something longer and more complicated. Gustave something. Hang on, let me see if I can remember it."

"Vern can check his ID when he gets there," Debbie Ann said. "Or we can check with the Inn."

"Yes," I said. "But I should be able to remember it."

I closed my eyes and searched my memory. Cordelia sternly telling the Gadfly to leave the Inn. She'd called him by his real name. Same initials as Godfrey Norton.

"Niedernstatter," I said finally. "Gustave Niedernstatter. But don't ask me how to spell it."

"And he is—was—staying at the Inn."

"Not any longer," I said. "Ekaterina kicked him out for bad behavior, around lunchtime yesterday. I had no idea he was still in town. Or why he was out here at our house."

"Vern's nearly there."

I nodded, then realized she couldn't see that.

"Right," I said. "I can see his lights."

Vern had his cruiser's flashing lights going, but no siren. I wondered if they did that out of consideration for the people who were still sleeping, or just to minimize the odds of nosy on-lookers showing up to complicate the crime scene.

"The chief's on the way, too," Debbie Ann said. "And your dad. And Horace. But stay on the line with me until Vern's there to secure the crime scene."

"Will do," I said.

"When Vern gets here, maybe you should go back inside," Michael said. "Check on Rose Noire and Delaney."

"Probably more useful if I stay out here, at least for a little while," I said. "Not that going back inside where it's warm doesn't sound heavenly, but at least I can tell Vern a little bit about who he is. And who might have had it in for him."

"Fair enough," he said. "But as soon as Vern gets here, I'm going back in to get your hat and gloves. And maybe a sweater to layer in under the coat."

"Great idea," I said. "And as soon as I've briefed Vern, I'm going back in to get dressed in something warmer." At least my coat had a hood, and nice, deep pockets into which I could shove my hands, but however cozy my flannel Christmas pajamas might be when I was tucked up in bed, they weren't warm enough for tonight's sub-freezing air.

Vern's cruiser had parked by the road, and it was light enough that we could see him striding rapidly across the yard toward us. And not that far behind him was the chief. Vern stopped in the middle of the yard and waited for the chief to catch up with him before continuing on to where Michael and I stood.

I realized, with relief, that I wouldn't need to brief the chief on who Norton was. I could go inside that much sooner.

Vern and the chief both nodded a silent greeting as they came up to stand beside us and gaze at the body.

"Poor soul," the chief said. "Any idea what happened?"

"No idea," Michael replied.

"Me neither," I added. "Rose Noire found him. She came out to open the doors to the chicken coops and scatter feed for the hens. But she didn't say a lot about what happened. She's pretty upset."

"Practically hysterical," Michael said. "Which isn't like her."

He sounded puzzled. I was puzzled myself. Not that the gory sight in front of us wasn't shocking enough to upset anyone. I was deliberately not looking at the Gadfly and not letting myself think too much about what I'd seen when I had looked. And Rose Noire hadn't had as much exposure as I had to Dad's enthusiasm for sharing the sometimes unsavory details of illnesses, crimes, and autopsies.

But she was nothing if not mellow and philosophical. And capable of any amount of empathy, not only for the victims of a crime but also for the perpetrator. Her usual reaction to a brutal crime was to say, somewhat tearfully, that a person had to have been hurt very badly to even think of doing something so cruel. Why did this upset her so badly?

I shoved the question out of my mind for now.

"You both look as if you're going to freeze to death," the chief said. "Why don't you go back inside, now that Vern and I have secured the scene. And we've got reinforcements on the way. As soon as your dad has pronounced and Horace gets started working the scene, I'll come in and interview you. And Rose Noire."

"Thanks," Michael said, through chattering teeth.

"Not going to argue with that," I said.

We walked briskly back toward the house.

In the kitchen, Rose Noire and Delaney were sipping steaming cups of tea. Delaney was rubbing Rose Noire's back with one hand. Rob was hovering nearby, looking anxious and awkward. He glanced up when Michael and I entered, and relief flooded his face. Rob was never any good at dealing with tears or tearful people.

"I'm going up to get dressed," Michael said. "Something tells me things will be a little busy around here for a while."

"I'll stay here with Rose Noire until the chief comes in," I said.

As I sat down at the kitchen table, across from Rose Noire and Delaney, I realized that Cordelia was here, rummaging in the refrigerator.

"If there's any of your fake vegetarian bacon in here, I can't find it," she said over her shoulder—talking, I assumed, to Rose Noire. "How about a nice hot bowl of good old-fashioned oatmeal?"

"That sounds wonderful," Delaney said.

I blinked in surprise. I'd never known Delaney to be a fan of oatmeal.

"I couldn't eat," Rose Noire said in a thin voice.

"I'm sure you don't want to," Cordelia said. "But you need to. You've had a shock. Tea helps, but you need solid food."

I wasn't sure oatmeal was what Dad would prescribe for shock. But Cordelia made it sound so logical and matter-of-fact that I wasn't the only one in the room nodding my agreement.

And Rose Noire did look better. Still trembling, but not sobbing hysterically. She looked up at me and tried to smile. She didn't quite succeed, but the effort reassured me.

"Meg, who is he?" she asked. "Who was he, I mean? And why did someone kill him in our backyard?"

"It's a guy named Gustave Niedernstatter," I said.

Cordelia froze, and turned around from the stove, a wooden spoon in one hand and a box of raisins in the other.

Chapter 13

"Gustave Niedernstatter?" Rob repeated. "Doesn't sound familiar. Do we know him?"

"He's—he was attending the convention down at the Inn," I said. "Remember how Cordelia and I were complaining about someone we called the Gadfly?"

Rose Noire nodded.

"That's him," I said.

"Oh, man," Rob muttered.

"Rose Noire, how did you happen to find him?" Cordelia turned back to her cooking, but I could tell her attention was on our conversation. A good thing she'd probably fixed oatmeal a few thousand times in her life. "Isn't it a little early to be out, even for you?"

"I have so much to do today," Rose Noire said. "And I woke up early, and I knew I wouldn't be able to get back to sleep, so I thought I'd start my usual chores. I went out to let the hens out, scatter food for them, and refill the bird feeders so Delaney could see her chickadees. Oh, dear. I didn't get to the feeders," she said. "Or the chickens. I should—"

"You should stay here and get some food in your system," Cordelia said. "It's only just getting light. The birds won't starve if they have to wait a little while longer."

"Rob, could you go out and do it?" Delaney asked. "It would make Rose Noire feel so much better."

"Right." Rob looked relieved to be given a job to do—one that didn't involve staying in the kitchen and dealing with a tearful cousin. He fled before Rose Noire could finish giving him instructions for how much of what feed to give the chickens and the chickadees.

"I'll go and help him." Michael had returned, dressed in jeans and a heavy fisherman's sweater. "Not sure he even knows where the chicken feed is."

"So, Rose Noire, go on," Cordelia prodded. She was alternating between stirring the oatmeal and chopping up the raisins, dried apricots, and walnuts she was going to add to it. "You went out to feed the birds and . . ."

"And he was lying there, behind the barn," Rose Noire said. "And I overreacted."

"Overreacted?" Delaney said. "I think it's perfectly reasonable to be upset, finding a dead guy in your own backyard."

"I just panicked," Rose Noire said. "I don't know what came over me. I should have had more empathy for his situation. Said a blessing over him or . . . something."

"Running in to sound the alarm sounds quite sensible to me," Cordelia replied.

"It hit you hard," I said. "Any particular reason?"

Rose Noire cocked her head as if listening for some small, inner voice.

"I was looking for an omen," she said finally.

Cordelia and Delaney reacted with puzzled frowns. But I'd known Rose Noire longer. I nodded my comprehension.

"Because today's not only practically Christmas, it's also the winter solstice," I said. "A day to make a new beginning."

"Exactly!" Rose Noire actually smiled at that. "It was so cold and dark, and I was trying to think positive thoughts. Honoring the shortest, darkest day of the year, while also thinking about the promise of the season. That today is the start of the return to light and love and warmth. And I'm having a little solstice celebration later today, with a couple of fellow Wiccans, and thinking about that made me happy. And then I saw him."

"You can do a cleansing later," Delaney said, patting Rose Noire's back again.

"Yes," Cordelia said. "The ritual will make you feel better."

"Actually, the ritual has already begun." I was peering out of the back window. Horace had joined the group by the side of the barn, and Dad was bouncing across the yard with his medical bag in hand. "Chief Burke and Vern Shiffley are standing vigil by the body. Dad's here. He'll pronounce the Gadfly officially dead, and then he and Horace will begin examining the scene. They're all playing their parts in the ritual. A secular one, of course, and one we'd rather never need. But it's some comfort, isn't it, to know the search for justice has already begun?"

"Yes." Rose Noire closed her eyes and let out a breath. "Yes. Thank you. That helps."

We heard a rap on the back door, which then opened to reveal Chief Burke. And Mother.

"Good morning, dear," Mother said, giving me a quick kiss on the cheek. "I came with your father." She repeated the greeting with Delaney, then pulled up a chair, sat down beside Rose Noire, and took both of her hands. "How are you doing, dear?" she asked.

"Better," Rose Noire said, in a voice that still quavered a little. "But it was pretty awful."

"May I take your coat?" I asked the chief.

"Give it a minute, if you don't mind," he said. "I need to warm up a bit."

"There's hot tea," Cordelia said. "English breakfast tea," she added as she filled a mug for him. The chief looked relieved at the news that we weren't trying to dose him with one of Rose Noire's allegedly healthy but definitely noxious herbal blends.

"Thank you," he said, wrapping his hands around the mug. "Meg, may I take over your dining room for a little while? For interviewing the witnesses and such."

"You'll have to take over the library instead," I told him. "We've turned the dining room into a bedroom until Delaney's allowed to do stairs again."

"Roger. The library it is." He seemed to be studying Rose Noire.

"Why don't you let Meg fill you in on what she saw?" Cordelia suggested. "While I get a hot breakfast into Rose Noire. She's had a shock."

"I'll be fine," Rose Noire said, with a tremulous smile.

"Eat your oatmeal," the chief said, smiling back. "We'll talk soon."

So the chief and I went down to the library.

"Rose Noire seems to be taking this rather hard," he said, when we were well out of earshot of the crew in the kitchen.

"It's the winter solstice," I said. "She thinks it's a bad omen, finding a body on the solstice."

"A bad omen at any time." He shed his coat and sat down at one of the sturdy oak tables. Then he took out his notebook and looked up at me expectantly. "And you could have knocked me over with a feather when Debbie Ann told me who the victim was. I'm going to do what I can to keep our investigation from interfering with your grandmother's conference—"

"But the murder investigation takes priority over the conference," I said. "She'll understand."

"Ah, but will the attendees feel that way?" he asked.

"If we spin it right, they'll be enchanted," I said. "At least ones who are here mainly because they're true-crime addicts. I bet a lot of them will be excited at being part of a real live murder investigation."

"We can always hope," he said. "So, I caught a little bit of what Mr.—" He glanced down at his notebook.

"Niedernstatter," I supplied.

"What Mr. Niedernstatter was up to at the conference," he said. "Let's make sure I know the whole of it. And do you have any idea why he was out here at your house last night?"

"After Cordelia kicked him out, he started calling and texting her," I said. "Alternating between pleading with her to let him back in and threatening what he'd do if she didn't. She blocked him, and then he started doing the same thing with Kevin, and after Kevin blocked him, it was my turn. I must have ignored half a dozen calls and who knows how many texts before I blocked him. So I expect he wanted to talk to one of us. Or all of us. And came out here to do it. No idea how he figured out where to find us. Or why he'd think we'd be willing to talk to him at all, much less in the middle of the night."

"He was probably killed before midnight," the chief said. "According to your father's preliminary estimate. That makes it a little less implausible."

"But no less annoying." I sighed. "That he'd come out here at all."

"Might help Rose Noire's state of mind," he said, "if we point out he was killed last night, not on the solstice itself."

"That's true," I agreed.

"And it would be nice to know where he was between the

time Ms. Cordelia kicked him out and his death," he went on. "I checked with the county attorney yesterday afternoon and she gave me the go-ahead to charge him with animal cruelty. I was going to haul him in and do that, but even though I had a countywide BOLO on him, we never found him."

"I bet he guessed you were after him," I said. "And made himself scarce."

"No doubt. And when I get his phone records, the pings may shed some light on where he's been keeping himself."

"And when he arrived here," I added. "He and his killer. Unless, of course, whoever killed him pays enough attention to the role cell phone data plays these days in catching criminals."

"True." The chief winced slightly. "Nowadays, anyone who pays the slightest attention to true-crime stories knows enough to turn off their phones before going on a crime spree."

"And most of the attendees pay a lot of attention to it," I said.

"So worst case, Mr. Nieder . . . Nieder . . ."

"Niedernstatter," I said. "But wouldn't it make sense for us to keep calling him Mr. Norton? Because most of the suspects and witnesses you're going to be interviewing won't have any idea of his real name."

"That makes sense." He sounded relieved. "Worst case, it's possible that Mr. Norton turned off his phone when he left the conference and his whereabouts for the last twelve hours will forever remain a mystery."

"That would be unfortunate," I said. "But I doubt if he did. Most people have trouble living without their phones for half an hour, much less half a day. I bet you'll be able to track him."

"Hope so." He opened his notebook. "So let's go over what you observed at the conference—because half the attendees there are going to be suspects. All the ones he was harassing, both before and at the conference."

"Yeah, pretty much the immediate world," I said.

"Which means this won't be an easy homicide to solve."

"Are they ever easy?" I asked.

"They can be," he replied. "Back in my Baltimore homicide days, so many of them were either drug- or gang-related. You knew who the players were and what beefs they all had with each other. Half the time you had confidential informants who were happy to curry favor by spilling everything they knew, and it wasn't hard to figure out who did it. Between those and the domestics, a lot of them were easy. This won't be."

I nodded. I could see what he meant. He had a hotel full of people who were mostly respectable, law-abiding citizens with a greater than average interest in crime. This was going to be tough.

"But maybe we'll get lucky." He deliberately replaced his frown with an expression of intent interest. "Fill me in."

"Okay—here goes."

I gave him everything I could remember about the Gadfly's clashes with Ezekiel Blaine, Amber Smith, Ginny and Janet, the redheads, Festus, Grandfather, Cordelia, and at least half of the hotel staff and conference volunteers. And I worked in the Gadfly's real name a couple of times, both so the chief could learn it and so I felt more comfortable pronouncing it myself.

"An equal opportunity jerk," the chief said when I'd finished.

"Maybe we're looking at a real-life replay of *Murder on the Orient Express*," I said, only half joking.

"I think if a crowd of Mr. Norton's detractors had convened behind your barn to do him in, you'd probably have noticed."

Someone knocked on the library door.

"Come in," the chief called.

Cordelia entered.

"I'm heading over to the Inn now," she said. "Obviously your investigation takes priority, but I'd like to do what I can to keep my conference on track. And you're not the only scheduled speaker who's going to be pretty busy with this investigation."

"Horace, Dad, and Kevin, for sure," I said.

"I've already arranged with Ekaterina to make a meeting room available for you to use if you want to interview people at the hotel," Cordelia went on. "I expect most of the people you'll be wanting to talk to will be there, so it will be a lot more efficient than ferrying them out here or even down to your station."

"And it will minimize the interruptions to your conference." The chief had a twinkle in his eye. "That does sound like an excellent idea."

"Chief?" Michael had appeared in the doorway between the library and the sun porch. "Horace and Meg's dad say they're finished with the body, and do you want to see it—him—one last time before the ambulance takes him away?"

"I probably should. Thanks."

Michael nodded and ducked out again. The chief stood and began struggling back into his wraps.

"I'll see you over at the Inn," he said to Cordelia, who nodded and strode out. "I'm sure with the dining room occupied, you'll want the library back sooner rather than later," he added to me.

"No rush," I said. "We're not having any big gatherings this year—not here at the house, anyway."

"Good to know," he said. "I'll stay till I've interviewed Rose Noire and anyone else who might have seen anything here, and I'll let you know when I leave for the Inn. Or will you be heading over there to do whatever Cordelia has on your plate?"

"I have no assigned responsibilities at the conference," I said. "In fact, the main job Cordelia gave me was to help keep Norton in line, but whoever did him in just took care of that. Unfortunately," I added, in case it sounded as if I was happy about his death.

"Alas," he said, before striding out through the sunroom. Michael returned.

"Of all days for something like this to happen," he said.

"Christmas day would be worse," I said. "Or Christmas eve."

"True," he said. "But are you still okay with me going up to Dulles to deal with Mom?"

"I'm fine with it," I said—although in truth I'd forgotten all about it in this morning's excitement. The last couple of years, Michael's mother had grown fond of taking a Christmas cruise, then joining us for a belated holiday celebration sometime in January. This year she was sailing out of Baltimore but hadn't found any cheap flights from Newport News to BWI. So she'd recruited Michael to pick her up at Dulles, take her to lunch, spend some time with her, and then deliver her to the Baltimore Harbor in time for her boarding. Michael had actually been looking forward to having a brief get-together with his mother— and also to whiling away the several hours of driving with a new audiobook.

"And don't forget, you'll be picking up Delaney's mother while you're up there," I added. "Give your mom my love and tell her we're looking forward to seeing her for New Year's."

"You're sure?"

"Just try to make it back for the concert," I said. "And the fireworks, of course."

"Keep me posted on what's happening here," he said. And then, after a quick farewell kiss, he hurried off.

I glanced at the craftsman-styled clock that sat on a nearby shelf. Nearly nine o'clock. Only nine o'clock. It had only been around two hours since Rose Noire's screams had awakened me, but it already felt like a day and a half.

And I should check on Rose Noire. And Delaney. And maybe even Rob.

Chapter 14

I took a few of the deep, calming yoga breaths Rose Noire would have recommended if she had been in her normal frame of mind, and headed for the kitchen.

I found all three of them sitting around the kitchen table eating some of Michael's planned-overs from the Shack. Normally, Rose Noire would have protested that it wasn't a suitable breakfast, but she was happily devouring corn on the cob, coleslaw, hush puppies, baked beans, macaroni and cheese, and—in a new culinary development—fresh fruit. I spotted mandarins, pomegranates, and grapes.

"Someone sent us a fruit basket?" I asked, snagging a grape.

"Caroline Willner," Delaney said. "And not just a fruit basket—more like a fruit crate. It arrived just now. And she says she's sorry she can't be here for Christmas, but she and her daughter are having a great time on their cruise, and she'll see us for New Year's. Have a pomegranate."

Just then the doorbell rang.

"Save one for me," I said. "I'll go see who it is."

"Probably more cops," Rob said.

"I think the whole county force is out there already," Delaney said.

I didn't hear Rob's reply—I was already halfway to the front door. I opened it to find a young woman standing on our front step. She looked nervous, or maybe anxious. And vaguely familiar. I had the feeling if I were more awake, I'd have recognized her.

"Ms. Langslow?"

"What can I do for you?" I asked. "And sorry—I know we've met, but I'm not quite awake yet—"

"Merrilee Rafferty," she said. "I'm—"

"Of course," I said, shaking her outstretched hand. "Iris's granddaughter. I heard you were staying with Iris, but I didn't get to see you when you dropped her off last night."

"May I bring in Gran?" Merrilee asked. "She wants to talk to Chief Burke, and she thought he might be here."

"He is," I said. "But he's pretty busy at the moment. You may not have heard—"

"That you had a murder here last night," Merrilee said. "I heard. And Gran heard—that's why she wants to talk to the chief."

"How in the world did she hear that already?" I wondered.

"Police band radio," she explained. "Her new hobby. And she thinks she has some information that might help the chief with his investigation."

Her tone suggested that she didn't think her grandmother's information would be all that helpful. I could understand her attitude. And I wondered how the chief would feel about having Iris as a possible witness. Had she really seen something, or would this turn out to be like the aliens and the exorcism?

Luckily it was the chief, not me, who had to figure that out.

"Okay if I bring her in?" Merrilee asked.

"Of course," I said. "Do you need any help?"

"Not really. She's pretty spry for ninety. That's part of the problem. If I turn my back for five minutes . . ." She let the thought trail off and shook her head. Then she hurried back down the walk to where she'd parked her car, right by the opening where our front walk ran through the hedge. Iris began getting out of the car before Merrilee even reached it.

While they were making their way back to the door, with Merrilee trying to offer her arm for support and Iris sharply elbowing her away and occasionally flourishing her cane, I texted the chief to let him know what was up.

"Merry Christmas," I said when they reached the front door.

"Same," Iris said as she strode inside. "Where's Henry Burke? I need to tell him about the ninjas."

"Ninjas?" I echoed.

"Gran thinks she saw ninjas last night," Merrilee said.

"And Merrilee thinks I was hallucinating," Iris said. "She'll see. Where is he?"

"In our library," I said. "Would you like to have a seat and—"

But Iris knew the way, and she was off, hobbling briskly across the front hall, with the rubber tip of her cane making muted thuds on the hardwood floor.

"They probably parked down by the creek," she said over her shoulder. "And then snuck back through the countryside. They were heading for your house."

"For our house? Last night?" I followed Iris. I knew better than to try to help her, but at least I could try to catch her if she fell. Or pick her up if catching failed. "What time?"

"Late," she said. "About the time the Johnny Carson show started."

"Gran," Merrilee said from behind us. "Johnny Carson isn't on the air any longer."

"Of course he isn't," Iris said. "Been dead for years. Decades.

But his show's still on. They've got some young whippersnapper taking his place. Never can remember his fool name. Doesn't hold a candle to Carson—nowadays half the time the show puts me to sleep. But maybe that's a silver lining."

She'd reached the library door, gave a perfunctory knock, and flung it open. Chief Burke and Horace looked up from the table where they'd been examining some bit of evidence.

"Mrs. Rafferty," the chief said. "Meg tells me you have some information for me."

"I do indeed." Iris stumped over to the nearest library table and sat down. "Should break your case wide open."

"I look forward to hearing it." The chief seated himself across the table from Iris, took out his pocket notebook, and sat with an expression of attentive anticipation, as if he really thought Iris's information would turn out to be useful. And you never knew—maybe it would.

"Last night, I'd already gone to bed," Iris said. "And I was watching Joh—watching one of those blasted late shows." She shot a "so there" glance at Merrilee. "And I heard noises in the backyard, so I got up and grabbed my binoculars and went to see what was up."

"And what did you see?" A good thing the chief was used to all her alien sightings—it would help him keep a straight face when he heard her answer.

"Ninjas!" Iris sat back in her chair with a triumphant expression, as if she'd delivered the telling blow in some verbal combat.

"Ninjas?" the chief echoed.

"Those Japanese assassin guys," Iris explained.

"Yes, I'm familiar with ninjas," the chief said.

"You've seen them, too?" Iris asked, eagerly.

"Not personally," the chief said. "But I know what they are.

How could you tell they were ninjas? I mean, can you give me a description?"

"Dressed all in black, of course," Iris said. "With one of those ski-mask things terrorists always wear."

"I see." The chief scribbled in his notebook. "How many of them were there?"

"I only saw the one," Iris said. "But they usually travel in groups, don't they? Covens. Isn't that what you call them?"

"I think that's for Wiccans," I said. "I don't know what you call a group of ninjas."

"A murder?" Iris suggested.

"That's for crows," I said. "Which they might greatly resemble, given the black outfit and all, but—"

"A skulk," Horace said. "That's what you use for foxes, but I think it fits."

"I think a skulk sounds very suitable," the chief said—a little hastily, since he was familiar with our family's ability to conduct hours-long discussions about collective nouns. "If we find out there's a better term, I can update the records. So you observed one ninja crossing your yard and deduced the presence of a skulk."

"That's right." Iris sat forward again. "Except he wasn't exactly crossing the yard—he was creeping along through the trees behind the house. You know how there isn't a clean line between where our backyard ends and the woods start," she added, looking at me. "It just gradually changes from no trees to some trees to mostly trees, and eventually you're in the woods. He was in the some-trees part."

I nodded.

"I see." The chief looked torn. On the one hand, this could very well be a useful bit of evidence. On the other hand, Iris, with all her talk of aliens, demons, and ninjas, wasn't exactly the most reliable information source in town. And she'd be a disaster on the witness stand. "Do you think you could identify the . . . er . . . ninja in a lineup?"

"Hell, no," Iris said. "It was dark, and my eyesight's not that good in the daylight."

"Understandable," the chief said, in a soothing tone. He sounded almost relieved.

"But you might be able to do something with the video." Iris pulled out a sleek new iPhone with a *Dr. Who*–themed case.

"You took video?" The chief sounded surprised.

"You didn't tell me that," Merrilee said.

"You'd be surprised what we old fogies can do." Iris was pushing buttons on her phone. "It's not going to be great—moon was only half full, and he was pretty far away. But maybe you can do all those magic computer things they do on *CSI*."

"I'm afraid network television often exaggerates what even the best of evidence technicians can do," the chief said. "But I can assure you, we'll do everything we can to identify the subject of your video."

Iris held up her phone and we all edged closer to get a better look. The video wobbled in and out of focus for a few seconds, then settled down. And yes, it did look as if someone dressed all in black was creeping stealthily through scattered tree trunks. Moving from left to right, which was the direction an intruder would be taking to reach our house if you spotted him from one of Iris's back windows. But did it really look like someone wearing a black ski mask? Or had Iris's words influenced me into seeing a ski mask where there was only shadow?

"Well, there was definitely someone there," Horace murmured.

"The trick is identifying that someone," the chief said.

"So you don't think it's going to be useful." Iris looked disappointed.

"Actually, it could be very useful," the chief said. "We may not be able to identify your . . . ninja from the video—though we'll certainly try. But assuming the time on your phone is reasonably accurate—"

"Reasonably accurate?" She snorted. "It's dead accurate. They tell me the damn thing checks with the stars or something and updates itself if it's gained or lost time. I don't even have to do anything when we go through that stupid time change twice a year. But how's that going to help you?"

"Anyone who can prove they were back at the hotel when the video was taken isn't going to be your ninja," the chief said.

"And isn't the killer," Iris added, in a triumphant tone.

"We won't know that for sure," the chief said. "We'd know your ninja came over here, but we'd still need to prove he was actually the one who attacked Mr. Norton."

"Yeah, right," Iris said. "What are the odds of two sinister intruders sneaking around out here in the boonies in the middle of the night?"

"Around here?" Horace murmured. "Higher than you'd think."

"Two unrelated intruders in one night would be quite a coincidence," the chief said. "And I'm not a big fan of coincidences when they come anywhere near my crime scene."

Iris nodded as if to say that this was more like it.

"But I'm also not big on jumping to conclusions." He glanced over at Horace. "Horace can check out your yard to see if the intruder left any trace. And to assess what kind of trace evidence he might have picked up."

"Yes," Horace said. "Remember Locard's exchange principle."

"Remember it?" Iris said. "I've never even heard of it."

"Edmond Locard was a pioneering forensic scientist," Horace said. "They called him the Sherlock Holmes of France. His exchange principle means that when someone commits a crime, they always leave something behind at the scene and take something away."

"Even if the only thing left behind is footprints, that could be useful," the chief said. "And even if we don't find footprints, we can also examine the footwear of our suspects to see if any of them have picked up trace evidence that would indicate they'd been sneaking through your yard. Can you send us that video?"

"No idea how to do that, but here." She shoved her phone into my hand. "You do it."

She rattled off her phone's passcode, and I navigated to the video in question.

"Is it okay if I send myself a copy, too?" I asked. "I could take a look and see if I recognize the ninja."

"That would be acceptable," the chief said. "Since I know you'll tell me immediately if you do identify the intruder."

"And copy Kevin with it," Horace said. "He's light years ahead of me when it comes to enhancing digital images. And he could—wait! Doesn't Kevin have security cameras set up here? If he caught the ninja on camera—"

"I've already asked," the chief said. "He does have cameras here, but they're mostly designed to spot anyone approaching the house. He's going to do a more in-depth search, but so far he hasn't yet found any trace of an intruder on any of last night's footage, which suggests that the killer struck before Mr. Norton got close enough to the house to be within camera range."

"Want to bet that by New Year's Kevin will have a whole bunch of new cameras set up?" Horace asked. "Covering every square inch of the backyard?"

"If you're betting it won't happen till close to New Year's, I'll take that bet," I said. "I'm betting he'll take time off from the conference to install them."

"The time when Mrs. Rafferty shot her video may help Kevin

narrow down his search in the video footage," the chief said. "Horace, why don't you go over now and work the scene in Mrs. Rafferty's backyard, And Meg, maybe you could go along, in case he needs an extra pair of hands. We're a little understaffed to begin with, and this is going to take a lot of my deputies' time."

"No problem." Actually, I realized that the chief wanted me along to watch Horace's back. When he was focusing on a crime scene, it wouldn't take ninja-level stealth skills to sneak up on him. He could easily ignore a herd of elephants crashing through the underbrush, and there was a killer on the loose. A killer with a history of creeping around our neighborhood.

"Do you need for us to be there?" Merrilee asked. "After all of last night's excitement, Gran's heart rate is a little wonky, and I want to take her into town to get it checked out."

"No use in that," Iris said. "Dr. Steiner's on vacation. Sunning himself in Florida, the lucky dog."

"Yes, I know," Merrilee said. "But we could see if someone down at the hospital could take a look at you."

"Hell, no," Iris said. "Damn place is probably a hotbed of germs this time of year."

"Isn't Dad dropping by pretty soon to brief you on his preliminary examination of the body?" I asked, turning to the chief. Actually, I was inventing this, but I knew Dad would gladly drop by if he thought there was any chance Iris needed him. "While he's here, why don't we ask him to check Iris out. Just to ease Merrilee's mind," I added, before Iris could interrupt.

"No need for all that fuss." Iris crossed her arms and scowled at us.

"Yes, but while he's doing that, he could see if you're a good candidate for that forensic hypnosis he's been working on," I said. "Wouldn't that be a good idea?" I added, turning to the chief. "It would certainly be a help if Iris could remember any more details about the ninja."

"It's definitely worth trying." The chief managed a straight face. "If Mrs. Rafferty is willing."

"Sounds like fun," Iris said. "Count me in."

Actually, Dad wasn't all that skilled at hypnosis, but occasionally he did manage to put one of his subjects under, and he and Iris would have fun trying.

"You got any more questions for me?" Iris said, turning to the chief.

"Not at present," he said. "But I'll come and find you if I think of any more. You're staying in town for the holidays, I presume?"

"Only sane thing to do," she said. "You seen how crowded the planes and trains get this time of year?"

"Very sensible," the chief said.

"So we'll stop bothering you and go wait for Dr. Langslow," Iris said, and led the way out of the library.

"Horace, let me know when you're ready to leave," I said. "I'll be in the kitchen grabbing a bite of breakfast."

He nodded and went back to showing the chief some interesting bit of evidence. I left them to it.

"Have you eaten?" I asked Merrilee, as we followed Iris down the hall to the main part of the house.

"I was just about to fix some breakfast when Gran came in to tell me she had to talk to the chief," Merrilee replied.

"Come have a bite with us, then," I offered. "No one's had any time to cook yet this morning, so it's not technically a proper breakfast—"

"Are you offering leftovers from last night?" Iris asked. "Count me in. It's from the Shack," she added to Merrilee. "What's not to like?"

So Iris and Merrilee joined us in the kitchen, and Rose Noire was sufficiently recovered from her shock that she insisted on heating the food and serving us.

"When you're up to it," I told her, "the chief would like to interview you before he heads over to the Inn."

"Oh, dear," she said. "I'm really not looking forward to reliving all that."

"The sooner you get it over with the better," Mother said, in her most soothing tone.

"Don't think of it as reliving it," I suggested. "Think of it as pouring out all this morning's negative experience into the chief's strong and capable hands."

"Ooh," she said. "I like that."

"You're getting really good at that whole glass half full thing," Rob commented.

"What are you telling the chief about?" Iris asked. "Did you see the ninjas, too?"

"Ninjas?" Rose Noire echoed.

"She found the body," Delaney said. "And it was very upsetting," she added quickly, seeing the look on Iris's face. "We've agreed not to talk about it just yet."

"I'll fill you in later," I said to Iris.

"Meg?" Horace appeared in the doorway. "You ready to go?"

Chapter 15

"I'm helping Horace out with something," I explained, as I grabbed a last segment of clementine and stood.

"You go on, dear," Mother said. "I'll keep an eye on things here."

"And Rose Noire, the chief's ready for you in the library," Horace added.

"Go on and get it over with," Delaney said, patting Rose Noire's shoulder.

Rose Noire stood, took a deep breath to center herself, and walked out of the kitchen, head held high. Iris looked disappointed. I decided maybe it was a good thing Horace hadn't mentioned where he and I were going, or we'd have Iris trying to join in the fun. Or at least watching us through her binoculars from her back windows, which Horace might find distracting.

But we managed to escape the kitchen, leaving Merilee picking at a small plate of barbecued chicken and potato salad, while Iris chowed down on a plate piled high with ribs.

"I'd suggest taking separate cars," Horace said. "In case I get another call while I'm working the scene. But pretty much any call I got, I'd have to go past your house on my way to it."

"And I could walk home if need be," I said. "Or call someone for a ride." The road that led past our house dead-ended at the bank of Caerphilly Creek several miles farther on, with Iris's house being one of the few houses between us and the creek. Walking to the creek and back was one of the things I sometimes did when something had angered or upset me and I needed to calm down.

I wondered, briefly, if the chief had thought of searching for Norton's car down by the creek. If I had been planning to sneak through the woods to our house, I'd probably have parked there, behind the Spare Attic, a former textile factory that had been converted into self-storage units. Behind the Spare Attic, or possibly among the cars belonging to the residents of The Haven, a formerly run-down motel that Rob had bought and converted into cheap apartments for many of his junior employees.

But the chief had probably already thought of this. In fact, just after Horace and I pulled into Iris's driveway, I saw another police cruiser pass by, with Vern Shiffley at the wheel. He and I waved at each other. Horace either didn't notice or was too busy to wave. He hopped out of the cruiser and was now focused on the contents of its trunk. I could hear him talking to himself, nearly inaudibly, as he rummaged through all his forensic tools and supplies, picking out the precise selection that he'd need for working a crime scene in the woods. Or at least in the "sometrees" part of the yard, I thought, smiling as I remembered Iris's description.

I stood looking up at the house. It was an attractive white-frame farmhouse. Old, though not as old as our house, and not the least bit run down. I guessed maybe late Victorian, maybe early twentieth century. And big, though again not as big as our house. Two stories, and I could see a few dormer windows indicating that there was an attic, and a set of old-fashioned slanted metal doors that obviously led to the basement. A wide covered porch encircled the building—open along the front and sides of the house and screened in along the back. The mother-in-law suite had been added onto the left side, but they'd done a nice job of making it look as if it belonged to the rest of the house. And the whole thing looked in excellent condition—you couldn't tell that the addition was new, since the whole house had been recently painted and showed no visible need for repairs. Which was more than I could say for our house when we'd bought it. In fact, the only reason we could say it now was that we practically had the Shiffley Construction Company on retainer to fix all the damage regularly wrought by age, weather, and the comings and goings of a large number of friends and relatives.

Iris had a nice house. If it had been on the market when Michael and I had been house hunting, we'd have jumped at it. And I could see why she was worried about what would happen to it when she no longer occupied it. I had no idea how plausible her fears were that either a developer might build a subdivision on her farmland or a corporation might turn it from an organic family farm into a profitable but pesticide-laden environmental menace. But I could see someone trying to build a golf course here. Or some wealthy outsider buying the property, tearing down the beautifully maintained but old-fashioned farmhouse and replacing it with a honking big mansion. It was way too good for a tear-down, in my opinion, but it wouldn't pass muster with a buyer who wanted something sleek and modern. A buyer who would almost immediately begin complaining about the proximity of Seth Early's sheep, our chickens and llamas, and Dad's heirloom sheep, cows, and goats.

I was starting to sound like one of the old-timers, complaining about people who aren't from around here.

The place might not be going on the market soon—at least

not if Iris had anything to do with it. But would she feel differently if someone she knew and trusted approached her with an offer?

Someone like, for example, Rob and Delaney?

Or would she resent the idea, feeling we were trying to kick her out?

I tucked away the idea for later consideration and focused on what I was here for—helping Horace.

Just then Vern pulled his cruiser up beside Horace's and got out to join us.

"Hey, Horace. Hey, Meg," he called out. "Chief sent me to help out. He figured while you were working the scene, I could see if whatever evidence you find makes it possible to follow the intruder's tracks. See if he really went from here to Meg and Michael's place. And don't worry," he added, seeing Horace's slight frown. "I know how to hang back and not trample any evidence before you can collect it."

"That's fine," Horace said.

"By the way, Aida located the victim's car," Vern said. "Abandoned on a side road not that far from the entrance to the Inn."

"Interesting," Horace said. "So maybe Norton came here with his killer."

"Or the killer used his car to get back to the Inn," Vern said. "Or maybe Norton was killed elsewhere and dumped here."

"Pretty sure he was killed where we found him," Horace said. "Too much blood at the scene."

"That fits, actually," Vern said.

"You were headed down toward the creek," I said. "Did you find anything there?"

"Some tire tracks in that muddy place behind the Spare Attic," he said. "They'll probably turn out to be how our murder victim got here. I took some photos of them," he added to Horace, who had come to attention at the mention of tire tracks. "And I rigged a cover over them, the way you showed me you like, so they'll still be there waiting for you when we finish up here. Any other season, I'd just assume it was young folks looking for some privacy, but in this weather?" He shook his head.

"We can compare the tire tracks to Norton's car," Horace said.

"Yup," Vern said. "A pity the snow didn't start last night. That would make tracking pretty darned easy."

"Did the chief show you the video Mrs. Rafferty took?" Horace asked.

Vern nodded and held up his phone.

"Good," Horace said. "You can help me figure out exactly where the alleged ninja went, because all I see in the video is trees."

"That I can do," Vern said. "There are some pretty distinctive trees in that video." Trees were one of Vern's passions.

"If you say so." Unless they held a clue to a case he was working on, trees were mere scenery to Horace. "Any chance you two could carry some of my gear?"

Vern and I each shouldered one of the two sturdy carrying bags in which Horace had loaded his gear, leaving him freer to work. We began slowly approaching the area he wanted to examine—slowly because both he and Vern were using Iris's video to figure out exactly where Iris's ninja had passed through. Actually, it was mainly Vern doing the figuring.

I glanced around to orient myself. On what would be the left side of the house if you looked at it head-on—the side farthest from town—I could see a field where in season Ben Shiffley raised organic vegetables. Now, it was planted with red clover as a cover crop, and around its edges were the tall, dead stalks of the bee balm he planted in summer to attract pollinators.

Across the street you could see one of Seth Early's sheep pastures, though there weren't any sheep there at the moment. Which was unusual unless—I pulled out my phone and checked the weather app. The chance of snow later today had crept up to sixty percent, which explained why this pasture was empty. Seth liked to keep his flock closer to the barn when there was any chance of snow.

To the right of Iris's house was a small barn, now serving more as a combined garage and storage shed, neatly painted white to match the house. And behind the house and barn and to the right of the barn the open yard gradually gave way to the woods. Neither the barn nor any other features in the yard, like the picnic table, the bird feeders, or the sad empty chicken coop, appeared on the video. Just trees and the ninja.

"I think we're getting close," Horace said. "See that tree that looks as if it's winking at us?"

"The scarlet oak right beyond the dead tulip tree?" Vern asked.

"The tree that still has a bunch of dead leaves on it," Horace said, frowning. "And has two knothole things side by side at around eye level, one bigger than the other."

"Yup," Vern said. "That's the scarlet oak."

"If you say so."

"And yes, the ninja passed right by it," Vern added.

"Good. Thanks." Any annoyance vanished from Horace's voice. He was focused on the ground.

We progressed slowly through the scattered trees, with Horace in the lead, bent over double, scanning the leaf-scattered ground for anything that might be evidence. Vern followed a few yards behind him, using a pair of binoculars to look ahead and to either side, hoping to find the ninja's trail. I brought up the rear, laden with Horace's gear. It occurred to me that if Vern was here, I was no longer needed to watch my cousin's back while he worked. But I hung around anyway, since my curiosity was roused. If anyone objected to my presence, I could always point out that I was still useful, since Vern could get called away at any time on some other bit of police business, leaving Horace vulnerable to the evil intentions of any lurking ninjas.

Was ninjas correct? Or was the plural of ninja still ninja? At any other time, I'd look it up. But what if Horace or Vern noticed me using my phone and asked what I was looking up? Wouldn't it sound frivolous? Then again—

"Man-made object to your left," Vern said. He pulled something out of his pocket and aimed it at a spot in the leaves. The red dot of a laser pointer appeared on the leaves—and on something small and silvery.

"Excellent," Horace said. "Let's check it out."

Chapter 16

Of course, checking out the object Vern had spotted wasn't as simple as merely striding over to where he'd pointed. The space between us and the shiny object was still part of Horace's search area, so he had to scrutinize every square inch of ground between us and it. When he finally got closer, he took a dozen or so pictures of the object in situ before picking it up in one gloved hand and holding it so we could see.

"It's a pen." His flat tone suggested that he wasn't overwhelmed by Vern's find.

"Odd thing to find out here in the woods," Vern said.

"Maybe if we were far out in the woods," Horace said. "This close to the house?" He shrugged. "Anyone could have dropped it. And it could have been here forever."

"Not forever," Vern objected. "Too clean for that. And can't you test it for DNA and stuff?"

"Of course," Horace said. "But even if we found someone's DNA on it, there's nothing to prove it was dropped here last night."

"There might be," I said. "Hold that thing up again, will you?"

Horace obliged.

"I think it's a combination pen and LED flashlight," I said. "Something Kevin and Casey ordered to promote their podcast. Take a closer look and see if it has *Virginia Crime Time* printed on the side, along with the podcast's website and email address."

Horace held it up, peered at it, and nodded.

"Should be useful, then—right?" Vern asked.

"A promotional item that they've given away by the hundreds." Horace shook his head in disappointment.

"Should I be insulted that they never offered me one?" Vern asked.

"Something they *will* be giving away by the hundreds," I said. "But the box of pens only just arrived yesterday morning. Kevin made a special trip back to the house to get them so he could start giving them away at the conference."

"I won't feel insulted, then," Vern said. "And I bet that makes it a lot more interesting to Horace."

"Yes." Horace was looking at the pen with a much more favorable expression. If it had been a dog, he'd have been patting its head and offering it a treat. "Because that not only narrows down the window of time when it was dropped, it definitely ties the pen to someone who was at the conference. Good information!"

We all beamed at the pen, and Horace had Vern don a glove and hold the pen flat on his hand so he could take a few more pictures of it. Satisfying to think that I'd made a contribution to the investigation. Of course, methodical as Horace and the chief were, they'd have eventually found out the source of the pen anyway, but I had probably saved them some time.

We continued on in slow motion through Iris's yard, although now Horace and Vern seemed to be cooperating better on our route, with Horace bent over to scrutinize the ground directly in front of him, and Vern searching the path ahead, looking for those telltale signs that an experienced tracker uses to follow a trail. Of course, not being an experienced tracker, I was clueless. Occasionally, Vern would utter a few words or just point to indicate a minor course correction to Horace. Very rarely, I could actually figure out what broken twig or partial footprint he'd spotted, but most of the time the clues were invisible to me.

At one point, Cordelia texted me.

"You still helping Horace?" she asked.

"Yes," I texted back. "You need me for anything?"

"No," she replied. "We're fine here. Just being nosy. Find some good clues!"

Horace bagged a few more pieces of evidence. For example, Vern pointed out where a small branch had recently been broken off a tree—recently enough that it could be the ninja who'd done it.

"Of course, he may have touched it, but what are the odds he wasn't wearing gloves last night," Vern said. "It got down into the twenties."

"Worth checking it out anyway for traces of fiber," Horace said, as he deposited the branch in one of his larger evidence bags.

"Good point," Vern said.

Aside from the pen, the other high point in our trip was when Vern spotted a footprint—only a partial print, but a good one that clearly showed the sole pattern. After Horace had taken a few dozen photos, he actually took a casting of it.

My excitement over the footprint faded during the half hour or so it took for the impression to dry. And by the time we resumed our trip, creeping over the forest floor like a trio of oversized snails, my initial enthusiasm had faded first into boredom and then into a curious sort of Zen state in which I stopped fretting about our slow pace and the racing clock and the penetrating cold and focused on trying to enjoy the moment. Appreciating the fading colors of the fallen leaves. Spotting the occasional interesting fungus. Listening to the birds' songs, the squirrels' chattering, and the crisp crunch of dead leaves underfoot.

I was actually surprised when we emerged from the woods and I found myself looking at our backyard. I was suddenly struck by how familiar and domestic the scene was. How welcoming. The copper-and-black Welsummer hens were busily scratching around the yard, and the bird feeders were swarming with customers. Mostly chickadees, titmice, and various little brown sparrows, but it made a lively show. Skulk, a gray-striped behemoth who was the larger of our two feral barn cats, was sunning himself atop one of the picnic tables. As I watched, Rose Noire, bundled up in her lavender wool cape, came to pour hot water into the bird bath to break up the ice, distracting me for just a moment as I wondered if she'd like the electric bird bath deicer I'd gotten her for Christmas. Then I focused back on the scene ahead of me. The llamas were ranged along the fence at one side of the pen, watching what we humans were up to. A charming scene.

Until you noticed what the llamas were watching. Sammy, another Caerphilly deputy, was standing guard over the crime scene. Well, not actually standing—he was pacing to keep warm, up and down the fence between our backyard and Rose Noire's herb garden. The ambulance and the Gadfly's body were long gone, but yellow crime-scene tape still surrounded the area, fluttering in the breeze, and if I got closer, I'd also see the drying pool of blood.

Would the blood disappear, or would we have to do something to get rid of it? It was organic, so surely something would eat it in time. But what? Would the Welsummers go after it when Sammy was no longer there to guard it? What about Skulk and Lurk, his fellow barn cat? Would the smell of blood draw them in?

And what about the chickadees and the rest of the feeder crowd? Not all birds were vegetarians—the chickadees relished suet, especially this time of year.

I thought of asking Horace, but he was still absorbed in his inch-by-inch inspection of the ground. A seasoned hunter like Vern might know, but he was wholly focused on figuring out the ninja's path, so Horace could examine all the right square inches.

I wasn't sure why I was so focused on when and how the blood would disappear. I could ask one of them later. Meanwhile . . .

"Mind if I peel off?" I asked. "I'd like to check on Delany, and then see if Cordelia needs any help down at the conference."

"That's fine," Vern said. "I can handle the rest of Horace's stuff."

I handed over the equipment bag I was carrying and Vern slung it over his shoulder.

"And your gran asked me to make sure Horace showed up for his afternoon panel," Vern said, in a tone low enough that Horace probably wouldn't hear it.

"Good," I said. "I know Horace will probably see it as a ridiculous interruption to the important work on the case—"

"He might," Vern said, with a grin. "If the chief hadn't given us all orders to spend as much time as we can down at the Inn, observing what all his suspects are up to. So Horace will be hoping to spot some behavioral clue that will crack the case."

"Good plan." I glanced over at where Horace was squatting down, scrutinizing a patch of dirt. "So have we been following the killer's path, or his victim's?"

"Both, probably," Vern said. "I can't prove it yet, but it looks to me as if two people passed this way along a very similar route."

"Together?"

"Maybe," he said. "More likely one following the other," he said.

"Or the same person coming and going?"

"Probably not. Directionality on both seems to be heading this way, and when I was guarding the crime scene earlier, I saw what I'm pretty sure were signs of someone leaving in the other direction, instead of heading back toward Mrs. Rafferty's yard."

"And that would definitely not be our victim."

"Right. Going to check that out when we eventually get there."

I was tempted to ask him to explain what subtle clues he'd observed to lead him to his conclusions, but I knew from past experience that I wouldn't understand more than half of what he said, and that was assuming he could even articulate the clues. I'd figured out that a large part of Vern's legendary tracking ability was based on the instincts he'd developed from his years of roaming the fields and woods of Caerphilly. And both he and the chief knew that "I could just tell" wouldn't fly in court, which meant that unlike Horace's finds, Vern's contribution wouldn't be admissible as evidence—never mind the fact that he'd successfully tracked down any number of lost people and animals over the years, not to mention the occasional dangerous fugitive and enough deer and other game to keep most of the Shiffley clan well fed in even the hardest winter.

"Oh, and that footprint we found," he added. "I don't think it's going to turn out to be our victim's. He was wearing athletic shoes, and that looks to me more like a boot print. But don't mention the footprint to anyone. We don't want the killer getting rid of the telltale footwear before we find it."

"Roger," I said. "Actually, given how focused everyone at the conference is on unjust convictions, I bet the killer wouldn't be the only one unloading suspicious-looking boots if word got out about what we'd found."

"You could be right," Vern said, shaking his head.

"Well, keep me posted if you find anything interesting," I said. "Like signs that the killer might still be lurking nearby."

"Roger," he said. "Chief already gave us orders to drive by here a lot more than usual, so there's that."

I glanced back at the house. Delaney was back in the sunroom, tucked up under a blanket on the chaise longue, with her binoculars trained on one of the bird feeders.

I felt a sudden surge of protectiveness. For Delaney, and my unborn niece or nephew. And Rose Noire, who should have been having a joyful solstice. And Dad and Horace and Vern and all the other deputies who would be suddenly pulling extra shifts during a season when they had a right to expect to spend some time with their families. Heck, I could probably even manage a little sympathy for the Gadfly if I worked at it.

My face must have given away what I was feeling.

"Don't worry," Vern said. "We'll find whoever did this."

"I know," I said. "But it can't happen too soon to suit me."

"Yup," he said. "I don't think there's any good season for a murder, but I have to admit, Christmas time's the worst."

He went back to hovering over Horace. Time for me to check on the household, and then maybe head down to the Inn. See what I could do to keep Cordelia's conference on track.

And maybe help the chief.

But for starters, I went out to the barn and unlocked the door to my office. I wanted to use my laptop to do a little snooping about the Gadfly and some of the people who might have it in for him. I probably wouldn't find out anything that Kevin, Festus, and Cordelia didn't already know—or anything the chief wouldn't be finding out. But I was starting to feel that everyone knew more than I did about the Gadfly—and why someone might want to do away with him. An unfamiliar feeling, and one I didn't like.

But my laptop wasn't on my desk where I'd left it. Since I normally kept my office locked, either a burglar with excellent lock-picking skills had broken into my office, taken the laptop, and then locked up again after himself . . . or, more likely, Kevin had taken it away for some kind of update or maintenance. So I headed back to the house.

Rose Noire and several of her Wiccan or pagan friends were in the kitchen, fixing the refreshments for their solstice celebration. When she saw me, her expression changed from relaxed and happy to anxious. It wasn't me, I knew, but the fact that my return reminded her of what she'd seen.

So I put on my most cheerful, optimistic face and gave her a thumbs-up sign.

"Have they caught whoever did it?" she asked, her expression suddenly joyful.

"No, but Horace and Vern both had useful finds," I said. "I'm sworn to secrecy, but they're definitely making progress. Is Kevin around?"

"In his lair," Rose Noire said. "He's doing some kind of forensic work for the chief." Her tone suggested that I should refrain from interrupting him, lest I impede the progress of the case.

"Just collecting my laptop," I said. "I want to take it with me when I go back to the Inn. So I can help the chief if the opportunity arises."

She nodded, as if giving me permission.

I was just starting down the basement stairs when she called out something.

"Can you check on Delaney before you go?"

I retraced my path back into the kitchen.

"Check on her?" I echoed. "Why?"

"I don't quite know." She frowned slightly. "She's suddenly being very secretive about something. If I walk into the room when she's on the phone, she hangs up. And she's been texting furtively."

I thought of pointing out that this close to Christmas, a lot of us had reasons for being secretive. At any given moment, most of the family were tiptoeing around plotting various holiday surprises. And for that matter, Delaney could be starting to feel the signs of impending labor. And while I had no doubt that she was grateful for all of Rose Noire's care over the last five months, if I were in her shoes I wouldn't be in a hurry to announce that I was starting to feel contractions and cause Rose Noire to escalate her ministrations.

"I'll see what I can figure out," I said. Then I descended into the basement and entered Kevin's computer-filled lair.

Chapter 17

I paused for a moment to let my eyes adjust to the dimmer light level Kevin preferred. After a few seconds I could see my surroundings. A long, wide counter ran along one whole side of the room, holding a dizzying array of computers, monitors, printers, keyboards, mice, and other bits of electronic gear that I'd be hard pressed to name. Widget, Kevin's Pomeranian, was lying sprawled on one of the few open spots on the counter— right beside Kevin's Christmas tree, a two-foot-high artificial pine decked with some of his favorite Dungeons & Dragons miniatures, along with a lot of random bits of gold- and silver-colored computer gear to add a more festive touch. Widget lifted his head when I came in, thumped his tail a few times, then lowered his head again and sank back into the contented sleep of a dog who has been well and recently fed.

Kevin, on the other hand, didn't immediately acknowledge my arrival. So, once I spotted my laptop on the counter, I sat down in the nearest of the half-dozen office chairs scattered up and down its length and pulled out my phone to check for any newly arrived texts, emails, or voicemails. Two could play at Kevin's game.

"Kind of busy right now," he said, after a few minutes. "Got a few things I need to get done for the chief before I head back to the conference.

"Understood," I said. "I just wanted to give you a heads-up about something."

"If it's not connected to the conference or the murder—" he began.

"It's connected to both."

He whirled around, a frown battling curiosity on his face. I reached into my tote and pulled out a pen—the *Virginia Crime Time* pen I'd picked up at the conference. I flicked the little LED light on and off. His face relaxed into a smile.

"Pretty cool, huh?"

"Very cool," I said. "Any minute now the chief's going to be asking all sorts of questions about it."

"Why?" The frown was back.

"Because Horace and Vern and I just found one out in the woods near Iris Rafferty's house," I said. "On a path that Norton may have taken to get to our house. Or maybe the path whoever killed him took. Could even be both."

"You're serious, aren't you?"

I explained about Iris's report of ninjas and the resulting forensic hike through the woods.

"So the chief is probably going to want to know when I got to the conference with the pens," he said. "And who I gave them to."

I nodded. He frowned slightly, pulled out his phone, and did something on it.

"Okay," he said. "Rose Noire called me at nine-seventeen a.m. yesterday to tell me that the box of pens had arrived. Really annoying, because they were supposed to come Wednesday. And I had to miss nearly all of Festus's talk to make the round trip home to fetch them. And it's no use asking me who I gave them to, because I don't remember, and Casey had a bunch, too, and we left a box of them out on the freebies table for anyone who wanted one."

"So anyone could have had one," I said.

"Including Norton," Kevin said.

"Yeah," I said. "He definitely had one. Cordelia had to get after him about not flashing it in people's eyes during that roundtable session he crashed. She took it away from him. And that wasn't long before she kicked him out, but he probably had enough time to grab another."

"Oh, he definitely grabbed another," Kevin said. "As soon as Cordelia's back was turned, he pulled another pen out of his pocket and started doing the same thing. So I took that one away from him and kicked him out of the session. And it was right after I did that he started tormenting Ezekiel's dog."

He was now gazing at the pen with a slight frown.

"Don't let the Gadfly spoil your enjoyment of the pens," I said. "It's not your fault he found a way to misuse them. And it's not as if the pen was the murder weapon."

"Yeah." He handed me back the pen. "I'll get over it. It's just galling, you know. Cordelia comes up with the great idea for a conference, and first the Gadfly tries to spoil it and then someone else . . ." He shrugged and let his words drift off.

"And neither the Gadfly nor his killer can spoil the conference if we don't let them," I said. "But please tell me you have an alibi for when the murder took place."

"The chief made sure of that before he let me start working any evidence," he said. "Good thing I've got a pretty thorough alibi for all of last night, since it doesn't seem as if he knows yet when the killer struck. Has Grandpa weighed in yet on that?"

"Probably before midnight," I said. "And Michael said Norton was pretty cold when we found him. What are the odds he'd come out here for a visit all that late?"

"Who knows?" Kevin grimaced. "He was pretty rude and enti-tled. And who says he was coming for a visit? What if he wanted to cause trouble? Egg the house, or set off firecrackers to wake us up, or cut the power lines or . . . Who knows? What if he to-tally lost his cool over being kicked out, and was coming out here to exact his revenge, and whoever killed him actually saved us from all having our throats slit last night?"

He paused dramatically. And then realized that perhaps his drama was a little over-the-top.

"Well, it's possible," he said.

"Getting back to my original question," I began.

"My alibi," he said. "Right. Some of the attendees asked me for some suggestions about where to eat, and I recommended Luigi's, but I warned them how crowded it got on Fridays, so they did takeout, and I ended up having a pizza dinner with a whole bunch of them in one of their rooms. And we'd been talking about whether or not Norton could sneak back into the hotel, and the idea made Amber a little nervous, so I walked her back to her own room."

He paused, and there was just a slight note of something in his tone—embarrassment?

"And how long can you and Amber alibi each other for?" I asked, making sure to keep my tone innocent.

"Only for the walk from the third floor to the fifth." He rolled his eyes as if this was a ridiculous question. "And I was worried the stress would give her a migraine—she has them pretty bad."

"I know." I decided it would be tactless to mention that the reason I knew was that a migraine had been part of her alibi for her husband's murder. Besides, he knew that, too.

"So before I left I made sure she had her meds handy. I think I probably annoyed her by fussing over her."

"Making sure she has her meds handy doesn't sound like

fussing," I said. "Just ensuring that she's taking good care of herself."

"Actually, I think it was offering to get Grandpa to look at her that kind of annoyed her," he said. "I backed off on that when I realized how she felt about the idea. But I wish she'd talk to him. He really is very good at migraines and headaches generally, you know. He keeps up with new research in the area pretty closely, so he can do his best for Grandmother."

"If he could get the county to outlaw polyester and paintings on black velvet, it would do a lot more to prevent Mother's headaches than any medicine they will ever invent," I said.

"Probably." He snickered. "Anyway, Amber said that as long as she could get to sleep before too long, she'd be okay. So then I went down to the lobby and ran into Casey, and we decided we really needed to start recording our latest podcast episode, so he followed me back here."

"I thought you'd recorded a couple of episodes in advance so you could take off time for the conference and the holiday," I said.

"Yeah, but someone at the conference suggested this really cool idea for an episode," he said. "A true-crime Christmas— the top ten cases that happened on or very close to Christmas."

"How festive," I said.

"Hey, we know our audience," he said. "It'll be a smash hit. Anyway, I'm not sure what time we got here—maybe nine or so? Horace would know; it was about the time he went off duty and he was here picking up Watson from Rose Noire's doggy day care. And then Casey and I got online to record for the podcast, and it was like three a.m. before we finished and he drove home."

I nodded. It sounded as if he was well alibied. And I found myself hoping that the earlier part of the evening, when he'd been with "a whole bunch" of conference attendees, would turn out to be the critical time period. If that were the case, late dinners and after-dinner get-togethers would give a lot of the attendees alibis. And even though Kevin's cameras hadn't detected the arrival of the Gadfly and his killer, at least they should enable him to prove that he hadn't left the house to skulk behind the barn and bump off anyone after Casey's departure.

Of course, if anyone was capable of eluding detection by our security system, it would be Kevin, since he'd designed it. And the hotel security system, too. But with luck, Dad would determine that the Gadfly had been killed well before Kevin's alibi ended.

"I hope it doesn't turn out to be one of the Keepers," he said. "The murderer, I mean."

"Ginny and Janet," I said. "Who are trying to exonerate their high-school friend."

"Right." He nodded. "The Keepers."

"Been meaning to ask you," I said. "Keepers of what?"

"That's just how I think of them," Kevin said. "Because they kind of remind me of the ladies in that documentary, you know? The one where the two little old—er, two retired women get fired up to investigate the murder of one of their high-school teachers. You haven't seen it?"

I shook my head.

"Man, you should check it out," he said. "Remember that argument Dad was having with Cousin Julian."

"No," I said. "Julian argues with everyone, so it's kind of hard to remember any of them in particular. And if you looked up mansplaining in the dictionary, you'd probably find his picture there, so it's not as if I listen if I can help it."

"Good thing he's only a cousin by marriage," Kevin said.

"What was he on about this time?"

"He was giving Dad a hard time about reading mystery novels

with amateur sleuths," Kevin explained. "Being a cop, Julian thinks they're completely unrealistic and kind of stupid."

"No more unrealistic than the kind of hard-boiled mystery where the cop goes rogue, constantly does things that would get his case thrown out of court in real life, and racks up a body count in the dozens. Isn't that the kind of thing Julian reads?"

"The kind of thing he watches." Kevin was snickering. "I'm not sure he reads anything other than menus and traffic signs. But getting back to *The Keepers*—you should watch it. It's a real-life story of some amateur sleuths investigating a case and cracking open the most enormous can of worms. They find out—"

"No spoilers," I said. "Let's get back to Ginny and Janet."

"Right." He assumed a look of ostentatious cooperativeness. Or was it a look of ostentatious patience with what he probably considered my deplorable lack of knowledge about the world of true crime? I was still trying to figure out whether it was better to ask questions or just ignore the occasions when he tossed off what was obviously a reference to a case he was following that I'd barely heard of. Okay, sometimes I had to ask, when he tossed out remarks like, "not sure if I buy the killer owl theory" or "well, that's what the egg lady juror claims."

"Ginny and Janet are genuine amateur sleuths, just like the ladies in the documentary," he said. "And pretty darn good at it, from what I've seen. I'm thinking of suggesting to Festus that he do a trade with them. Maybe he could take on their friend's case pro bono in return for them doing some of the investigative work for some of his other cases. On top of being good at it, they're kind of like a stealth weapon—everyone underestimates them for some reason."

"Because they're women of a certain age," I said. "If they were my age or younger, they might be more likely to call out someone who ignores or undervalues them or suggests they go back to their kitchens. They just smile and get the job done, whatever it is."

"Yeah," he said. "And I'm glad Casey and I haven't ticked them off. You should see their takedown of Norton."

"Define 'takedown,'" I said. "Because if you said that about anyone else, I'd have suggested that maybe I've already seen that takedown—behind the barn this morning."

"When he went after them online, they did their research thing and published a blog all about his many lies and half truths," Kevin said. "In a sane world, that blog would have ended his career as a true-crime influencer, but you know how the internet works. 'A lie travels around the globe while the truth is putting on its shoes,' as someone said. Probably not Mark Twain, although he usually gets the credit."

"Not Twain," I said. "I tried to look it up once, and no one knows. Jonathan Swift said something similar in 1710, but I prefer to quote Terry Pratchett. Who definitely said it in one of his books, although he didn't claim to have invented it—he credits the ever-useful 'they say.'"

"Good to know." Kevin rotated his shoulders, as if he'd suddenly realized that he'd been hunched over his computer too long, and then segued into a full stretch. "Anyway, the ladies pegged him. I'll text you a link to what they said, if you want to read it."

"I'd love to," I said. "But later. For now, I'm headed to the Inn."

Chapter 18

"I'll be heading over to the Inn myself pretty soon," Kevin said. "Running out of things I can do to help the chief. At least until we get access to the Gadfly's iPhone."

"Okay, gruesome as it sounds, doesn't the chief have access to his body?" I said. "Or Dad. Can't they use facial recognition or Touch ID, whichever he has?"

"Nope," he said. "Apple thought of that. Touch ID uses the body's natural electrical charge, which vanishes after death. Facial recognition's a lot more complicated, but I could give you the details if you like."

"Or you could just tell me what those details add up to."

"They've built in a lot of protections. You might be able to use it to unlock a dead guy's phone if you could prop his eyes open just right, but it'd be a long shot. We're hoping Norton's got his password stored someplace."

"And if he doesn't?"

"We can still get a lot of the info from his carrier," Kevin said. "Calls and texts, for example. But that takes time—more time than usual, given the season. And we'll get a lot more if we can get into his phone."

"I'll keep my fingers crossed that he's got a bad memory, then, and has written down his password."

Kevin nodded and turned back to the computer he'd been working with. I spotted my laptop on the counter and went over to collect it.

Widget lifted his head, as if hoping perhaps I would feel inspired to give him a treat, to console him for my departure. Behind him, on a monitor, I could see Rose Noire chucking feed to the Welsummers.

Something occurred to me.

"Do your security cameras capture sound or just pictures?"

"They have audio capability," he said over his shoulder. "But I usually keep it turned off, 'cause I figure you don't want anyone eavesdropping on every single thing that's said in the yard."

"But hasn't Delaney been using the audio from the security cameras to listen to the birds?" I asked.

Kevin whirled around to stare at me for a few seconds.

"You're right!" he said. "I showed her how to do that weeks ago. Of course, I also showed her how to turn off the sound when she was finished."

"But maybe she didn't bother," I said. "She doesn't have a lot of energy for inessentials right now. In which case, even though no one was listening to it at the time—"

"The cameras might have recorded the gunshot that killed the Gadfly." Kevin's fingers were flying over his keyboard. "Let me just check the camera that's closest to the barn. She likes that one because it also lets her watch the llamas at closer range and—"

A scene of our backyard appeared on one of the monitors. Chickadees and titmice flitted to and fro by the feeder. Sammy paced up and down by the fence. The llamas were lined up inside their pen, watching whatever was going on behind the barn, sticking their necks so far over the fence it was a wonder none of them had toppled over.

But no sound.

"So much for that idea," I said.

"Don't give up that fast," he said. "Wait a sec . . . I don't usually keep the sound up on that monitor. There!"

Suddenly we heard birds chirping. Sammy slapping his arms against his chest and going "brrrrrr!" And the faint strains of Jethro Tull's "Ring Out, Solstice Bells" coming from Rose Noire's combination greenhouse and herb-drying shack, where she and her merry band of pagans were starting their Yule celebrations.

"So maybe it was capturing sound last night?" I asked.

"Maybe," he said. "Probably." His fingers danced over the keyboard again and the picture on the monitor changed from the luminous gray of a bright but cloudy day to mostly darkness. We watched in silence for some seconds until a bloodcurdling scream rang out. We both started then laughed.

"Foxes, right?" he said.

"Yes." I nodded. "It's their mating season. That's probably some dapper young fox singing the vulpine version of 'Baby, It's Cold Outside' to his favorite vixen."

"Not my favorite Christmas song, even when humans sing it," he said. "The gunshot won't be that dramatic—maybe just a pop. But if the microphone caught it . . ."

"Then you can pinpoint when the killer struck," I said. "Always assuming the clock on your camera system is accurate."

From the way he rolled his eyes I gathered this was an annoyingly silly question.

"And I was kidding, you know," I said.

"I should hope so," he said. "I'm setting it up so some of the chief's deputies can review the security cam footage from down at the station. I'll tell them to listen as well as look."

"Good idea."

"None of them are city slickers, right?" he asked. "Like I was when I first moved in, and called nine-one-one on the foxes?"

"I don't think so," I said. "But I'd remind them, just in case."

He nodded and returned to his rapid-fire typing.

I felt triumphant as I mounted the stairs with my laptop in hand. Maybe Kevin would have thought to check the audio feed later. Or maybe whoever the chief had reviewing the footage would have. But I'd been the first to think of it. While I wasn't exactly a Luddite, I also wasn't known for being tech-savvy, so this felt like a small but sweet victory.

Upstairs, I found Mother in the kitchen.

"Good afternoon, dear." She brushed my cheek with a kiss.

"Afternoon already?" I said. "Good grief. Are you sticking around to decorate something?"

"To visit with Delaney," she said. "So Rose Noire and her friends can have their celebration."

"Where's Rob?" I asked. And then, lest this sound like a criticism, I added, "Not that he's required to stay by her side twenty-four seven, but he's pretty much been trying to lately."

"Keep your fingers crossed," she said. "Jeanine may have found something."

Jeanine Shiffley was the real estate agent Rob and Delaney had been working with.

"Fingers and toes," I said. "The house in Westlake?"

"I think they lost out on that one." She shuddered slightly. "Not a great hardship, really. The sellers had absolutely appalling taste and way too much money."

"A lethal combination."

"Absolutely," she said. "We'd have had to gut the place."

"Jeanine found someplace better?"

"Well, someplace," Mother said. "It's not even officially listed yet, so who knows if it's better. But I would think almost anything would be better than Westlake. Jeanine has arranged a sneak preview. I do wish we could convince Rob to relax and wait until spring. There just isn't going to be that much on the market this time of year. Are you going over to the Inn to help your grandmother?"

"Or Chief Burke. Whoever needs helping most."

"I'll probably see you this evening, then. If Delaney feels up to it, I'm going to take her over to the Inn to hear the concert."

"Is Dad okay with that?"

"He brought over a wheelchair, so she doesn't have to walk a step, and we've arranged a room where she can nap if she gets tired."

She picked up a tray with what I deduced was lunch for her and Delaney—more of Michael's planned-overs from the Shack—and left the kitchen. I hesitated for a moment, then reminded myself that there would also be plenty of food down at the Inn.

Though I did decide to look in on Delaney before I took off. I knew she'd be more than fine in Mother's capable hands. Not that Mother was apt to do anything that resembled nursing or cleaning, but she was superbly capable of organizing people on a moment's notice to do anything strenuous that needed doing. And she was perfect for handling what I thought was needed most right now—amusing Delaney, cosseting her, and providing the sort of informed sympathy that only another woman who had actually given birth could provide.

I found them sipping tea, nibbling corn bread, and gazing through matching binoculars at the half-dozen bird feeders visible from the sunroom.

"I see your chickadees are out in force," I said.

Delaney lowered her binoculars.

"Oh, yes!" she said, beaming at the window through which we could see two feisty little chickadees battling over one of the feeders. "They've been such comforters to me these last few months. I wish I could—wait! I've got it! We could name the sprout after them! Wouldn't that be nice?"

Mother closed her eyes and almost managed to suppress a gentle sigh. Rob and Delaney's ongoing search for baby names—and some of the eclectic suggestions they seemed to like—had been a great trial to her lately.

"No, it wouldn't be nice at all," I said. "Chickadee Langslow? How could you do that to a defenseless baby?"

"Well, I suppose it might not work that well," Delaney said. "Perhaps as a middle name?"

Mother shook her head firmly.

"I know!" Delaney exclaimed. "We use their scientific name. As the middle name," she added, looking at Mother.

I had already predicted this next suggestion and picked up the Peterson Field Guide that was sitting on a nearby table.

"Latin names can be so musical," Delaney added, waving her hand as if air-conducting a sprightly symphony. Something festive by Mozart.

"The chickadees' Latin name isn't," I said. "*Poecile carolinensis* for the Carolina chickadee and *Poecile atricapillus* for the black-capped one. We get both here. And don't ask me if that's the correct pronunciation because I have no idea. And neither will little Poecile's teachers when he or she goes to school."

"Ah, well." Delaney sighed, and cast me a reproachful glance, as if I were to blame for the chickadees' less than musical scientific name. "Atrica or Atricus, perhaps? That might sound rather distinguished."

"No, dear," Mother said firmly.

I left them to it. I could see that Mother was already pulling out her phone, probably to call in reinforcements. Perhaps our good friend Robyn Smith, the rector of Trinity Episcopal, could weigh in on the virtues of the kind of good, old-fashioned, familiar names she and her husband had given their own two little ones. And remind Delaney at how delighted Grandfather and Dad had been that we'd named the boys after them. Mother had thoroughly approved of Joshua Blake Waterston and James Langslow Waterston.

Delaney had also pulled out her phone and glanced at it, in what I had to admit was a rather furtive manner. But then she smiled and tucked it away again. I saw that Mother, too, had noticed. Perhaps I should tell Rose Noire to stop worrying about Delaney's secretiveness. Mother was on the case, and a secret she couldn't ferret out wasn't worth knowing.

I made my escape before they sucked me into the never-ending discussion of what to call the expected bundle of joy and set out for the Inn.

Chapter 19

Once I hit the road, I turned on the Caerphilly College radio station. This close to Christmas most of the students who worked there had left town for the holidays, so the skeleton staff left behind tended to play long, uninterrupted blocks of Christmas music. And they were responsive to requests, so by this time in the season, I could usually count on hearing a few of my favorites. They were really hitting my playlist hard today. I caught most of Odetta's "Children, Go Where I Send Thee," followed by Loreena McKennitt's version of "The Wexford Carol" and Carnie and Wendy Wilson's glorious "Hark the Herald Angels Sing."

I was in a downright festive mood by the time I turned into the Inn's mile-long driveway, flanked on both sides by white-painted fences decorated with evergreen boughs, red ribbons, and twinkling lights. My mood persisted as I steered the Twinmobile to an open space in the Inn's spotless white gravel parking lot. The day might be gray and overcast, but you almost forgot that when you saw the soaring glass walls of the Inn with all the lights, tinsel, evergreen, and colored glass within. Enrique, the bell captain, was in his bright red holiday uniform with gold braid trim and a sprig of holly on the lapel.

My festive mood didn't even sour when I walked into the lobby to find the chief talking to Vern and Amber Smith. Although it did occur to me that I was walking into a crowd that probably contained Norton's killer—along with all the chief's main suspects. After all, while I had no doubt that the Gadfly made enemies wherever he went, here in Caerphilly he hadn't spent much time anywhere but at the Inn. At the Presumed Innocent conference. So whoever killed him was almost certainly here.

And I'd almost certainly met the killer. I ran through my short list of subjects. Ezekiel. Unable to prevent his exoneration, Norton had done what he could to poison his new life of freedom. Amber, whose bid for permanent freedom Norton was bent on thwarting. The Keepers, Ginny and Janet, who wanted to help the high-school friend who'd been in prison almost as long as Ezekiel. Norton had only been getting started on their case, but anyone could already see how vicious his opposition was going to be. And the same went for the redheads, Madelaine and Ellen—Norton would almost certainly have argued that Madelaine's mother had committed murder rather than manslaughter and should die in prison.

I'd keep my ears open for other cases that might have caught Norton's eye and inspired his murder. In the meantime, I hoped those six had good alibis for last night—because as much as I liked all of them, I had to admit that they were all suspects.

I stopped just inside the lobby and did a mental exercise Rose Noire had once suggested, pausing to relish the joyous, peaceful mood the carols had created, and then imagining myself tucking it away in one of my brain's closets, where I'd have no trouble finding it again when I'd finished whatever practical tasks I'd need to do to help with the conference or the investigation.

Then I strolled over to where the chief was standing, right by the wall of glass. He and Vern were looking up at the sky. Amber was watching their faces.

"I think he's pretty much finished with it," Vern was saying. "He's going to send a few bits of evidence down to the Crime Lab in Richmond, and then he can come out here to work this part of the scene."

Evidently they were talking about Horace. I wondered what they wanted him to work on here at the Inn.

"Good," the chief said. "As long as we do our best to wrap this up before the snow starts."

"Are we definitely getting snow?" I asked. "Last time I looked there was only a sixty-percent chance."

"It's up close to a hundred percent now," Vern said. "But Judge Jane says it should hold off at least a few more hours."

"Do you need permission from the court to have a white Christmas around here?" Amber asked. "What happens if the snow starts early—will they charge Mother Nature with contempt of court?"

"If anyone could do that it would be Judge Jane Shiffley," Vern said, with a chuckle. "But no, she doesn't try to control the weather—she just predicts it. Her left knee is more reliable than the weather service. And I'll check in with Great-uncle Jasper to see if his shoulder concurs," he added, turning back to the chief.

"That would be helpful," the chief said.

"Do you need me for anything else?" Amber asked.

"Not at the moment," the chief said. "Thank you."

"You know where to find me if you think of something." She nodded to me and headed away. I thought she was heading for the conference room but then she veered over toward the little side area where the fireplace was. Ezekiel was standing in front of the fire, warming his hands, and Ruth had her front paws up on the hearth as if to get closer to the welcoming heat. I watched as Amber spoke to Ezekiel—asking permission to pet Ruth, no doubt—and then knelt to scratch the dog behind her floppy ears. I smiled at the relaxed look on her face. Then I turned back to Vern and the chief.

"Did Kevin tell you what he and I just figured out?" I asked.

Vern and the chief both shook their heads. And from the hopeful looks on their faces, I suspected they would welcome some good news.

"Maybe you can act surprised when he does," I said. "Thanks to Delaney's chickadee-watching, our home security system's audio was on last night, on top of the video. So whoever reviews the feed—"

"Might detect the gunshot that killed Norton," Vern finished.

"Excellent," the chief said. "We've agreed on calling him Norton, by the way," he added to Vern. "Since most of the people we're interviewing only know him by that name."

"Makes sense," he said. "And only takes half as long to say as Niedernstatter."

We all chuckled at that.

"If the crew checking the video finds anything they think might be a gunshot, I'd be happy to take a listen to it," Vern said. "I'm pretty good at telling the difference between gunshots and car backfires and all the other noises people sometimes panic over."

"Good idea," the chief said. "My experience in that area's pretty exclusively urban. Sound works differently out in the country."

"Meanwhile, I'll go see what I can find outside." Vern strode off, putting on his coat as he walked.

"Is he looking for something connected with the case?" I asked. "I thought it was pretty definite that Norton was killed where we found him."

"Absolutely," the chief said. "But most of the people in town who might have it in for him—in fact, most of the ones who have any idea who he is—would have been here at the Inn."

"Except when they were over at our house actually committing the deed," I said.

"Exactly," he said. "And so, speaking of security systems, we need to figure out if it was possible for Norton's killer to leave the Inn without being detected. So I've given the boys an assignment. Adam, Josh, and Jamie, that is."

"An assignment?" I echoed. "Not because of some transgression, I certainly hope."

"No, no." He smiled. "Not a punishment detail. I've challenged them to see if they can find a way to sneak out of the hotel without being spotted on any of those security cameras."

"Ooh, fun," I said. "But if the idea is to keep them out of mischief, I'm afraid it will just change the kind of mischief they get into."

"It's not busy work, if that's what you're thinking," he said. "It might make a solid contribution to the case if they manage it, because a whole lot of the attendees are on record as never having left the hotel. And Kevin's set it up so we can scan all the hotel security footage from last night—I've sent Sammy back to the station, so he can help George with that as well as the footage from your house. But I'd like to make sure the cameras really do cover all possibilities."

I thought of pointing out that Kevin had designed the system, and he was pretty good at it. But the chief knew that.

"Good idea," I said. "Because Kevin would have been designing the system to keep intruders out, not to keep guests from sneaking out to commit crimes."

"Exactly," he said. "If the boys can sneak out without appearing on camera, someone else could, too."

"I bet they jumped at the idea."

"They did." He smiled. "Right now they're scouting out the whole hotel, trying to figure out where all the cameras are and exactly what area they cover."

"Ekaterina couldn't just give them a plan of the system?"

"She could, but if someone wanted to sneak out of the hotel for some nefarious purpose, I doubt if they'd blow their cover by asking for specs on the security system. What use would a blind spot or a gap in the coverage be if you can't deduce its existence without the plan?"

I nodded.

"Eventually, when they think they've discovered some holes in the system, we'll have a test. Ekaterina's getting her office set up so we can watch the feeds from all the cameras, and we'll see if the boys can pull off their invisible exit."

"So are you hoping the boys can't pull it off?" I asked. "Since that would whittle down the number of viable suspects. Or is there someone you're hoping will turn out to have holes in their alibi?"

"Hard to say." He took off his glasses and rubbed his eyes. "If they can't pull it off, it won't prove that it can't be done. Only that it's pretty darned difficult. But if they can, I can think of several people who made rather intemperate statements about Mr. Norton. Frankly, from what I've learned, I don't blame them, but if they try to claim hotel security as an alibi, I'd like to know if it's valid."

"Who in particular has been badmouthing Norton?" I thought I knew the answer, but I was wondering who he had in mind.

"Well, Ellen Mays and Madelaine Taylor, for example."

"The redheads," I said. "Who want to exonerate Madelaine's mother."

"That's them." He rubbed his forehead, as if feeling a headache coming on. "I talked just now to the police chief of the town in which Mary Campbell, the mother, was convicted. If I listened to him, I'd probably want to arrest both of those ladies, alibi or no alibi. According to him, they're both dyed-in-the-wool troublemakers trying to manufacture fake evidence to free a bloodthirsty killer. He even hinted that he wishes he could have found enough evidence to prove they were accomplices to the crime."

"Wow," I said. "But you said if you listened to him. I gather you're skeptical."

"I overheard some of their side of things yesterday. I'll need to interview them, of course—even if they're fully alibied—and check out their story about what Norton did to them, since it could have some relevance to other suspects' motives for wanting to get revenge on him."

"And what was their story?"

"That there was ample evidence showing that Mary Campbell was the victim of over ten years of domestic abuse." His expression had gone grim. "Supposedly the judge refused to admit any of that evidence into court."

"Supposedly," I repeated. "You don't know for sure yet?"

"I have a call into Mary Campbell's defense attorney," he said. "We'll see what she says."

"That's good," I said. "But even if it's true, what does that have to do with Mr. Norton?"

"In their roundtable session yesterday, Ms. Mays and Ms. Taylor asserted that Mr. Norton poisoned the judge against their relative's side of the case. And they could have a point. I have been able to determine that Mr. Norton did carry on a remarkably intense online campaign to paint Mary Campbell as a mentally unstable person who wanted to do away with her husband for his life insurance. The local paper took the same line in covering the case, although I don't yet know if the paper influenced Norton or the other way around or if both got their view of the case from a third source."

"Like maybe that local police chief?"

"It's possible." He sighed and pinched the bridge of his nose—another clue that the case was already giving him a headache. "It's a very small town, and the police chief and the late Mr. Campbell were both lifetime residents, within a year or two of the same age. And maybe it's just a wild coincidence that the judge is married to a woman whose maiden name was Campbell, but . . ."

"Yikes," I said. "Sounds like they have a great case for an appeal."

"Festus thinks so. But he also thinks that the local authorities are going to do everything they can to derail the appeal, so it's not going to be easy. Ah. There's my next interview subject. If you need me, Ekaterina has me set up in the staff meeting room, right next to her office."

I saw Ginny Maynard looking around as if lost. Or maybe she just looked that way because I was so used to seeing her as part of a pair, her short, plump figure contrasting with Janet's tall, lean one. The chief strode over to greet her and led her toward his temporary office.

I was heading over to greet Ezekiel and Ruth when my phone dinged to let me know I had a text arriving. From Michael.

"Safely arrived at Dulles," it read. "And we just claimed Mom's luggage. What's the name of that Thai restaurant she liked so much the last time she was here?"

Not that I'd been overly worried, but it was reassuring to know that something was going as planned. Multiple somethings— his drive, his mom's flight, her baggage, and giving her a lunch she'd adore. I texted back the restaurant's name and address, along with a greeting for his mother, and then went over to the fireplace to see Ezekiel and Ruth.

Chapter 20

"Afternoon," Ezekiel said, standing to greet me. "I do hope you weren't too upset—finding that poor man dead in your backyard."

"Having a doctor for a dad helps," I said. "I'm not as shockable as many people. And my, how things change—now he's 'that poor man'?"

"Just trying to remember that even he didn't deserve what happened to him." He sat back down on the hearth. "When I heard about it, I admit, I had a hard time with it. I knew the right thing to do was to feel sorrow for him and to pray that he made his peace with his maker before he passed. But doing it still comes hard. Even in a season like this, when we should be filled with the spirit of peace and goodwill to all mankind."

I nodded. No doubt the Gadfly had friends and family members who would mourn his passing. No sane person would expect Ezekiel to be one of them.

But he was clearly troubled by his own reaction to the news.

"No need to feel guilty," I said. "It's not as if you jumped for joy when you heard."

"No," he said. "What I felt wasn't joy. Not any kind of joy. But it was . . ."

"Maybe relief?" I suggested.

"Yes. Relief." His face relaxed with the obvious pleasure at being given exactly the right word. "That's it. Relief. Naming it does help. I won't have to worry about him hurting Ruth ever again. Or trying to poison people against me. Or doing his best to put obstacles in the way of another innocent person's quest to regain their freedom."

"Festus is fond of quoting what Clarence Darrow once said in a similar situation: 'I have never killed anyone, but I have read some obituary notices with great satisfaction.'"

Ezekiel smiled at this.

"There's something to that," he said. "But I'm worried. It seems all too clear that someone took the law into their own hands. Probably someone here at the conference. And that's not all right."

"No," I said. "It's not. But maybe it's understandable."

"Not to me," Ezekiel said. "Oh, I understand the impulse. The temptation. But I can't understand someone giving in to it. Something like that comes into your mind, you shove it aside. You recognize it for the evil temptation it is and you pray it away. You don't give in to it. Only some poor soul did. And for all we know, maybe they're tortured now. Realizing what they've done. Realizing, maybe, that they gave way to a moment's anger and did something they can never take back. Something they're eventually going to have to answer for, one way or another."

I nodded and kept quiet. Would it make him feel better or worse to know that whoever killed the Gadfly probably hadn't given in to a moment's anger? Because if what Vern had learned from his tracking efforts was true—and I'd bet it was—the person who killed the Gadfly had stalked him through the countryside and waylaid him behind our barn. Not exactly something that could be explained away by a momentary fit of anger.

"Maybe it will turn out to be self-defense," Ezekiel said. "Although what I've heard so far doesn't fit in too well with that idea. And when you come right down to it, isn't whoever did it just doing the same thing that's been done to so many of us?"

My face must have showed my puzzlement.

"A lot of unjust convictions come about because of racism or corruption," he said. "But I've seen just as many happen because the cops or the prosecutors think they're doing the right thing. They think someone's guilty, and they're frustrated because they can't prove it, so they do whatever they need to get a conviction. To get a bad man off the streets. They think they're protecting society and saving lives. I think that's why it's so hard to get a conviction overturned sometimes. Because they don't want to admit that they were wrong."

"And that was what Norton was doing, too, wasn't it?" I asked. "I've heard more than one person say he played fast and loose with the truth in his efforts to prevent exonerations. Spread lies, forged documents—"

"Oh, he did all that," Ezekiel said. "And he never gives up, not even when someone he thinks is guilty gets set free. Never gave up, I mean. He got me kicked out of the first apartment Festus found for me. Spread rumors that I was a stone-cold killer who'd gotten off on a technicality, and would probably murder them in their beds. Got the other tenants in the building so riled up that they started making complaints about me. That I came home drunk, that I'd hassled some of the ladies in the building, and that Ruth was barking all night. Fake, all of it, but it cost us our home. Of course, I landed in clover—Festus was so mad at what happened that he insisted that I move into the apartment over his garage till I get on my feet again. Which is going to be a lot easier now, without Norton trying to poison the well every time I apply for a job or an apartment."

"You're making it harder for me to feel sorry for Norton," I said.

"If turning the other cheek was easy, the man upstairs wouldn't have to tell us to do it." Ezekiel shook his head. "Maybe whoever killed Norton did it because they wanted to stop him. To keep him from hurting anyone else. But you just can't do that."

"No, vigilantism's never a good thing," I said.

He nodded.

"So I don't think you're the killer," I said. "And I bet the chief doesn't, either. But please tell me you have a solid alibi for last night."

"Depends what time we're talking about," he said. "I had dinner with Festus and a bunch of people from the conference. But a couple of the Innocence Project people wanted to have a meeting with Festus after dinner, and I told him not to worry about me and Ruth—we'd be fine for an hour or two. I took her out for a nice, long walk across the golf course. When Festus finished his meeting, he called me, and I met him back in the lobby, and he drove us out to his farm. He probably knows the times better than I do—I don't think his meeting was much over an hour and a half, if that. Of course, I've got no proof that instead of strolling across the golf course I didn't steal a car, drive out to wherever your house is, and bump off Norton during that time, so let's hope that's not when it happened."

"Here's hoping," I said. I decided not to mention that the hotel's security cameras would probably record exactly when he and Ruth had gone out and when they'd returned. With luck, the audio on our home system would peg the exact time of Norton's murder and it would turn out to be during a stretch of time when Ezekiel was accounted for.

And that could be the kind of thing Vern was looking for out in the hotel grounds—signs that might show how someone had managed to leave the hotel and kill Norton. Even if someone managed to sneak into a car in the parking lot or the valet garage without being seen, they couldn't drive it off the grounds without being spotted by the bellhop on duty in addition to the security cameras. And if someone had parked a car somewhere nearby and hiked across the golf course to it, Vern would find signs.

And I rather doubted that Ezekiel was up to making a hike like that. He got around well enough, but slowly, and he tended to sit down to rest rather often.

"Well, I'm going to get myself a good seat for the next session." Ezekiel heaved himself up from the hearth and steadied himself on his cane. Had he been using a cane yesterday? I didn't remember it. But yesterday had been a relatively strenuous day—I had several older relatives who kept a cane around for days when their hip, knee, or foot problems were acting up and happily did without on good days.

"What is coming up next?" I asked.

"One of your local deputies," he said. "Talking about the challenges of being a woman in law enforcement."

"That's my friend Aida," I said. "I should definitely go, if only to give her moral support. I'll see you there."

He nodded, and headed for the door to the conference rooms, with Ruth almost touching his right leg.

If I were a regular conference attendee, I'd have hurried along with him to get a good seat. But Aida would see me just as well—maybe better—if I ended up standing along the back wall, ready to dart out and deal with any kind of kerfuffle. So

I began making my way toward the Hamilton Room, but in a leisurely fashion.

I ran into Cordelia in the Gathering Area.

"How was your morning with Horace?" she asked. "Find any useful clues?"

"Yes," I replied. "But nothing that's going to blow the case wide open. How's it been going here?"

"A little subdued," she said. "I could have prevented this, you know. I should have kicked Norton out the minute I found out who he was."

"You couldn't have predicted what would happen," I pointed out.

"I predicted he'd cause trouble," she said. "I just thought we could handle it. If I'd kicked him out Thursday, maybe he'd still be alive today."

"And maybe that would only have been a temporary reprieve," I said. "Unless this was the only time he ever left his computer, sooner or later he'd have run into someone who had it in for him. If not here, then somewhere else. I'm not saying he deserved what happened to him, but is anyone all that surprised?"

"No." She sighed. "He was a nasty, toxic, unpleasant person. But he didn't deserve to die like that. And you know what I'm most afraid of?"

I shook my head.

"That his pigheadedness may have driven some perfectly nice person over the edge. I'm going to focus on keeping the conference on track. Keep me posted if you learn anything. No, I take that back. Don't tell me too much. I don't want to accidentally spill anything the chief wants kept quiet. Just keep an eye on things for me."

"Will do," I said.

She nodded and strode off toward the ballroom. Probably checking on lunch.

I paused to peer inside the Lafayette Room. Although there wasn't a formally scheduled session going on in there, I could see people having quiet discussions at several tables—including one where Amber Smith appeared to be giving an informal tutorial to two other women on what a grand jury was and how it worked. I stopped to listen and nodded my approval. Not that I was a lawyer, but I'd listened to Festus often enough that I could tell she was probably giving good information.

As I watched, she glanced down at her cell phone and nodded slightly, as if confirming that yes, it was time to get a seat for the next session.

"So don't worry too much at this point," she said, by way of wrapping up the conversation. "All the grand jury indicting your cousin means is that the case is probably going to trial. That grand jury didn't hear one smidgen of the exculpatory evidence you just told me about. Exculpatory's the high-falutin' way of saying evidence on your cousin's side," she added, seeing their frown at the word. "So don't panic yet—just make sure his lawyer is the best you can find."

The discussion trailed off at that point into thanks on the women's part, and assurances on Amber's that they were welcome to email her if they had more questions. Evidently they found whatever she'd told them reassuring. They scurried off to the next session in the Hamilton Room. Amber followed more slowly, and I fell into step beside her.

"You're pretty good at that," I said. "I don't know that much about your story—are you a lawyer or did you just pick all that up dealing with your own case?"

"Picked it up," she said. "My husband was a lawyer—the one they think I killed. But it's not as if he ever talked to me about his work. And he did real-estate stuff, not criminal defense. How he'd laugh if he could see me now—talking about briefs and motions as if I was Perry Mason or something."

"Well, however you learned it, it's great that you're helping out other people with what you know."

"A lot of people have helped me," she said. "I feel like I should pay it back. Or would it be paying it forward? Anyway, I just hope I don't have to make use of my knowledge of the legal system for myself this weekend. And don't pretend that puzzles you," she added, seeing my expression. "Your local police chief is no dummy and neither am I, so I know he's got all of us here at the conference pegged as suspects."

"No, I get that," I said. "I was just puzzled at the idea of you having to use what you've learned yourself. I mean, didn't I hear you yesterday telling someone else that the first thing you should do the minute a police officer wants to talk to you is find a good lawyer and then shut up and do what the lawyer tells you?"

"You think that sounds suspicious?" She paused and looked around, but we were in a quiet part of the Gathering Area, as most of the people were hurrying to get seats for the session that was about to start.

"No," I said. "It sounds smart. It's exactly what Festus has always drummed into the heads of any family member who'll listen to him. And I gather you've already got a good lawyer—or does the one you're working with only do appellate work rather than trial work?"

"He does both," she said. "And his firm also has a department that does civil cases, like trying to claim my share of my husband's estate so I can actually pay them. But until they can pull that off, I'm flat broke, and not all that happy about the possibility of going even deeper into hock for another criminal case. So let's hope the chief finds whoever did away with Norton before I have to rack up too many more billable hours. Do you know if he's looking at anyone in particular?"

"If he is, he's keeping it close to the vest," I said.

"Figures," she said. "Meanwhile, what do you want to bet that as soon as the news gets out, the trolls will start saying someone did us a favor?"

"Did us a favor by making us all suspects in a murder case?" I asked. "Seriously? You think someone really will say that?"

"Yes, I know." She laughed ruefully. "No one wants that. But you just wait. As soon as the news gets out, I bet one of Norton's minions will say that, and the rest of them will chime in with the hate."

"Actually, my dad has been thrilled on a couple of occasions when he thought he might be a suspect in a murder case," I said. "But I think that reaction was pretty unique to him. And it's because he reads mysteries by the bushel. Mysteries in which the real killer is always caught by the last page and gets his comeuppance."

"Must be nice to be a suspect in one of those," she said. "In real life, you can get cleared of all charges and have the real killer tried, convicted, and put away, and people online will still be saying you got off on a legal technicality."

"As if actual innocence were a technicality." I nodded my agreement.

"Yeah," she said. "I've stopped worrying about my reputation."

"'Reputation is an idle and most false imposition,'" I quoted. "'Oft got without merit, and lost without deserving.'"

"Is that another of the Dickens quotes Kevin says you're good at this time of year?" she asked.

"Shakespeare," I said. "From *Othello.* My husband appeared in a production of it a few years ago. Nothing like helping an actor learn his lines to help you memorize things. Which is useful, since I come from a family of competitive quoters."

"Must be nice." We had reached the door of the Hamilton Room. "You coming in?"

"I'm going to slide in at the last moment," I said.

"See you later, then." She joined the stream of people entering the room.

I'd spotted someone else I wouldn't mind talking to— Madelaine Taylor. She was sitting by the glass wall at the other end of the Gathering Area, staring out and looking rather down in the mouth. Although even her unhappy expression didn't spoil her looks. She had the translucent porcelain complexion that went with her vivid red hair, though I'd have called her pretty rather than beautiful. Even though she and Amber were probably within a few years in age, she looked a lot younger. Maybe it was her waiflike, orphaned air. Which was understandable. I tried to imagine how I'd have felt if Mother were locked up for murdering someone.

"You look glum." I took a seat beside her.

Chapter 21

"Not sure how I feel," she said, glancing over at me before returning her gaze to the bleak winter landscape. "Glum? I don't know. Should I feel glum? Or maybe guilty? It's not like I'm glad the Gadfly's dead—I don't wish anyone dead. But I'm not going to go around pretending to be all sad and solemn."

"You're allowed not to feel all that much grief," I said. "And even relieved that you don't have to deal with him anymore."

"At least I don't have to decide whether or not to report him." Glum wasn't the right word. Madelaine looked more angry than anything else. "But I'm a little ticked that now there's no use reporting him."

"Reporting him for what?"

"He showed up at our door Thursday night," she said. "Around nine. Aunt Ellen was still down in the restaurant with those two ladies who are trying to exonerate an old friend of theirs."

"Ginny and Janet?" I asked.

"Yeah, I think that's their names," she said. "She really hit it off with them. I like them, too, but I was kind of socialed out. Conferences are hard on us introverts. So I told them I needed to get to bed early, and bless her heart, Aunt Ellen didn't ruin it by pointing out that, normally, midnight is early for me. She realized I just needed some space."

I nodded.

"So I came back to the room and put on the TV, and I started watching *Forensic Files.* It was either that or one of the Christmas specials, and I wasn't quite in the mood. It's weird, you know. I travel a lot for my job, and at every hotel I've ever been in, they have a channel on their cable system that shows *Forensic Files,* and half the time I end up watching it because I can't figure what else is on. And besides, it's kind of a comfort watch, weird as that sounds. Anyway, Norton showed up at the door."

"Damn," I said. "I hope you called hotel security."

"I should have," she said. "But seeing him at the door caught me off guard, and he pushed his way into the room before I could stop him, and I'd left my phone on the charger on the bed-side table and he was between me and it. And he started talking about how he could do good things for my mom's case if I made it worth his while."

"Good grief," I said. "Did he mean that the way it sounds?"

"I think so," she said. "Only, stupid me—I thought at first he was trying to ask for money. And when I figured out what he really meant, I went after him. I threw things at him and . . ."

"And," I prompted, when her pause looked likely to stretch on indefinitely.

"And I may have scratched his face," she said.

"Did you tell the chief?" I asked.

"It didn't have anything to do with his murder," she said. "It was the night before, and—"

"Tell him," I said. "What if they find your DNA in the scratch? I have no idea how long DNA sticks around in circumstances like that, but you never know. You might be able to find someone who remembered seeing the scratch on his face Friday, but what if no one noticed it? Or what if he told someone about the encounter and you don't? That might look suspicious."

She winced and closed her eyes.

"Did you at least tell your aunt?"

"I didn't want to upset her," she said. "She was already pretty nervous, just seeing him at the opening reception."

"Tell her," I said. "And then tell the chief."

"Yeah." She nodded. "Your chief probably already has us pegged as suspicious characters, given what Norton was doing to us."

"Just what was he doing?" I asked. "Apart from never missing a chance to gloat that your mother was convicted of murdering your stepfather? I know you were doing a roundtable about her case this morning, but I was still at home, dealing with the investigation."

"And I bet that wasn't a lot of fun," she said. "I heard he was shot—it wasn't inside your house, was it?"

"Behind the barn," I said. "Couldn't even see it from the house. A cousin who lives with us went out to feed the chickens and found him."

"Is she okay?"

"She will be."

"Good." She nodded. "I had a really hard time going back in the house after Mom shot my stepfather. In spite of how much I hated him. I only did it maybe twice, to bring out things Mom needed. Then I let Aunt Ellen arrange to have everything else packed up and the place cleaned out, and we sold the house so we could afford to pay her lawyer."

She took a deep breath and closed her eyes. I wondered if she remembered my question. Should I ask again what Norton had been doing to her and her aunt?

My phone dinged to announce the arrival of a text, but I resisted the temptation to check it. If I just waited patiently . . .

Madelaine opened her eyes again and launched into her story.

"My stepfather was a controlling jerk," she said. "He wasn't usually physically abusive—I think he figured out early on that he'd get in trouble for that. But Mom couldn't lift a finger unless he gave her permission. He wouldn't let her get a job, wouldn't let her have any money or make any decisions, like when he decided they should move from Wisconsin to his hometown in Virginia, away from all her friends and family. By that time he'd cut her off from them anyway. I grew up hardly knowing any of my grandparents or any of Mom's or Dad's family. Just his creepy family. It got so Mom wouldn't even leave the house, because when she got home, he'd interrogate her about where she'd been and who she'd talked to. And he'd search her phone and check the car mileage. It was like being in prison."

"Did he treat you the same way?"

"He wasn't quite as hard on me," she said. "But same idea. I left home the day I turned eighteen. Maybe that was a mistake. At least when I was there, she had someone else. And he tried to keep her from even seeing me. Maybe that doesn't sound like abuse—"

"It sounds exactly like abuse," I said. "They even have a name for it now—coercive control. They've passed laws about it in England, defining it as a type of domestic abuse. Most parts of the US haven't caught up to them on that."

"Wish they would." She sighed. "Anyway, Mom endured more than ten years of that. Then one day she was decorating the Christmas tree, and happy because she knew I was coming to the area and she figured one way or another she and I could sneak in a visit. She was humming a Christmas carol, which always annoyed him, so she wouldn't have done it if she'd realized he was in the dining room, cleaning his guns. He liked to do that—he'd spend hours oiling them or whatever, and when he finished he would pretend to be aiming at something—her china cabinet, or the TV set, or maybe even her. He heard her humming and he lost it, and stormed over and knocked over the tree, and he was stomping on the ornaments and yelling that he'd show her, and she just picked up one of the guns and shot him with it."

Somehow that last part took me by surprise, and I just blinked for a few seconds.

"So yeah, she killed him." Madelaine stuck her chin out defiantly. "But it wasn't murder. I'm not sure how much of what she felt was fear and how much was just being pushed beyond her limits. Not sure it matters. It wasn't murder."

"Sounds to me like either self-defense or voluntary manslaughter," I said.

"I think her attorney tried for one or both," she said. "But the judge wouldn't let in any evidence of abuse."

"Wouldn't let it in? How could he get away with that? He or she, but under the circumstances, I'm betting it was a he."

"Yeah." She uttered a snort of mirthless laughter. "Not only a he, but an old friend of my stepfather's family. I'm sure that had nothing to do with it. And before you ask, yeah, Mom's lawyer tried for a change of venue. I have no idea why that got turned down."

"I seem to recall that changes of venue are at the judge's discretion," I said. "And I get the impression that even if judges don't like the idea, a lot of the time they grant it—at least if they're smart—because not doing it can be grounds for overturning a conviction. So that's one more thing that could help her case for appeal."

"In theory." She nodded. "But that takes time. And maybe I'm all wrong on this, but nowadays it seems as if you have a lot better chance of getting your appeal heard and having it succeed if you've got public opinion on your side. So we've been trying to get Mom's case out there in social media. Get people to understand that he was abusing her, even if he was careful never to leave bruises. That she wasn't trying to deny killing him—only that it wasn't murder. And Norton kept trying to sabotage it."

"Sabotage it how?"

"By promoting lies." She grimaced slightly. "I don't know if he made up stuff, or just took lies other people wrote and amplified them. Stuff like a story that Mom killed him to get a million dollars in insurance money, which is ridiculous. He had an insurance policy at one time, but he'd stopped paying on it years ago. There was no insurance. Or that she killed him because she couldn't afford a divorce lawyer. Also nonsense. She knew I'd found a nonprofit group that works pro bono for women who want to divorce their abusers—she just wasn't ready to give up on the marriage. She's very Catholic. Norton even tried to use that against her—that she killed my stepfather because she wanted out of the marriage but didn't believe in divorce. The worst was when Norton put something out in his blog that we're pretty sure he just completely made up—an interview with a woman who claimed she was a friend of my mother's, and helped her plan my stepfather's death, and that the police would never figure out who she was because she and Mom got prepaid cell phones and only ever called each other on those. It's total nonsense, but we can't disprove it, and the police have been driving us crazy, trying to get us to tell them who the friend was, and they never listen when we tell them that we have no idea, and either the woman's lying or Norton completely made her up."

"That must be maddening," I said.

"Maddening, yeah," she said. "But not a motive for murder. He could slow the process down, but Aunt Ellen and I are in it for the long haul. We accept that she has to serve some time for what she did. But not life without possibility of parole."

"Manslaughter's no more than ten years," I said. "Big difference."

"Yeah," she said. "Really hoping we can get her sentence reduced by the time ten years have gone by. But this isn't going to help—Norton getting murdered. What if people start thinking he's some kind of martyr who was killed because he was trying to protect society from dangerous criminals like Mom? Because I've already seen someone online saying that."

"Then we do our best to get the truth out there," I said.

Not until it came out of my mouth did I realize that it sounded as if I were pledging myself to help their campaign.

And maybe I was.

"Thanks," she said. "Let's hope it doesn't get quite that bad. Look, I'm going to lie down. Tension headache coming on."

"Do you need anything for it?" I asked.

"No, but thanks." She stood and gave me a weak smile that was probably intended to show that she was basically fine. It only made me more worried about her.

"If you need a doctor, my dad's on call for the conference," I said. "And he's very sound on headaches."

"Thanks. I'll definitely keep that in mind if the Excedrin lets me down." Her smile grew a little more believable, and she headed for the door to the lobby.

My phone dinged again, and I looked at the text—Michael asking what Thai dishes he should bring back for me and the boys to eat tomorrow. I texted him some suggestions. He replied with a thumbs-up and a selfie of him and his mom. I was glad to think that he was coming back by bedtime—with or without pad Thai. Between his run to the Shack Friday and the Saturday night banquet here at the conference, we weren't short on delicious food. In fact, not just coming back by bedtime, but still planning to get here in time for the banquet, the concert, and the fireworks. I smiled as I tucked my phone into my pocket.

Time for Aida's panel.

Chapter 22

When I reached the Hamilton Room, instead of sitting in the
audience, I pulled a chair over to the back wall and sat there.
Under the circumstances, Aida would probably understand if I
multitasked by checking up on a few suspects while listening to
her talk. And Kevin had helped out by sending me a link to a
page where he had collected a bunch of links, not only to stories
about the Keepers, but also to Madelaine's mother's case, Ezekiel's, and Amber Smith's.

He'd helpfully labeled the links as either "good source" or
"troll source." Or "good source if I say so myself" in the couple
of cases where the link was to the *Virginia Crime Time* website. I
noticed that the troll sources included *Godfrey for Justice* and *The
Real Scooparino.* I pulled out my notebook and jotted a reminder
to ask Kevin if he knew the Scooparino's real name. From what
little I'd seen, he and Norton seemed to spend almost as much
time attacking each other as analyzing cases—what if whoever
was behind the Scooparino alias was here at the conference?

I learned that Ezekiel had been alibied by seventeen people
who could all testify that on the evening in question he'd been

helping bus tables and wash dishes in his cousin's bar, not robbing a gas station an hour's drive away. But since all of the witnesses were either related to Ezekiel or alleged to have been inebriated when the crime took place—not an unusual condition for the occupants of a bar between midnight and two A.M.—the prosecutor disparaged the testimony of the six who took the stand, and obviously the jury didn't believe them. Why only six? Did some of them refuse to testify? Were some of them intimidated out of testifying? Did the defense think some of them wouldn't make credible witnesses? And maddeningly, the police did not act in time to get hold of security camera footage at either the gas station or the bar. Not that grainy security footage from the eighties would necessarily be all that useful, but you never knew.

Ezekiel would probably still be in prison if the doomed gas station worker hadn't pulled a gun from under the counter and exchanged gunfire with the robber. They'd tested the blood shed by the wounded robber: B negative. I remembered the statistics Dad was so fond of quoting. B negative was relatively rare, accounting for only about two percent of the human population—only AB negative was rarer. Unfortunately, they hadn't arrested Ezekiel until several months had gone by—time enough for a minor wound to heal. And he was also B negative, which was the last nail in his coffin. But fortunately the blood samples they'd taken from the gas station floor were still in the police department's evidence locker, and after many long years of legal skirmishing to force the authorities to allow it to be tested, Grandfather's labs were able to demonstrate that the gas station robber may have shared a blood type with Ezekiel, but his DNA was different. They were even able to identify the owner of the DNA—a man who'd died in prison after killing the clerk at a liquor store he was robbing.

I glanced around and spotted Ezekiel, sitting at the far end of the front row, beaming as Aida deftly fielded questions about her work as a deputy and her experience as a Black woman in law enforcement. Was he thinking that perhaps, if he hadn't been railroaded, he might have had a daughter like her? Or was he able to set aside might-have-beens and enjoy the sight of a strong young woman with a passion for justice making a good career for herself?

This was his first Christmas of freedom in nearly fifty years. Nothing we did could make up for those lost years—his stolen life. But we could damn well do our best to make this Christmas a merry one. I scribbled a reminder in my notebook to ask Festus what Ezekiel wanted or needed.

I moved on to the links about Amber—whom the Gadfly had dubbed the Black Widow of Virginia Beach. Most of the information tracked with what Amber had shared, both about her side of the story and what the trolls were promoting. About the only new bit of information was that she had grown up "on the wrong side of the tracks," according to the prosecutor. I'd have said grown up poor in an abusive family and given her full credit for doing well enough in school to get a scholarship to Tidewater Community College. But only a partial scholarship—she still had to juggle a job along with her classes. So maybe instead of calling her a gold digger for marrying a wealthy older man, might the prosecutor want to consider that perhaps she saw her husband as the white knight who rescued her from a life of unending labor at minimum wage? And that maybe the last thing she'd have wanted was to kill the goose who was continuing to lay golden eggs at a rate of at least half a million dollars a year?

I decided that I was provisionally on Team Amber in this case. Although I'd need more time to consider whether I approved of her as a romantic interest for Kevin. She was only a couple of years older than him, but she almost certainly had a lot of baggage. So I'd wait and see. If Kevin was serious, he'd bring her to some family gatherings. Seeing how she handled that would give me much more scope for assessing her. And if Kevin was smart, he'd realize the same thing. Maybe I should start preparing Mother for meeting Amber at Christmas dinner. I got the impression she didn't have any family of her own to celebrate with. Better yet, maybe I should start preparing Amber for surviving Mother's scrutiny.

Not something I needed to worry about just yet. I focused back on Aida's talk. She was currently fielding an annoyingly misogynistic question from a man in the audience.

"No, I don't agree that I'm less capable of dealing with the physical requirements of the job than a male officer," she was saying. "Physical combat isn't that big a part of the job most days, and when it is—you want to arm wrestle? Compare our times on the hundred-yard dash? See which of us can bench-press more weight? Go down to the gun range and see who's the better shot?"

The audience tittered slightly, probably because the heckler was a pudgy-looking thirtysomething man with the stereotypical pale complexion and bad posture of someone who spends more time online than anything else.

"Shouldn't this clown at least wait till Norton is decently buried before trying to assume his mantle?" said a voice, almost in my ear. I started when I realized it was Amber. Had she been looking over my shoulder while I read up on her case?

"I should warn you, though," Aida went on. "I can still fit into the uniform I wore when I was all-state in track and field, it's been a while since I placed below the top ten in a statewide law enforcement marksmanship contest, and I hold a black belt in kenpo."

"I'm not trying to cast aspersions on your qualifications," the misogynist said. "Only—"

"Yeah, you are," Aida said. "But I'm used to it."

She smiled the sort of smile mothers use to warn their darlings that they are on very thin ice. Probably an expression the misogynist had seen a lot of in his time on this earth. He clamped his mouth closed and sat down.

Someone else was waving his hand in the air. Josh. Why weren't he and the others busy with their quest to figure out how to escape the Inn without being seen? And what was he up to now?

"Deputy Butler," he said, when she nodded at him. "Could you demonstrate some kenpo? Like what you'd do if a bad guy got the drop on you?"

"I might be persuaded," Aida said. "If you and your buddies will serve as my ukes."

Josh, Jamie, and Adam all leaped up and hurried to the front of the room.

"Uke?" Amber said, in a low tone.

"Literally, Japanese for 'receiver,'" I said. "In martial arts, it's the person who pretends to attack the instructor and gets thrown or punched or kicked or whatever."

"The fall guy," she said.

"It actually requires a certain amount of skill," I said. "You have to know how to take a fall or a punch. A good teacher makes sure the uke has the expertise to keep from getting hurt."

"So I gather your kids have had some training."

I nodded. I could have added that I had, too, but it would sound like bragging, and anyway Aida was starting to explain what she was about to do and I shut up so I could hear her. And pulled out my cell phone so I could record what the boys were up to for Michael.

The audience watched in rapt fascination as Aida demonstrated what she would do if a thug—or a gang of up to three thugs—tried to punch her, choke her from behind, grab her gun arm, or slash at her with a knife—with the roles of gun and knife being played by a stapler and a large carrot, respectively. Josh, Jamie, and Adam happily mugged for the crowd in their roles as thugs.

The demonstration proved to be a big crowd-pleaser. I noted Cordelia scribbling something in her notebook. I suspected she was making a note to have Aida do a longer demonstration at her next conference. Maybe a self-defense course—Aida had plenty of experience doing that.

And maybe we could do it on short notice at this conference, if the needs of the murder investigation made it difficult for Chief Burke to do anything else he was scheduled for. I thought of taking out my program to see when those were, but I didn't want to make it look as if I was impatient for Aida's star turn to end.

Aida and the boys finished their demonstration and took bows. A good third of the audience surged up to the front to ask more questions. Another third or so were staying put, or moving up to get better seats for the next session—a presentation by one of the Innocence Project attorneys.

I stayed put long enough to email the video to Michael, then joined the remaining crowd, who were swarming out into the Gathering Area to hit the coffee, tea, and soda station. But once I got there, I realized that I was feeling a sudden strong disinclination to staying among the conference attendees. When I followed my impulse and stepped out into the relatively uncrowded main lobby, I felt an overwhelming sense of relief.

Why?

It wasn't just that any of the people in the chattering crowd could be the Gadfly's killer. No, it was more that any of them could be one of the trolls I'd seen in the sites Kevin had steered me toward. Most of the people who posted and commented seemed like nice, decent people who just happened to be fascinated with true crime. But there were a few whose words were drenched in vitriol. I didn't want to find out that one of these pleasant, smiling, friendly people in the Gathering Area was actually KinkySeeker or Avenger4zt or any of the other screen names that the worst of the trolls hid behind. And even after the chief caught the one person who'd killed Norton, there would still be plenty of trolls to carry on his nastiness.

I glanced toward the door of the staff conference room, where Chief Burke had set up his command center. The door opened, and someone came out. I recognized the faded red of her hair—Ellen Mays, Madelaine Taylor's aunt. The chief strolled out with her, and they shook hands, smiling. I found myself hoping the smile meant that he'd eliminated her as a suspect.

The chief went back into the conference room. Ellen closed her eyes and took a deep breath, as if to steady herself. She suddenly looked older and more faded, as if her hair had gone grayer overnight. I tried to imagine her shooting Norton and couldn't.

Then she opened her eyes and looked around as if unsure where to go.

I went over to join her.

"Are you all right?" I asked.

"I'll be fine," she said. "Your chief seems to be a nice man, and I gather from what Kevin has said that he's a straight arrow. But after my sister's experience with small-town law enforcement—well, being interviewed by the police is just a bit unnerving. Brings back bad memories. And what if he decides I'm a prime suspect?"

"You're probably in good shape," I said. "Didn't you go into town with Ginny and Janet to see the Christmas lights?"

"I did," she said. "But I didn't end up coming back with them. We parked someplace and walked around, visiting shops and listening to the strolling musicians and eventually ending up by the big Christmas tree in the town square. And there was such a crowd! We got separated, and I wandered around for what seemed like forever, looking for them."

"I gather you didn't have their number," I said. "Or you could have called them."

"I didn't even have my phone," she said. "So I couldn't have called anyone. It ran out of juice by the end of the day's program, so I took it to my room and left it there to charge while we had dinner. When they suggested going to see the Christmas lights, I thought about running up to get it, but I didn't want to hold them up, and I didn't exactly expect to get lost. I couldn't even call a cab."

"What did you do?"

"I went into the diner in the town square and had a cup of coffee to warm up," she said. "And I started talking to the very nice lady behind the counter—her hair and mine were exactly the same shade of red."

"That would probably be Muriel," I said. "She's the owner."

"Yes, it was," she said. "And she was so nice that I got up the nerve to ask if I could use her phone to call for a cab. And she said not to bother about a cab, she'd find me a ride. And in a few minutes, a nice young African American woman in a deputy's uniform came in—"

"That would be Aida Butler," I said, nodding.

"That's right," she said. "I wish I could have seen her session, but I didn't want to put off Chief Burke. And I wanted to get my interview over with. Anyway, once she got her carryout coffee mug filled, she brought me back to the Inn. So all's well that ends well. Thank goodness this is a small town. If we were in the city, I bet I'd have gotten mugged or something. But I have no idea what time it was when all this was happening. It was getting late by the time I got home. Do they know when he was killed?"

"Not yet." Which wasn't a lie. Dad hadn't officially weighed in yet, and the chief probably wouldn't appreciate my sharing anything I'd overheard while he and Dad and Horace were discussing the case. And had Sammy and George had any success finding the gunshot on the security footage? I shoved the question aside and focused back on Ellen, who still looked shaken. I reminded myself that this wasn't necessarily the reaction of a guilty person. More likely the reaction of someone who'd had way too much personal experience of injustice.

"Muriel will remember when you came into the diner," I said. "And while the town doesn't have any kind of organized security system, the college does, and a lot of the shops, restaurants, and homes have their own systems. Even if it's only a video doorbell, if one of those caught you at the right moment, you'd be alibied. And I bet the chief is already rounding up as much video as possible."

"That's a little reassuring," she said. "But I won't rest easy until I know they've apprehended whoever killed Norton. Because until they do, I'll be worrying that maybe they'll decide it was me."

I nodded my agreement. And didn't say aloud what ran through my mind—that leaving her phone in her room and getting separated from the Keepers when she went into town with them would be a pretty good way to muddy the waters if she had wanted to sneak away from the hotel to kill Norton. The fact that I had a hard time believing she could be a murderer didn't mean she wasn't.

"If it helps, the chief has a lot more experience with homicides than your average small-town police chief," I said. "He spent over a decade as a homicide detective in Baltimore."

"Also encouraging," she said.

"And he's not the kind of cop who'd let an innocent person take the rap for someone else's crime," I said. "Or he wouldn't have Festus's seal of approval. He's actually helped with a couple of exonerations."

"I'll try to relax, then." Her smile was brave and a little forced, but maybe she'd feel better when she put more time and distance between herself and her police interview.

"If you hurry, you can get a good seat for the Innocence Project people," I said, mostly to distract her.

"Goodness! I do want to see them. Thank you!"

She bustled off toward the conference area. I was about to follow her when—

"Mom?"

I turned to find Jamie standing behind me.

"What's up?" I asked.

"We're ready to see if we can sneak out of the hotel without you guys catching us," he said. "Can you meet Ekaterina in her office?"

"Sure thing," I said.

"Great!" he exclaimed and raced off.

Chapter 23

Horace and the chief were already in Ekaterina's office. Ekaterina had set up a semicircle of chairs facing her desk and credenza. She had shoved aside her small Christmas tree—festooned with a selection of antique, hand-painted Russian Christmas ornaments—to make room for a collection of nearly a dozen monitors. Except for the largest one, each showed the coverage from nine of the Inn's security cameras, stacked in a three-by-three grid pattern, with a little label to indicate which camera that picture belonged to and what area it covered—#03: LOADING DOCK or #07: MAIN PARKING LOT or #14: SIDE DOOR #3. The largest monitor showed a video feed of the lobby.

"Looks like a bunch of tic-tac-toe games," Horace commented.

"More like the set for *Hollywood Squares* before the players arrive," the chief said. "Pictures are pretty small."

"Our system stores the full-sized picture for each of the cameras," Ekaterina explained. "So Sammy and George can see them as large as they like."

"Or at least as large as their monitor permits," Horace said. "Kevin has set up a feed to the station," he explained, looking at me. "Sammy and George are back there reviewing all the footage from the last twenty-four hours."

"And here, we can switch to a closeup of what's on any camera at any time." Ekaterina demonstrated, making a few swift keystrokes on her computer. The large monitor switched from the lobby to a view of the loading dock, where a slender young man in chef's whites sat on the edge of the concrete apron with his back to us, gazing moodily into the distance through the plume of smoke drifting up from his cigarette.

"We even have some ability to change the camera focus." Ekaterina rattled the keys some more. The picture slowly zoomed in until it was focused on the chef's left ear. More keystrokes and it pulled back again. It must have made a slight noise—the chef turned his head and stared up at the camera. Then the camera panned left until he was almost out of the picture . . . right again so we only saw half of him. The chef took another deep drag on his cigarette, blew out the smoke, and then gave a rather perfunctory and slightly sardonic wave at the camera with his free hand.

"We do not make any particular effort to hide the security cameras," Ekaterina said. "The staff are accustomed to having them around, and their visible presence seems to be reassuring to the guests while acting as a deterrent to thieves and other would-be intruders."

"And you have all the entrances covered?" the chief asked.

"Yes," she said. "All the entrances, and also the entire parking lot. Many of our guests drive expensive vehicles that would otherwise be tempting targets for larceny."

Nice to know the ancient Twinmobile was well protected while I was here.

"How long do you keep the tapes?" the chief asked.

"Tapes? We do not use tapes!" Was there just a slight note of reproach in her voice? "That would be so very twentieth century.

Kevin has set us up with a large amount of online storage. We retain the data automatically for a year, and if we have any reason to suspect a security breach, we have the ability to flag that day's data so it will be stored indefinitely. Or until we decide to release it."

"Impressive," the chief said. "Isn't all that rather expensive to operate?"

"It pays for itself over time," Ekaterina said. "Only six weeks ago, for example, a guest complained that his Lamborghini had been stolen from our valet parking. Fortunately our camera system captured the real story, and we were able to prove that the guest himself entered the valet parking garage with stealth and used a spare key to remove the vehicle. It does not take very many occurrences of that kind to make our security system pay for itself."

"You should have reported that," the chief said, with a frown.

"The incident would not have enhanced the Inn's reputation." Ekaterina's tone was prim but decisive. "We would have called you in if he had not been cooperative. But he signed a full confession, and he is unlikely to offend in Caerphilly County again, since we have banned him permanently from the Inn. As we had with Mr. Niedernstatter."

Her tone implied that the banning was by far the direst punishment either miscreant could possibly incur, and the Gadfly's demise only a sad but minor footnote to the story.

"And we did call upon Deputy Shiffley to make sure he did not linger in Caerphilly," she added.

"Ah," the chief said. "I do recall Vern mentioning that he escorted a misbehaving guest off the Inn grounds and over the county line." He nodded with satisfaction. I'd heard him say, more than once, that if most of the other local businesses were run the way Ekaterina managed the Inn, his job would be much less demanding.

I studied his face, trying to get a clue about how the case was going, but his expression was neutral. Guarded. Not surprising with Ekaterina nearby, since she was a civilian. Technically, so was I, but he sometimes forgot that. And was he really expecting the boys' project to help with his case, or was he just humoring Josh, Jamie, and his beloved grandson Adam? I couldn't tell.

My phone rang.

"Mom?" It was Jamie. "Are you guys ready?"

"Whenever you are," I put the phone on speaker. "So are you going to tell us where you're making your first escape attempt?"

"No!" he said. "That would make it too easy. Just say, 'ready, set, go!' And then we'll start."

"Ready when you are," the chief said.

"Remember," Ekaterina said, pointing to the larger monitor, "if you want to get a closer look at something, just tell me which camera and I'll show it there."

"Good," the chief said.

Horace merely nodded.

"Ready, set, go!" I said into the phone. And then I muted it so Jamie couldn't hear anything we said while watching for the Great Escape.

For several minutes nothing happened. The four of us sat there, our eyes shifting from screen to screen. Occasionally movement would catch our eyes. A uniformed hotel employee retrieving a car from the valet parking garage. An energetic terrier emerging from a side door, dragging a man in a bulky down coat over to the hotel's canine exercise yard. The larger of the Cobalt Cab Company's two taxis arriving at the front door and disgorging a brace of well-dressed women.

"Camera twelve," Horace said pointing at the screen in question.

But Ekaterina had already spotted it and pulled up the picture from camera #12 on the larger screen. We could see a section of the flagstone path that led to the three cottages that provided the Inn's most luxurious quarters: the Jefferson, Washington, and Madison Cottages, which were scaled down replicas of Monticello, Mount Vernon, and Montpelier, respectively. The path was lined with evergreen bushes that were either dwarf varieties or had been cowed into remaining small by frequent vigorous pruning.

"Thought I saw some movement in the shrubbery," Horace said.

We all stared at the monitor. A full minute went by. Maybe two. It felt like a couple of hours.

"I could zoom the camera in," Ekaterina murmured.

"No." The chief, too, kept is voice low, as if whoever might be rustling the shrubbery on camera #12 could hear us. "That would not be a fair test."

"There it is again." I pointed. "Right near the bottom of the screen."

The shrubbery moved, then stilled—but now we could make out bits of clothing through the leaves. A pair of dark jeans, a khaki camouflage jacket, and a patch of black with a Nike Swoosh logo on it.

My finger hovered over my phone's mute button.

"Shall I tell Jamie we can spot whoever's doing that?" I asked. "Or do you want to watch a little longer?"

"Just another few seconds," the chief said. "I think—yes. It's Adam. Go ahead and tell them."

I unmuted my phone.

"Tell Adam we've spotted him," I said to Jamie. "He's wriggling through the shrubbery outside one of the cottages."

"Darn," he said, and then he shouted to the others. "No dice, guys!"

On camera, Josh appeared in the frame, and held aside some of the holly branches so Adam could crawl out from behind the bushes.

"An impressive first attempt," Ekaterina said. "He almost succeeded in evading detection."

I made sure Jamie relayed her compliments to Adam. Josh made a gesture clearly intended to say "Curses! Foiled again!" Jamie and Adam were laughing gleefully and waving at the camera.

"He's scratched his face," the chief said. "I hope it's not too bad, or Minerva will skin me alive for letting him do this."

"Okay, we're heading for test site number two," Jamie said on the phone. "I'll call you back when we get there."

"We wouldn't have spotted him if we hadn't been watching closely," Horace said. "That area by the cottages looks like a possible point of vulnerability."

"Perhaps we need more cameras," Ekaterina said. "I can ask Kevin to take another look at the system."

"I think if we look closely, we'll be able to spot anyone who slips in or out of the hotel that way," the chief said. "Unless the boys find a bigger hole in the system, it will do fine for our purposes today."

Ekaterina nodded, but I suspected Kevin would still be hearing from her.

My phone rang again.

"Ready for test run number two?" Jamie asked.

"You may fire when ready, Gridley," I said.

"Who's Gridley?" he asked.

"Look it up later," I said. "Start your test." And I muted my phone again.

Ekaterina, Horace, the chief, and I all leaned forward and stared at the monitors again. Nothing much happened for a couple of minutes. A bellhop drove up in a sleek black minivan. As he hopped out, a man in a business suit strode out of the front door, handed him a folded tip, and drove off. A housekeeper with a knit cap on her head and a puffy jacket over her uniform emerged from the Jefferson Cottage, pushed her cart down the flagstone path to the Washington Cottage, and let herself in. On the loading dock, the chef stubbed out his cigarette and checked his watch. He pulled out a pack of Gauloises cigarettes and lit another one. Then he glanced up. Was he glancing at the camera out of guilt, because he was overstaying his break?

No. He wasn't quite looking at the camera. He seemed to be looking a little to the right of it.

"Can you show camera number three on the large screen?" I asked. "That's the loading dock, right?"

The figure of the cigarette-smoking chef appeared on the large screen. He was definitely leaning back slightly so he could stare at something overhead. And frowning slightly, as if he wasn't quite sure what he was seeing but knew he didn't exactly like it.

"Are you doing something with the camera again?" Horace asked. "Something that would attract his attention?"

"No," Ekaterina said.

"Then what's he looking at?" the chief mused.

"The loading dock is an obvious area of great vulnerability," she said. "So we have more than one security camera in that location. Let's see if we can get a better view."

She glanced along the row of monitors, then typed something in her computer. Another view of the loading dock appeared on the large monitor, this one from near ground level and near the open roll-up door. Now we could see the chef, half turned so he could stare up and behind him at where Josh appeared to be crawling along the ceiling of the dock area.

"Oh, my God!" I exclaimed. "What is he doing?"

"Do not be alarmed," Ekaterina said. "There is a sort of metal grid attached to the ceiling, to assist in loading and unloading large or bulky objects, like refrigerators and mattresses. He appears to be anchoring himself to that."

Yes, he was. He was using climbing gear—probably the gear Rob and Delaney had acquired for the rock-climbing trip they'd taken last year to the Southwest. He was wearing a climbing harness, and there appeared to be ropes and pitons anchoring him to the metal grid. I still didn't like it.

"Is that a camera you normally monitor?" I asked.

"Of course," Ekaterina said. "We pay a great deal of attention to the loading dock. I suspect they failed to detect the presence of the second camera because it is down near the floor, instead of up by the ceiling, like most of the cameras."

"Then we've legitimately detected their second attempt," the chief said. "You can tell him to come down from there."

"Let me take a few deep breaths first," I said. "So I can tell him very calmly."

I unmuted my phone and took one last deep breath.

"You can tell Josh to stop crawling over the ceiling of the loading dock like a human fly," I said. "But don't startle him."

"Darn!" Jamie exclaimed.

I flinched at how loud he was.

"You can knock it off," Jamie called out. "They spotted us somehow."

The chef said something while looking up at Josh. It was too soft for Jamie's phone to catch it, and if these security cameras had audio it wasn't turned on. But the chef also pointed toward the camera with his free hand.

"A little far-fetched to think that any of the conference attendees came equipped with climbing gear," the chief said.

"I think if someone were desperate he could probably make that climb with his bare hands," Horace said. "Or maybe with a rope. It'd be pretty nerve-racking, but doable."

"But we would still have detected him, thanks to the second camera," Ekaterina said. "And most of the time the loading dock door is closed after dark."

We watched a little anxiously—at least on my part—while Josh made his way back to the side wall of the loading dock area, where a metal ladder ran up, no doubt to give hotel staff a way to use the ceiling grid for the freight-handling purposes it served. I breathed a sigh of relief when Josh was back on the floor of the loading dock.

"Okay, that was a bust," Jamie said over the phone. "But we've got a third exit route. Third time's the charm, right?"

"It always is in fairy tales," I said. "Please tell me route number three isn't as scary as this one."

"Don't worry," he said. "It's much easier. I'll call you back when we're there."

I hung up and took another few deep breaths.

"Relax," Horace said. "He'll be fine."

"And it appears as if Josh was taking all the proper safety precautions," Ekaterina said.

"And they're not toddlers, and they're pretty reliable and responsible for their age, and I can't keep them wrapped up in cotton wool for the rest of their lives," I said. "I know. And I didn't freak out on the phone, did I? So just let me freak a little now, while I won't embarrass them."

"I know how you feel," the chief said. "If I'd known they'd do anything risky—"

"It's okay," I said. "Jamie says the next one is much easier. And he's a lot more risk averse than Josh. And—"

My phone rang again. This time it was Josh on the line.

Chapter 24

"This better not be anything like that last escape attempt," I said.

"Hey, Mom," he said. "Sorry if I scared you. It probably looked a lot more dangerous than it was."

"Glad to hear it," I said. "Since you're calling me, does that mean Jamie's going to play Houdini this time?"

"Yeah," he said. "Only fair, since he figured out this one. You guys ready?"

I glanced over. Horace and Ekaterina were both studying various monitors, but the chief nodded.

"Ready when you are," I said.

Then I muted my phone and fixed my attention on the row of monitors.

The hotel was quiet—at least the part of it we could see through the cameras. The occasional guest arrived or departed from the front door. Ezekiel took Ruth out to the doggie exercise yard and watched her romp happily. A housekeeper pushed a cart down the walk to the third of the cottages.

But no sign of Jamie on any of the monitors. No sign of Josh or Adam, either. I was just glancing down at my phone, thinking of asking Josh if there was some kind of holdup when—

"There he is," Ekaterina said. "But he's not going out—he's coming back in."

She tapped some keys and brought up the feed from the camera that covered the front door. Jamie was walking in, saying something to Enrique, the bell captain.

"Did anyone spot him?" Horace asked. "Because I sure didn't."

"Not me," I said. Ekaterina and the chief merely shook their heads. Well, they also frowned. I suspected Ekaterina would have already been on the phone to Kevin if the rest of us weren't there. And the chief probably wasn't happy that his suspect pool had just grown instead of shrunk.

A minute later Jamie appeared at the door of Ekaterina's office.

"Hi, Mom," he said, leaning against the doorframe in a pose that only looked casual. He was grinning from ear to ear over his victory.

"So how did you pull it off?" I asked.

"You know how some of the rooms have sliding glass doors instead of windows?" he said. "With no balcony to walk out on, only a ledge for flower pots? We just went out one of those."

"But none of the rooms on the first floor have those sliding glass doors," Ekaterina pointed out. "Only the ones on the upper floors."

"I know," Jamie said. "We went out one on the far side, where the first floor's like kind of almost a half basement, so the drop from the second floor wasn't that bad."

"But all of those rooms have screens in the windows," Ekaterina said. "And the screens do not open—we cannot have guests falling out of the windows all the time."

"They may not open," Jamie said. "But they're designed to

come out easily so you can wash the windows. All you need is a screwdriver and you can pop them right out. And pop them right back in again, no problem," he added quickly, seeing Ekaterina's face. "You absolutely can't tell it was ever removed. The window cleaners do it all the time."

"But how would you have gotten back in again?" the chief asked. "Because the hotel security system only works as an alibi if you can not only get out but also back in again without being seen."

"We did it with a rope," Jamie said. "We brought one along, because we knew we could have made one with bedsheets but we didn't want to mess up the sheets." Said with a cautious glance at Ekaterina. "We tied our rope to the balcony, and then we all climbed up and down a few times. And if he didn't want to leave the rope dangling from the balcony, he could take it with him and then kind of lasso the balcony when he wanted to get back in. The way the ground slopes, some rooms you wouldn't even need the rope—you could just jump up, grab the balcony rail, and pull yourself up."

"Does this mean I will need to have Kevin add a camera to cover every single window?" Ekaterina demanded. "On every floor? Do you realize—"

"Of course not," I said. "You only need to make sure that you've got a camera covering the base of every outside wall. Because no matter what room they're in and how high up, if they're using the balconies to make an illicit exit, they eventually have to reach the ground and walk away, right?"

She nodded and looked a little mollified.

"And you kind of have to know where the outside cameras are," Jamie said. "Because it wouldn't do you any good if you got out of the hotel without getting caught and then walked right past one of the cameras guarding the parking area."

"Horace," the chief said. "Can you make sure Sammy and George are looking at the footage from all the cameras? Not just the ones covering the exits."

Horace nodded, picked up his phone, and began texting.

"So merely being in the hotel at whatever turns out to be the time of the murder no longer constitutes an alibi," I said.

The chief sighed.

"I'm sorry," Jamie said. "We didn't realize—"

"Don't apologize," the chief said. "You may have saved us from making a dangerous error."

"And you have alerted me to a hole in our security." Ekaterina had pulled a card out of her desk and was writing something on it. "I expect your strenuous efforts have given you an appetite. Please take Josh and Adam to the restaurant with you and present this to your waiter. He will bring each of you the dessert of your choice."

"Even the chocolate volcano cake?" Jamie asked.

"Even that."

"Thank you." He took the card and glanced at me, and then at the chief.

"Good work," the chief said. "Go enjoy your reward."

"Your very well-earned reward," I added.

Jamie grinned at us and walked out. He waited until he was out of sight—but not out of earshot, before uttering an ecstatic "woohoo!" Followed by what I deduced was his half of a phone conversation. "Meet me in the lobby! I have great news!"

"Of course, there are other challenges a hotel guest might face if he or she wanted to commit the murder," the chief said. "Getting from here to your house without being detected— because it's too far to walk, and we are, of course, going to check out any cars coming and going from the hotel grounds."

"Just getting out of the immediate vicinity of the hotel itself without being spotted will have been somewhat challenging," Ekaterina said. "Although not as challenging as it will be soon," she added under her breath.

"And another thing," I said. "Even if someone was able to escape from the hotel last night without being seen, won't we be able to see them on camera yesterday, prowling around the hotel to scope out where the cameras are?"

"Alas," Ekaterina said. "They would not have needed to explore the hotel to learn that. Some of the guests—particularly the female ones—were expressing anxiety over whether Mr. Niedernstatter could gain reentry to the hotel. I explained the thoroughness of our security system to them and pointed out some of the cameras. I even brought them here to show them the system in operation."

"I see," the chief said.

"And—perhaps I am overly suspicious," Ekaterina went on. "But some of the guests were power walking in the hallways Thursday and yesterday."

"Power walking?" the chief repeated.

"For exercise," she explained. "Apparently our weather over the last few days has been more severe than they are accustomed to." And then, in a show of unusual restraint, she closed her mouth and pursed her lips. Normally, if someone complained about the weather in Caerphilly, she would pull out her phone, consult her weather app, and inform us what the temperature was in Moscow—or, if Moscow's weather didn't sound sufficiently daunting, in Yakutsk, where the average winter temperature was in the minus thirties.

"So they've all been marching up and down the hallways en masse," the chief said.

"Only eight or ten of them," Ekaterina said. "Some of them with hand weights."

The chief frowned. I looked up from my phone but decided it would not improve his mood if I announced that in Moscow, the temperature was minus twelve Fahrenheit. And minus thirty-eight in Yakutsk.

"Do you happen to remember which guests were involved in this power walking?" he asked.

"No," she said. "But we can determine that from the security video, if you think it will be relevant."

"Who knows?" he said. "Can you get Sammy and George the video from the day or two leading up to the start of the conference? Starting whenever the first conference attendees arrived— I seem to recall that some of them came early to do a little sightseeing."

"I will ask Kevin to make that video available to them as well." Ekaterina began typing on her phone.

I'd been staring at the monitors, and something occurred to me.

"You've got cameras covering the pathways to the cottages," I said. "What about the private terraces behind each of the cottages?"

Ekaterina blinked and frowned.

"No," she said, after a pause. "We do not have security cameras covering the terraces. That would invade the privacy of the guests who stay in the cottages."

And it went without saying that, since the cottages were the most expensive and luxurious of the Inn's accommodations, the guests who stayed there were VIPs who valued their privacy. Grandfather had stayed there often, before Mother and Dad had bought their sprawling farmhouse and set aside a ground-floor suite for his use.

"Naturally, all of the doors leading from the terraces into the cottages are equipped with burglar alarms," Ekaterina went on.

"The doors and windows. But our focus, of course, is on protecting our guests from intruders. We've never had to worry before about protecting anyone on the outside from our guests."

"No reason you should have worried about it," the chief said. "You're running a luxury hotel, not a penitentiary. But Meg's right—if whoever killed Norton was here in the hotel, that could be how they managed to slip out of the hotel without being noticed. I assume the cottage guests have the ability to shut off the alarms so they can go out on the terrace and turn them on again when they turn in."

"Of course," she said. "And our security staff can monitor whether the system is engaged. If the hour grows late and the console shows that a cottage's system is not activated, they drop by to remedy that."

"Who's in the cottages now?" he asked.

"The Washington Cottage has been serving as the conference office," she said. "And I believe Dr. Blake is occupying the bedroom, to spare him the difficulty of commuting to the hotel every day."

"And also because he never passes up a chance to stay someplace with room service," I added.

"The Jefferson is occupied by two elderly German tourists," Ekaterina said. "Among the few current guests not connected with the conference. And the Madison is under renovation. A pipe burst, and the entire floor was badly water damaged."

"So we might see workmen coming to and fro," the chief said. "But not guests or housekeeping."

"And not workmen, either, until the new flooring material arrives," Ekaterina said, with a frown. "Which may not be until after the new year."

"If I were trying to sneak out of the hotel," I said. "I'd probably make tracks for either the Washington or the Madison. Turn off the burglar alarms, exit through the terrace, and plan to be back before the security staff come by to turn the alarms on again. Do the cottage guests know about that routine?"

"Yes," Ekaterina said, with a frown. "There is a notice informing them that if the burglar alarm has been turned off, the security staff will rearm it at midnight."

The chief nodded and turned to Horace.

"Tell Sammy and George to pay particular attention to anyone coming and going from those cottages—what are the camera numbers?"

"Seventeen and eighteen," Ekaterina said.

"Roger." Horace was texting briskly.

Just then we spotted Janet and Ginny lurking outside in the main lobby.

"My next interview is here," the chief said. "My next two interviews. I'll see you later."

He hurried over to greet the new arrivals.

Chapter 25

"This is very unsatisfactory," Ekaterina said. "While our security system has been able to provide the chief with some information, so far all of it is information he has been able to determine from other sources."

"That doesn't mean it isn't useful," I said. "Remember, when he catches the killer, he'll need to take the case to court, where a defense attorney will try to poke holes in it. So having confirmation from your security system of the evidence he's gathered elsewhere could be invaluable."

"That is reassuring to hear," she said. "I wonder if he has found a skilled lip reader."

"Is he looking for one?" I asked.

"I would if I were him," she said.

"Why?"

Instead of answering, she sat down in front of her keyboard again and, after a few flying keystrokes, pointed to the large monitor. It showed footage from the camera that covered anyone arriving at the Inn's front entrance. The time stamp in the lower right corner indicated that it had been taken at 12:27 P.M.

yesterday. As I watched, someone stormed into the picture. He had a carry-on bag over his shoulder and was dragging a large suitcase behind him. He turned around, evidently looking back at the door, and I recognized him as Norton.

"This is when he was kicked out?" I asked.

"Yes," she said. "Now watch closely."

Norton's mouth began moving. From the look of it, he was shouting. He let go of his suitcase, which toppled over behind him, and raised his middle finger in the familiar rude gesture.

"What a jerk," I muttered.

"Might it not be useful to learn what he is saying?" she asked.

I nodded, although I rather doubted anything he said would provide a hot clue. More likely, it would demonstrate how boringly blue and repetitive his vocabulary was. Still, you never knew.

Behind him, a car pulled up under the porte-cochere—a beat-up gray Toyota Corolla. I could see a hotel staffer hopping out of the driver's seat.

Norton finished his invective with what I gathered was a final mighty bellow. Then he turned and pulled out his cell phone. The timing of the gesture suggested that he was using his phone to avoid meeting the gaze of the staffer—who might be hoping, in vain, for a tip.

"You see?" Ekaterina said. "If we could find someone who reads lips—"

"Robyn Smith does, I think," I said. "Or call the Caerphilly Assisted Living. I bet they've got a few residents who can."

"Excellent," she said. "I will—"

"Wait," I said. "Can you back up and play that last little bit again?"

"Of course." The picture on the screen paused. "From when he walked outside?"

"No," I said. "Just from when he pulled out his phone."

She looked puzzled, but she obliged, and we both peered intently at the screen.

"Bingo!" I said.

"Evidently you see something I do not," she said.

"Your security camera caught him typing the passcode to unlock his phone," I said. "I can't quite tell what it is from this distance—"

"But you're thinking that Kevin could enlarge that part of the picture and discover it."

"It's worth a try," I said. "Can you send him a clip of that part, or tell him where to find it?"

"Of course," she said. "And then we can discuss the upgrades that will be needed to the system."

"No long discussion needed, if you ask me," I said. "Just tell him what the problem is, and he'll fix it as soon as possible." Which might not be until after the conference was over and the murder solved—or at least until the chief had run out of cyber evidence for Kevin to analyze. But I didn't think Ekaterina was in the mood to hear this. In her mind, her beloved Inn was in dire peril, and she would expect Kevin to treat this as the emergency she considered it.

Ekaterina nodded absently and turned back to her keyboard.

I left her to it, but as soon as I was back in the lobby, I pulled out my phone and began texting Kevin, both to let him know about my useful discovery and to warn him that Ekaterina was on the warpath about what she saw as flaws in the security system. I had just hit SEND when—

"There you are."

I looked up to see Aida standing in front of me, coffee in hand.

"Good presentation," I said.

"Yeah, right," she said. "What did I say that was so off?"

"Off?" I was puzzled. "I don't recall thinking you said anything that was off. I thought it was great, and so did Cordelia."

"You were frowning at something," she said. "If I said something that you didn't think went over well, let me know so I can fix it next time I do something like this. It was when I was talking about how we all need to qualify in firearms every year. I know you're not a big fan of guns, but it's a professional requirement that—"

"Good grief," I said. "I wasn't frowning at what you were saying, not about guns or anything else. I was multitasking. Kevin had just sent me a bunch of links about some of the people who might have it in for the Gadfly. Links to the facts about their cases, and then the demented things he was saying about them. You probably happened to look at me when I was reading about the seventeen alibi witnesses whose testimony didn't save Ezekiel from being convicted."

"Well, if that's—wait. Seventeen alibi witnesses? Good lord. They really did a number on that poor man, didn't they?"

"They did indeed," I said. "Look, if you happen to talk to him, see if you can figure out what he needs."

"What he needs? Are we talking about Christmas present fodder, or big, important life stuff, like a job and a place to live and a big fat settlement from whatever town or county sent him up river for fifty years."

"Either," I said. "Both. He hasn't had a very merry Christmas for a few decades, and he needs help now, not in a few years, which could be how long it takes Festus to wring a settlement out of the county."

"At this festive season of the year," Aida intoned, beginning my oft-quoted favorite passage from Michael's annual one-man reading of Dickens's *A Christmas Carol*. I joined in, and we finished the quotation in unison.

"It is more than usually desirable that we should make some slight provision for the Poor and Destitute."

We both laughed, and then Aida's face sobered.

"And he is pretty poor and destitute," she said. "Put Ezekiel's case on your list of things we go back and fix when Kevin and your boys invent that time machine. Meanwhile, yes, I'll keep my ears open. Doesn't he have any relatives to help him?"

"According to him, the respectable ones won't help and the wayward ones aren't around any longer," I said. "So evidently not."

"Poor soul," she said, and headed back toward the conference area.

I checked my program. Apparently the chief had asked the Keepers to come for their interview right after the session they were doing about their high-school friend's case. A pity I'd missed that, but I could probably find some time to talk to one or both of them about it later—and if I couldn't, Festus or Kevin could fill me in. The next session should be good—Stanley Denton, Caerphilly's leading (and only) private investigator would be talking about investigative tools. A fascinating subject, and Stanley was always a good speaker.

But my mind kept circling back to those links Kevin had sent me. I wanted to check out the ones I hadn't yet had time to look at. And I didn't want to demoralize Stanley by scowling in the middle of his presentation, as I had during Aida's.

So instead of returning to the conference rooms, I found a seat in a corner of the lobby, near the fireplace and the main Christmas tree, and pulled my laptop out of my tote bag.

I'd been in the middle of reading what the Gadfly had to say about Amber's case when I'd put my phone away to watch Aida and the boys do their self-defense demonstration. I opened up my phone . . . and couldn't find the links Kevin had sent me. Had I somehow managed to delete them from the page where he'd been collecting them? Or was I going to the wrong page? Figuring that out was above my pay grade.

I fired off an email to Kevin, apologizing for bothering him and asking if he could resend the links.

But I realized that he might be a little busy at the moment, so instead of waiting until he responded, I did a few searches on my own.

I started with Amber Smith's name in combination with various words like "Virginia Beach," "murder," and "trial."

About the only new thing I learned from the resulting newspaper articles and web pages was that the local papers had really hated Amber. Article after article described her as a trophy wife from the wrong side of the tracks. Neighbors described her as "bitchy" and "standoffish." Several country club members said that she was loud and didn't fit in. "She was trash," one woman said. "She wore nothing but tight, skimpy clothes and big, gaudy jewelry."

I'd have wanted to stand off from that one, too. And the bit about her clothes and jewelry—that didn't sound like the Amber I'd met. Today she was again wearing jeans—well fitting, but not outrageously tight—a baggy sweater, and small plain silver hoop earrings. Had Amber changed? Or was the woman making it up?

Or—sad thought—maybe while her husband was alive, Amber had dressed to please him. The tight, skimpy clothes could have been his taste. And now that he was gone she had reverted to her own better taste.

I glanced up from my phone and saw the Keepers, Janet and Ginny, strolling through the lobby. The chief must not have kept either of them all that long.

Ginny looked pleased and enthusiastic about something, with a beaming smile and a spring in her step. Janet seemed less cheerful. In fact, she looked as if only good manners were keeping her from rolling her eyes in disbelief.

"What's so exciting?" I asked when they drew near.

"Okay, this is going to sound ridiculous," Ginny said, with a giggle.

"It *is* ridiculous," Janet muttered.

"You know you feel the same way." Ginny frowned at her friend before bursting out in giggles.

"Not quite the same way," Janet insisted.

"The same way about what?" I asked.

"We're suspects!" Ginny exclaimed. "Isn't it exciting?"

"Exciting's not the word," Janet said. "Interesting, perhaps."

"Interesting!" Ginny repeated. "She's excited, I can tell. She's just pretending to be blasé."

"And I can't help but wonder if she uses 'interesting' the way my mother does," I said. "It's her go-to adjective when she can't find anything nice to say. She just murmurs 'interesting.'"

"A sensible woman," Janet said. "Because I agree that it's interesting, after all the work we've been doing, learning about how the criminal justice system works, to be more directly involved in a case. But I'm not exactly excited about it."

"You'll see," Ginny said. "Once you get over the initial shock of it, you'll start to enjoy it."

"You sound like my father," I said. "He's such a mystery buff that he's never happier than when he gets to be a suspect, or at least has to prove his own alibi. I gather neither of you has one?"

"Well, yes and no," Janet said. "We were together all evening, which under most circumstances would constitute a perfectly solid alibi. But even we have to admit that we both disliked Norton."

"Really, really, *really* disliked him," Ginny said.

"So Chief Burke has to consider the possibility that we joined forces to rid ourselves of him." Janet pursed her lips as if the thought were distasteful.

"It's only sensible," Ginny said. "I'd be the first to admit that if Janet needed to bump off anyone, I'd absolutely help her. And hide the body, too."

Janet winced slightly.

"And Janet—well, she'd definitely get me a really good lawyer," Ginny went on.

They exchanged smiles, and I deduced that this was an old joke with them.

"So we're rather hoping your chief finds whoever actually killed Norton pretty quickly," Janet said. "Because we might have a hard time proving that we both spent the evening strolling through Caerphilly."

"And buying cups of hot chocolate and gingerbread cookies," Ginny added with a blissful smile. "And window shopping, and listening to the carolers, and taking pictures of the tree, and—"

"Sounds as if you hit all the high points," I said. "Many of those shops have security cameras, and the chief can check the footage. And think how many of the tourists are walking around with cameras or cell phones in their hands. The chief could send out a call for pictures taken last night."

"That sounds more like something our defense attorney would do after we're charged with murder," Janet said.

"You don't know the chief," I replied. "He's amazingly thorough."

"Doesn't really matter how thorough he is," she said. "He can't track us every minute of the time we were wandering around downtown Caerphilly."

"He doesn't have to," I said. "He just has to track you as being in downtown Caerphilly at a time that makes it impossible for you to travel to or from the murder scene at the critical moments."

"That's so." Janet looked pleasantly surprised at the thought. "Assuming the circumstances allow him to pin down the time of the crime with reasonable accuracy."

"You see?" Ginny said. "It will turn out all right. I just feel bad that we got separated from poor Ellen. We'd have been back a lot sooner, but we spent at least an hour going around asking people if they'd seen her."

"That's good," I said. "People might remember you doing that. More alibi fodder."

"But if we'd managed not to lose her, *she* could have been our alibi," Ginny said.

"And maybe the chief would believe her," Janet said. "But what if he decided she shared our motive for wanting to do away with Norton? I'm sure even if we had her to bolster our alibi, the trolls would say we were probably in cahoots."

"I'm sure the trolls are already convinced the whole lot of us ganged up on Norton and did away with him en masse, like a remake of *Murder on the Orient Express,*" Ginny said.

I decided not to mention that I'd had the same thought.

"Or that's what they'll say when they learn about it," Janet said. "Depressing thought. Let's hope the news hasn't hit the true-crime community yet. Well, let's go see what's happening with our fellow suspects."

"And what's happening outside!" Ginny exclaimed. "Look! It's snowing!"

Chapter 26

Ginny and Janet hurried across the lobby to the wall of glass and stood, peering out at the snow.

I rose to follow them, then paused long enough to close my laptop, in case anyone got nosy enough to spy on what I'd been up to.

Outside, the snow had indeed begun falling—rather heavily. I joined a small group of people who were staring out the glass wall of the lobby.

"The snow isn't going to interfere with the fireworks, is it?" a man asked.

"I don't think so," I said. "Unless it's a complete blizzard, they should work fine. The firm that's handling the show just needs to be careful to keep the fireworks inside where it's dry until right before they set them off. And they absolutely know that."

"Will we be able to see them from indoors?" Ginny asked.

"Yes," I said. "Although the view will be better from the patio."

"Guess I'll have to settle for the inferior view from in here," Ginny said, glancing down at her feet.

"You didn't bring your snow boots?" Janet asked. I deduced

from her tone that she'd recommended doing so and was exasperated, though unsurprised, that her advice had been ignored.

"I didn't expect to need them," Ginny said.

"You and me both," Amber said.

"The boots you were wearing Thursday aren't waterproof, then?" I asked.

"Boots I was wearing?" Amber frowned. "You must be mixing me up with someone else."

"Bother," I said. "Because the boots I remember someone wearing were very cool, and I was going to ask the wearer where she got them. Of course, that was Thursday, when I was still trying to attach names to faces. I wonder who it was."

"I bet it was Madelaine," Ginny said. "She also dresses very nicely."

"Probably," I said. "I should have asked when I saw them. Well, whoever it was, maybe they'll be wearing them tonight. But you shouldn't really need boots for the fireworks. They'll be shoveling the patio. Look, they're at it already."

I pointed to where Enrique and Jiro, one of the porters, had arrived with bright orange snow shovels and were beginning to clear the patio.

"That could keep them very busy," Ginny said.

"And they'll keep at it," I said. "If it gets very bad, they'll bring around a little tractor with a snowplow attachment."

"And if you're still worried, put on your warmest shoes and maybe a second pair of socks," Janet said to Ginny. "And then wrap plastic bags over it all."

"That would work," Ginny said. "Except I don't have any plastic bags."

"Ask at the desk," I said. "Last time I was here in a snowstorm, I suggested to Ekaterina that they should lay in a supply of disposable boot covers, and she thought it was a great idea."

Enrique looked up, saw us watching him, and waved cheerfully. Most of us waved back.

I was heading back to resume my online research when I saw the chief striding through the lobby. He appeared to be in a hurry—and he was headed in the direction of Ekaterina's office. I grabbed my laptop and headed that way—dawdling a little, in the hope that I could think of a good reason to show up there. A reason other than my well-known nosiness.

I arrived at the office before I thought of anything, but when I stuck my head in, I was greeted warmly.

"And here she is!" Ekaterina exclaimed.

"Good catch on Mr. Norton's cell phone," the chief said. "Kevin believes he will be able to determine the passcode from the video Ekaterina sent him and—"

"I'm in," Kevin said, through the speaker of Ekaterina's desk phone. "Ekaterina, go to that page—"

"I have," she said, and pointed to the large monitor. So far, it was just showing a mostly blank web page.

"Looks as if he was calling and receiving calls from a cell phone," Kevin said. "Calls and texts. I'm doing some searches on it, but it looks as if it's going to turn out to be a prepaid cell phone."

"Is that what they call a burner phone?" Ekaterina asked.

I nodded.

"I'm sending you screenshots," Kevin said.

Images began appearing on the screen. The chief moved closer and began peering over his glasses at it.

"If you want the highlights," Kevin went on.

"Yes, please," the chief replied.

"After Norton exchanged a couple of phone calls with the unknown phone, they began texting each other. I gather the unknown phone's owner claimed to have some information that would supposedly convince Cordelia to let Norton back into the conference, so they were going to meet him and go out together to confront her. And they arranged for Norton to pick them up just outside the Inn's front gate."

"They?" Ekaterina echoed. "You think more than one person was involved?"

"No," Kevin said. "I'm using 'they' because we don't know the gender of the culprit. Normally I'd say 'he,' but a lot of our suspects in this are women."

"It would actually be quite useful if there were more than one suspect involved," the chief said. "Criminal conspiracies have such a convenient tendency to fall apart. What time were these texts exchanged?"

"Last text was nine twenty-two," Kevin said. "At nine eighteen Norton said he was waiting in a side road near the entrance to the Inn."

"Probably that abandoned dirt road where we recovered his car," the chief said.

"And at nine twenty-two our unsub texted 'I'm here,'" Kevin added.

"Unsub?" Ekaterina repeated.

"Unknown subject," the chief explained.

"The killer?" Ekaterina asked.

"We don't know that," the chief said.

"Possibly the killer, though, no?" she said. "Can you trace this burner phone?"

"If by 'trace' you mean find out who owns it, good luck," Kevin said. "You can buy those things for cash pretty much anywhere. Walmart, Target, drug stores, supermarkets, 7-Elevens . . ."

"Yes," the chief said. "We can track the signal from a prepaid cell phone, just like any other cell phone. But as Kevin explained, even if we are able to read the texts its owner sent to Mr. Norton and use cell phone tower information to figure out where it went, tying it to a particular person can be difficult if not impossible. And even tracking where it went won't be doable immediately. I've already got a request in for information, both on Mr. Norton's phone and for traffic at the nearest cell towers. I'll start preparing a warrant so we can add the prepaid phone to the request. But responses to such requests can be slow at the best of times. At this season . . ."

His voice trailed off and he studied the small Christmas tree on Ekaterina's desk with less enthusiasm than he would normally have shown.

"You could call the number," suggested Ekaterina. "And see where it rings. If you went into the conference area, where most of the suspects are—"

"Not advisable," the chief said. "We don't want to alert the phone's owner that we are aware of its existence."

"Because then they could get rid of it," I said. "If they haven't already."

"If the killer's smart, they already did that, as soon as they bumped off Norton," Kevin said. "Turned it off, traveled to someplace in the middle of town, and dumped it there."

"And if he's very smart, he'll know about the possibility that we might recover DNA or fingerprints from it, and he'll have discarded it someplace where we'll never find it." The chief's tone was gloomy.

"I thought we were using 'they,'" Ekaterina said. "Since we have agreed that murder is an equal opportunity crime."

"True," the chief said. "*They* will have discarded it someplace where we'll never find it. So it seems probable that Mr. Norton picked up the unsub shortly after that last text and then they went straight out to Meg and Michael's neighborhood."

"About a fifteen-minute drive," Kevin said. "Unless they took some wrong turns and got caught up in the tourist traffic."

"Did Mr. Norton use his cell phone after he received that text?" the chief asked.

"Hang on a sec," Kevin said. "No. That's it. Always possible that he turned his phone off once he met up with the unsub. That'd be the smart thing to do if he thought they'd be getting up to something that wasn't quite aboveboard and didn't want us to be able to trace him."

"Also possible that the unsub instructed him to do so," the chief said. "Especially if the unsub was planning to do him in. Well, at least this lets us narrow down the time frame a bit. We can have Sammy and George start listening for the gunshot at, say, nine thirty."

"Pretty early in the evening," I said. "A lot of the conference attendees would still have been at dinner then, or hanging out together in the hotel together."

"Yes." The chief sounded pleased. "With luck we should be able to eliminate quite a few of them."

"The entire busload who went to Temple Beth-El did not return until nearly eleven," Ekaterina said. "And—"

Just then my phone dinged to signal that I had a text. Ekaterina and the chief watched with interest while I pulled out my phone, as if hoping I was about to produce some other useful tidbit of information. I hated to disappoint them, but—

"It's Michael." I held up the selfie he'd taken with his mother.

"That's not our tree," the chief said.

"It's the national Christmas tree," I explained.

"In Washington?" Ekaterina sounded displeased. "He is out of town? I have him listed as attending the banquet tonight."

"He's planning to be back for it," I said. "And for the holiday concert and the fireworks, of course. He'll be dropping off his mother at the Baltimore Harbor for her cruise anytime now, and then heading straight home to bring Delaney's mother here."

Ekaterina nodded her approval.

"So, Chief," she began. "Why—"

And then her phone must have vibrated. She pulled it out of her pocket, frowned, and typed a brief reply.

"Speaking of the banquet," she said. "I must go and sort out a confusion. Unless you need me—"

"Go on," the chief said. "We don't want anything to spoil the perfection of tonight's event."

She nodded and dashed out.

"Chief?"

It was Kevin's voice from the speakerphone. Both the chief and I started—evidently he, too, had forgotten Kevin was on the line.

"Yes, Kevin," he said.

"Sammy and Vern think they've identified the gunshot. At ten eleven. Want to hear it?"

"Please."

The resulting noise didn't sound much like a gunshot to me. More like a popgun. But I wasn't the expert. The chief nodded thoughtfully.

"Pretty faint," he said.

"It was behind the barn," Kevin said. "And Vern thinks they might have used a suppressor. And it was a quiet night—there's nothing else that sounds even remotely like a gunshot until well after the end of the range Grandpa calculated for the time of death."

"Yes." The chief was frowning. Was he thinking, like me, that the sound we'd just heard would be hard to sell to a jury as a gunshot?

"Chief?" Vern stood in the doorway.

"Good work on finding that possible gunshot sound," the chief said.

"Thanks, Chief," Vern said. "And about that 'possible' bit—me, I'm pretty darned sure it's a gunshot, but I bet you'd like to increase your comfort level. What if Horace and I do a little test? We get ourselves some sandbags and a couple of guns of the same caliber the killer used—a twenty-two, wasn't it?"

The chief nodded.

"Then we go out behind Meg's barn and fire off some rounds, with and without a suppressor."

"That would be useful, yes," the chief said. "Although wouldn't it be more scientifically accurate to do it under the conditions that prevailed last night? Same time of night, and without the snow, which can significantly alter acoustics."

"True, boss," Vern said. "Horace already mentioned that. So if we think we might end up relying in court on the sound Sammy and I found, we absolutely would need to set up an official test so the defense can't pick holes in it. We can do that as soon as the snow melts and we get some conditions that are close to what we had last night. But right now, if you want to feel better about eliminating suspects who have alibis for ten eleven—"

"Your test definitely would make me feel more confident," the chief said. "Sounds like a good idea. If Meg's okay with it—"

"Fine with me," I said. "And the llamas will love it—they've been rather bored lately, with most of us over here at the Inn. Just make sure whoever's in the house knows what you're doing. And that none of the critters are anywhere near your sandbags. The chickens would have gone to bed by ten fifteen, but keep an eye for the barn cats and the dogs—they're all nosy. And Seth's sheep—you know how often they wander over into our yard."

"Will do." Vern nodded at me, raised a finger to his temple by way of an informal salute to the chief, and ambled out.

I was about to follow suit when it occurred to me that if I was going to continue my research about Norton and the various people whose cases he had been talking about online, Ekaterina's office might be a safer place to do it. No danger that I'd get so wrapped up in reading about one of our suspects that I didn't notice that very person peeking over my shoulder.

"Mind if I stay for a little bit, to do some computer stuff in greater comfort?" I asked.

"No problem at the moment," he said. "I've interviewed everyone I need to interview for now, and I can always kick you out if I need to do another one."

Chapter 27

I glanced over the chief's shoulder at the large computer screen. Evidently Kevin was continuing to post information from Norton's phone for the chief. I assumed wherever he was posting the stuff was secure from cyber eavesdropping. After all, this was Kevin. And I decided it would be diplomatic to make it obvious that I wasn't trying to spy on what they were doing.

In addition to the desk, the credenza, and an impressive row of oak file cabinets, Ekaterina's office featured a small, round oak table with three comfortable chairs. I settled in there and turned on my laptop.

It was curiously peaceful. The same soft, instrumental Christmas music you could hear in the lobby was emanating from a couple of well-camouflaged speakers. A bowl of seasonal potpourri sat in the middle of the table, and the mingled scents of cinnamon, clove, and spruce raised my spirits. I resisted the temptation to raid her bowl of miniature candy canes—she had both the red-and-white peppermint and my favorite green-and-white wintergreen ones. But I didn't want to spoil my appetite for whatever the Inn's kitchen was preparing for tonight's feast. I hadn't heard what the final menu was to be, but I had overheard Cordelia fretting about whether to choose ham, turkey, or roast beef for the carnivores, and Ekaterina asking why not serve some of each. And they'd roped in Rose Noire to sign off on the vegetarian options. For all I knew, Ekaterina might have offered to have the kitchen prepare multiple options there, too. And I'd definitely be sampling any of those they served—the perfectly grilled portobello mushrooms, the risotto aux fines herbes, the seven-cheese ravioli. I'd long ago decided that I might possibly be able to stick to a vegetarian diet if I ate at the Inn every day.

And Ekaterina had promised a special Christmas dessert buffet featuring plum pudding.

Maybe I should have a candy cane after all, to get my mind off food and back onto our suspects.

The chief's suspects, I reminded myself. He was being very patient with my kibitzing, probably because so far I'd been reasonably useful. And maybe because exposure to some of the overeager self-proclaimed internet sleuths at the convention had made me look deferential and unobtrusive by comparison. None of them were quite as obnoxious as the Gadfly had been, but there were a couple who would seriously have gotten on my last nerve if I were a detective working a case with a high profile on the internet.

I looked at my phone, to see if I could get back to the page of links Kevin had sent me . . . and instead of the links, I saw the screenshots from Norton's phone. Evidently Kevin was posting them in the same presumably safe space he'd used for the links he'd gathered for me.

After scrolling up a dozen times and still finding nothing but screenshots, I decided to do my own searching. I'd already asked Kevin to resend the links—he'd almost certainly do that when he had the time. I opened up a browser window and prepared to type in potentially useful combinations of words. I could start with Godfrey Norton, murder, and one of the potential exonerees.

No, wait. What was that name Amber had mentioned—the screen name for Norton's archrival. The Real Scooparino. I added that to my search terms.

Bingo! In addition to holding forth on his own website, in the links I'd already visited, my search found links to posts Norton had made in quite a few true-crime discussion groups and Reddit threads. And conducted any number of pitched battles with people who disagreed with him—especially whoever was behind the Scooparino screen name. Good heavens, but the man had been busy. Just scrolling through my search results made me feel tired. And did I really need to read more of his venomous lies? Maybe I should move on to another case. Ezekiel's case, or Mary Campbell's or—

Suddenly a phrase caught my eye: "a just reckoning at Presumed Innocent." Was that about the murder? And those words "just reckoning"—was someone suggesting that Norton deserved his fate?

But no—the post couldn't be about Norton's murder—it was dated three days before the conference began.

Still—it was probably about the conference. I clicked through to see what Norton had to say.

"Yikes," I exclaimed, when I saw the page.

"Something wrong?" the chief asked.

"I don't know yet," I said. "Take a look at this."

He came over to the table and I turned my laptop so he could see it, too.

"Good grief," he muttered.

The link I'd found showed that Norton had been bragging about his plans to "invade" Cordelia's conference "under a nom de guerre that I will not be revealing here." Which wasn't exactly the truth—he'd registered under his own name. It was the one he used online that was the pseudonym.

"This is unsettling." The chief pulled up a chair beside mine and motioned for me to scroll down. "We've been operating under the theory that while many people might have had it in for Mr. Norton, only attendees at the conference would have reason to know he was here. But if he announced his intentions to come to Caerphilly this publicly . . . Wait, just how public is this post of his?"

"Posts," I said. "Quite a lot of them. And it appears to be a Reddit thread."

"Does that mean anyone could see it?"

"Even me," I said. "And I do not ordinarily hang out on Reddit. Worse, this seems to be a pretty . . . combative discussion. One step away from being a flame war. Norton has allies here, but also a lot of people who really, really dislike him. Especially this Scooparino person."

"What's going on?" Kevin said through the speakerphone.

"Can you send him a link to that page we're looking at?" the chief said, as he rose and returned to the desk. "And copy me."

"Roger," I said.

"Meg has found some unsettling information," the chief told Kevin. "She's sending you a link. It appears that we may need to widen our pool of suspects."

"Like it isn't already big enough," Kevin said.

After that we all fell silent for a while as we scrolled through Norton's Reddit fulminations.

"Oh, great," Kevin said after a few minutes. "He's doxxed us. That means—"

"Yes, I know," the chief said. "Published personal information you'd rather not have out there for the whole world to see. How much information did he share?"

"Only the addresses," Kevin said. "And a few phone numbers."

"What do you mean, 'us'?" I asked.

"Well, he doxxed me," Kevin said. "Only the address and phone number, but it's still annoying, and it's like doxxing you by proxy. And he also got Festus, and Horace—"

"And me." The chief's voice had that tight, precise tone that suggested he wanted to cut loose and give someone what for. And was frustrated that the logical target of his wrath was permanently beyond his reach.

"Doxxing's illegal in Virginia, you know," Kevin said.

"Only a misdemeanor," the chief said.

"A misdemeanor for most of us," Kevin said. "A class six felony for doxxing a law enforcement officer. One to five years."

"True." The chief smiled slightly at that thought. "Of course, Mr. Norton's beyond our reach now."

"But I'll definitely be scouring Reddit to see if anyone else pitched in with the doxxing," Kevin said. "Or re-shared any of the information Norton published."

"If you see anything that looks actionable, get it to the county attorney," the chief said. "But I think it's more urgent to identify some of these people on Reddit—the ones who seem particularly hostile to Mr. Norton."

"So we can figure out if any of them were in Caerphilly last night," Kevin said.

"Yes," the chief replied. "Obviously any one of them would have known he was here for the conference. They'd even have known how to find you."

"Yeah," Kevin said. "I'll work on it, but it's not going to be easy."

"And I'd give this Real Scooparino person a high priority," the chief said.

"Already trying to figure out who he is, even before the

conference," Kevin said. "He or she. One of the worst trolls in the whole community. No luck so far, but I'll keep trying."

It occurred to me that Kevin's research might also be useful if the chief decided to press charges against the doxxers. Or if Festus wanted to file a civil suit of some kind. But obviously, finding Norton's killer came first.

"Has word about Norton's demise gone out to the public?" I asked.

"Not officially," the chief said. "We haven't yet identified his next of kin, much less notified them. And I've given everyone here at the conference a stern warning not to go public with it. No telling if they'll listen though."

"Then maybe I should also keep an eye open for anyone online who announces his death," Kevin said. "Because that might mean they know more than they should."

"Or just that they know someone at the conference who ignored my warning," the chief said. "But yes, do keep your eyes open."

"Meg, can you maybe help with that?" Kevin asked. "Keep reading through the posts and feed me any names of people who seem particularly hostile to Norton?"

"Can do," I said.

So I started scrolling through the various Reddit discussions Norton was involved in, texting Kevin the names of anyone who seemed particularly combative. Kevin, meanwhile, did the harder work of trying to identify these new suspects.

"It's not illegal for you to unmask them?" I asked at one point. "That doesn't count as doxxing?"

"Only if I make them public," Kevin said. "And giving them to a law enforcement agency for good reason is not making them public."

"So I'm not aiding and abetting a felony," I said. "That's good to know."

"I'm pretty sure doxxing these clowns would only be a misde-meanor," Kevin said. "No way any of them would pass whatever psych screening any sane police department would require."

"Amen to that," the chief muttered.

He sounded discouraged. Or was I projecting my own dis-couraged feelings onto him? Figuring out who killed Norton had begun to seem—well, not easy, but manageable. He'd probably begun to think that he was working with a fixed set of suspects—a large set, of course, since it originally included all two hundred or so of the convention attendees. But still a fixed number, and the various dinner parties and after-dinner gatherings seemed to be gradually eliminating quite a few of them. Not, unfortunately, some of the ones I knew and liked and hoped were innocent. And now this discovery, opening the door for any number of plausible suspects that he would need to identify, track down, and interview.

"Well, the case isn't going to solve itself." He stood up, stretched, and headed for the door. "I'll be back later. Lock up if you leave."

"Will do," I said.

And as soon as I was all alone in the office, I felt restless. What good was I doing here? It had been a while since I'd found any new names for Kevin to research. All I was seeing were the same all-too-familiar screen names saying the same things over and over again. I knew which few would make thoughtful, courte-ous, non-judgmental comments and which ones were just full of sound and fury and signifying even less than nothing. The online equivalent of mob justice—like that scene from the movies where the angry, torch-waving villagers threaten to burn down Drac-ula's castle. Only it wasn't Dracula the online mob was after. It was Ezekiel. And Amber. Madelaine's mother. The Keepers' high-school friend.

Just then my phone buzzed. I picked it up and saw a text from Rob.

"You wouldn't happen to be back at the house, would you?"

Back at the house. Suddenly that was where I wanted to be. Back home. For the moment, the fascination of the conference faded and the luxurious but somewhat impersonal surroundings of the Inn had lost their charm. I wanted to be home, where I could kick my shoes off, put my feet up, and declare myself in for the evening. Home with my family around me, or at least expected soon. Home, where I could enjoy Mother's beautiful Christmas decorations. Home, where the only crime I was apt to witness was the squirrels stealing seed from Delaney's beloved chickadees.

"No, not at the house," I texted back. "But I can be pretty soon. Why?"

"Delaney left behind a bunch of things she might need," he texted back. "Can you—"

"Left behind? She's not at the house? Where is she? Is—"

"She's with me and she's fine," he texted back. "Baby not arriving. We're running an errand and then coming to the hotel for the dinner and the concert. But we left some stuff behind. Can you—"

"Text me the list," I replied. "I'm on my way."

So it wasn't just Delaney who was being secretive. But whatever she and Rob were up to, they were together, and she'd be fine. I advised Kevin that I was running some errands, shoved my laptop into my tote, and headed for the coat check.

The snow was steadily falling, but the roads weren't yet bad, thanks to the diligent work of Beau and Osgood Shiffley, who drove the county's two snowplows. For the final stretch of road that led to the house, I even followed Beau, who had a set of ten-point antlers festooned with twinkling holiday lights mounted atop his snowplow's cab. I didn't spot Osgood's snowplow with its life-sized Rudolph the Red-Nosed Reindeer, but I knew he was also hard at work somewhere. Comforting.

As I hurried up the front walk, I glanced through one of the living room windows. Rose Noire and her solstice celebration crew were gathered around the fireplace, sipping cups of tea and nibbling gingerbread persons. It was so blasted heartwarming and normal that I paused on the porch for a moment to blink back tears.

Then I pulled out my key, unlocked the door, and hurried inside—only to find myself surrounded by a flock of chickadees. They swooped and fluttered around my head as if joyfully welcoming me. What the—?

Not real chickadees, I realized, after a few seconds. Very realistic model chickadees, but they were soaring rather than flapping their wings. And real chickadees would be serenading me with "chickadee-dee-dee," not a tinkling music box version of "The Carol of the Birds." It was an elaborate mobile.

"Meg!" Rose Noire hurried to help me with my coat. "Do you like it? We waited until Rob and Delaney left to put it up, so we could surprise them. Do you think Delaney will like it?"

"She'll love it," I said, as I disentangled one low-flying chickadee from my hair. "Could you maybe hang it a foot or so higher, so it won't poke taller folks like Rob or Michael in the eye?"

"Oh! I never thought of that! I'll fix it right away." She started to dart away, then turned back. "You're here to pick up those things for Delaney, aren't you?"

"I am," I said. "And where is Delaney, anyway? And Rob? I can't believe he took her out in this weather."

"They wouldn't tell me." Rose Noire wore a look of mingled worry and disapproval. "He got a phone call, and then they rushed out and wouldn't tell me where they were going."

"They're probably working on some kind of Christmas surprise," I said, in my most reassuring tone.

"Finding out if they're having a boy or a girl is enough of a surprise if you ask me," Rose Noire said. "Don't run off. I'll go and get the ladder and you can help me adjust the chickadees."

She dashed off, so I didn't get a chance to suggest that maybe Rob had received a hot tip on a newly available house. Probably just as well. I'd noticed that even mentioning the possibility that Rob and Delaney might be moving upset Rose Noire. I wished they'd wait until the holidays were over before bringing it up again.

But there was nothing I could do about that, so I focused on collecting the things Delaney was asking for. Her favorite water bottle. Some dry socks. Her lip balm. All the small, practical things she'd normally never have forgotten. Rose Noire had already collected most of them in a red-and-green Christmas tote that sat in the hall, at the foot of the slender Christmas tree that filled one corner—right beside Delaney's go bag, the one that had been packed for weeks now with everything she wanted to take with her to the hospital when the new arrival began arriving. How had they ever forgotten that?

I ducked into the living room to exchange assorted holiday greetings with the solstice crowd. Then I carried Delaney's things out to the Twinmobile and came back to gather a few things of my own. Snow gear, for example, not just for me but also for Michael, Cordelia, and the boys.

As I was in the front hall, realizing that I'd probably need to make a second trip to carry everything, Rose Noire reappeared—followed by Kevin, who was carrying the household stepladder.

"Just see if you can lift it up about a foot," she said. She did something with her phone and the chickadees overhead glided to a halt.

"Right." His mind was obviously still on the case—he didn't even bat an eye at the birds' sudden appearance. "Meg, are you going back to the hotel soon?"

"As soon as I load the car," I said. "You want a ride?"

"Please."

So I steadied the ladder while he raised the mobile, and then he took the greater half of the snow gear I'd collected and hauled it to the car for me.

"Got to prep for my panel," he said, as I eased the Twinmobile onto the slightly icy road. "Will it bother you if I practice a couple of things out loud?"

"Go for it," I said. So I turned the volume down on my usual seasonal soundtrack of carols and focused on giving him what I hoped was useful feedback on whether he was making his topic intelligible to his largely non-technical audience.

And the panel went over well. I suspected some of his comments were even more pointed than usual, thanks to how we'd spent the past few hours. He hit particularly hard at the damage that even well-meaning people could cause by sharing unsubstantiated rumors—or genuine information that the police wanted to keep confidential.

"For example," he said, "I know Chief Burke warned all of you not to say anything to anyone outside this conference about Godfrey Norton's death. And that's not because he's worried about the effect on Caerphilly's tourist trade. After all, what we lose in regular tourism we would more than make up for with true-crime fans like me."

The crowd laughed at this, and a few people called out "and me!" from various parts of the audience.

"It's because the chief is having trouble notifying Norton's next of kin," Kevin went on. "In fact, we have no idea who his next of kin is."

"Either Sauron or Voldemort," someone called out.

"No, Darth Vader," came another voice.

"We'll see what we can do with those suggestions," Kevin said, deadpan. "And if anyone else has information that could help the chief find Norton's family, please see him after this panel. And everyone else please continue respecting the chief's request."

"You think Norton would have respected the chief's request?" someone called out. "If it was someone else who got killed here?"

"No," Kevin said. "He'd have been posting to that website of his five minutes after he heard the news. We can do better. There's a lot we need to fix about this true-crime community of ours, and doing a better job of respecting the feelings and privacy of victims and their families is high on the list. So let's not treat Norton the way we think he deserved. Let's treat him the way we wish he had treated others."

The audience greeted this statement with applause and scattered cheers. I wondered if the chief had put Kevin up to making this statement. Or was it just a coincidence that the chief was seated along the side of the room, near the front, where he could easily scan the faces of the audience to see if any of them were showing signs of guilt?

Definitely not a coincidence that Amber was sitting front and center, where she could give Kevin encouraging smiles and a thumbs-up from time to time. She was definitely growing on me.

Kevin's presentation was the last one of the day, so it was all the more impressive that the Hamilton Room was still packed by its end. And he earned the loud applause that followed, having done a great job of explaining any number of highly technical topics.

I texted Michael to remind him that the banquet was about to start and ask if he would be back for it.

"Getting close!" he texted back. "But we might be a little late—don't wait for us."

I didn't need to be told twice.

"I'll try to save you a few scraps of food," I replied.

And then I headed for the Madison Ballroom.

Chapter 28

In the ballroom, the buffet was set up along the left and right sides of the room, with tables for the diners in the middle of the floor and, on the far wall, the risers where the choir would stand for the after-dinner concert. The tables were all covered with bright red tablecloths, on which stood centerpieces that combined purple candles, gold tinsel, and greenery in the form of magnolia leaves and evergreen fronds. Mother was there, inspecting the centerpieces and making small but (I assumed) critical tweaks to how they were arranged.

Just inside the ballroom door, I spotted Cordelia. She was standing close enough to the door to nod and smile to all the new arrivals, but far enough away that they'd have to make an effort to come over and talk to her. And most were too intent on getting a good place in the buffet line to do so.

"Not hungry?" I asked. "Or just not in the mood for conversation?"

"I figure as the host it's bad manners for me to rush to the front of the line," she replied. "And it's not as if Ekaterina will let any of us starve."

"If they run out of anything you particularly want, I bet she'll have the kitchen whip up another batch," I said.

"Exactly," she agreed. "And it's nice to see things working like clockwork. Check another completed item off my conference to-do list."

"Last panel of the day completed," I said. "Check. Delicious banquet deployed for the delight of the attendees. Check. I think you can safely leave devouring the banquet up to the attendees."

"Yes," she said. "Well, at least one plan didn't quite work out the way I hoped, but we're managing."

"Which plan is that?" I asked.

"My plan for scheduling the conference this weekend."

"You deliberately scheduled it this close to Christmas? I just assumed this was the only weekend you could get, or the only weekend when it was affordable."

I refrained from reminding her of the somewhat caustic comments she'd made when Grandfather had scheduled a conference dedicated to owls almost as close to Christmas. "Any true ornithologist would jump at the chance to celebrate the season among fellow lovers of Strigiformes," Grandfather had said. To my astonishment, he'd been correct. Evidently the same went for true-crime fans.

"Yes, it was deliberate," she said. "I thought this close to the holiday season—Christmas and Hanukkah overlapping like this—the only people who would come would be people genuinely interested in exoneration. People who were already facing the holidays without a loved one and were willing to give up some of the usual festivities of the season in the hope of having their loved one with them next year. But it turns out Kevin was right. Having it this close to the holidays probably cut down the number of sightseers, as he calls them. But it didn't eliminate them."

"I think a lot of the people interested in true crime are pretty serious," I said. "And care about truth and justice and such. But you probably did weed out a lot of the people who are only in it for entertainment."

"Exactly," she said. "Because that was the plan. But you know who we may not have weeded out?"

I shook my head, although I suspected what she was about to say.

"The real nutcases."

"Like Norton," I said. "Are there any others like him? I confess, I've spent more time helping Chief Burke than helping you. I haven't had time to get to know that many of the attendees."

"Isn't Norton enough?" She closed her eyes and shook her head, slowly, a time or two. "There don't seem to be any others quite as bellicose as he is. But there are a couple who look a little . . . intense. I had to stop one woman from trying to record sessions with her cell phone—pointed out that by registering, she had agreed to refrain from unauthorized video or audio recording."

"And that shut her down?"

"No." She sighed. "So I sicced Festus on her. He explained that I had retained him to protect the privacy of the conference participants, and he'd be filing suit against anyone who broke the conference rules."

"And that straightened her out."

"Curiously, no," she said. "The woman got all huffy about Virginia being a one-party consent state and we were infringing on her rights. Fortunately Kevin dropped by just then and took care of it."

"Kevin took care of it when you and Festus couldn't?" I exclaimed. "What on earth did he do?"

"Convinced her that he'd set up some kind of anti-recording security field in the hotel that would suck up all the contents of her phone and replace it with malware."

"And she bought that?"

"Well, obviously she wouldn't have if I'd said it like that." Cordelia chuckled. "But you should have heard him when he got going with his explanation. I almost bought it myself."

"Are you sure it isn't real?" I asked. "I mean, if anyone could figure out how to do something like that, it would be Kevin."

"He said it was a fake, but who knows?" She shrugged. "Maybe he was just trying to reassure me. It did sound like the sort of Big Brotherish thing computer companies would love to develop. Anyway, he asked me for her cell phone number. It was on her registration form. I gave it to him, since he was going to do something to keep the story going. Nothing nefarious," she added, seeing the look on my face. "I think he planned to text her things from a number with an official-sounding name attached to it, to make it seem as if she was under surveillance. She's been looking rather jumpy ever since, and I haven't once caught sight of her cell phone."

"And what if it turns out she was only pretending to be discouraged and taped things after all?" I asked.

"Then I ban her for life from all future conferences and turn Festus loose on her." She smiled as if she wouldn't mind seeing this. "And frankly, while I can't say that I've heard every word of every session, so far I haven't heard anything said that should embarrass the speaker or cause trouble for the conference. Just a lot of excellent information from the experts and thoughtful, heartfelt comments from the attendees. At least since I kicked the Gadfly out. Speaking of which, is the chief making any progress identifying the culprit?"

So I filled her in on what I knew about the investigation as we watched the attendees file past. Including the newly revealed information about how many of Norton's online enemies might have known where to find him this weekend.

"Oh, dear," she said. "I was hoping the chief would have this solved before the conference was over."

"There's still time," I said. "I'm hoping he manages to strike some of the people I really like off his suspect list."

"I hear you," she said. "I'm starting to worry about those two women Kevin calls the Keepers."

"Ginny and Janet? Worry about them in what way?"

"The chief's been gathering footage from every security camera and video doorbell in town," she said. "He's been able to eliminate a few people that way, but there's no sign of them from the time the cab dropped them off near the town square to the time it picked them up again. How do you suppose they managed to spend more than three hours wandering around downtown without once showing up on camera?"

"Oh, dear," I said. A picture suddenly sprang into my mind: Ginny and Janet, furtively reclaiming a car they'd parked somewhere in town and heading for a fatal rendezvous with Norton. "Could just be their bad luck," I said, as much to reassure myself as her.

"Could be," Cordelia said. "But you won't see me going off for a tête-à-tête with them anytime soon—or any of our other attendees, for that matter. It's turning into a very un-merry Christmas for the chief and the rest of his department. Well, the line's almost gone—let's dig in."

We grabbed our bentwood trays and began filling plates with ham, turkey, roast beef, risotto, pasta, and at least two dozen vegetables and sides. Even the freshly baked dinner rolls smelled heavenly, and I realized that except for grabbing a plateful of Michael's planned-overs from the Shack for breakfast, I hadn't eaten today.

Michael and Holly McKenna, Delaney's mother, joined us, along with the boys, who had worked up an enormous appetite having snowball fights on the increasingly snow-clad grounds of the Inn. And we were all delighted to see Rob and Delaney.

Though not as delighted as Delaney was to be there for the banquet and the concert.

"I think it's been three weeks since I've left the house for anything other than a doctor's appointment," she said.

"And Grandfather already gave us his key card to the Washington Cottage," Rob added. "So if Delaney starts feeling tired, we just wheel her over there, instead of having to take her all the way home."

"I can see the concert," Delaney said. "Maybe I can even stay up for the fireworks."

"Only if you feel up to it," Rob cautioned. "If need be, we can get Kevin to video the concert and the fireworks."

"Not the same as being there," she said.

"But better than missing it entirely," I pointed out.

"So are you finally going to tell us what you're naming the kid?" Josh asked.

This started a general discussion of baby names, with various family members and friends making pitches for their favorites. I leaned back and listened. I was pretty sure Delaney and Rob had already picked out both a girl's name and a boy's name, and our chances of changing their minds were pretty close to zero. Festus favored Atticus for a boy, after his beloved Atticus Finch, the inspiration for his crusading legal career. Cordelia suggested that Noelle would be a lovely name for a late-December girl. But why wasn't Kevin here, making ridiculous suggestions, as usual?

I spotted him sitting by himself at a corner table. Strange that he wasn't besieged with conference-goers. Maybe everyone he'd been sitting with had gone back for seconds. Or thirds.

Or maybe the morose look on his face scared them off. That and the Greta Garbo body language. I abandoned the baby-name discussion to go over and take a vacant seat across the table from him. He glanced up and nodded at me.

"You look glum," I said. "What's wrong?"

"Just kind of worried about Amber," he replied. "She's coming down with a migraine."

"Again? Poor thing."

"She gets them a lot," he said. "She basically has to lead a pretty regimented life—eat regularly, watch what she eats, get enough sleep, avoid stress. If anything disrupts her schedule, her migraines are apt to kick in. And the snow's the final straw."

"Sounds as if she knows her triggers, then," I said. "According to Dad, that's the first step to dealing with a migraine."

"Yeah," he said. "Traveling's really hard for her."

"And avoiding stress probably went out the window, first with the Gadfly showing up and harassing everyone—and her in particular. And then the investigation into his murder."

He nodded, then looked down at his phone. He smiled fleetingly, typed something into the phone, and stuck it back in his pocket.

"She's hanging in there," he said. "Meds starting to work a little."

Then he frowned again and poked at the bit of pumpkin pie remaining on his plate. I tried to remember the last time I'd seen him fail to finish dessert.

Was he worried about Amber? Or maybe worried about what he would be getting into if he started seeing someone with so much baggage. Health baggage, legal baggage, and possibly even relationship baggage. I liked Amber. But did I like her for Kevin? If you asked me, Kevin needed someone who would shake up what was already a rather regimented life, between his demanding day job and his demanding podcasting career—not someone for whom he'd need to impose even more structure on his world.

And nobody had asked me. It was arguably none of my business. So I bit back half a dozen wise yet potentially discouraging things I wanted to say and just nodded.

"Let's work on getting her to talk to Dad about migraines," I said instead.

"Won't fly," he said. "She doesn't want to talk about it."

"Then let's engineer a setting in which she can overhear him having an intense informational discussion with someone about headaches," I said. "Cordelia would go along with it, I bet."

"Could work," he said. "Let's think about it when we're past all of this."

He waved his arm in a sweeping gesture.

"Past all what?" I asked. "The conference? The holidays? The murder investigation?"

"All of the above." Then his phone dinged. He looked down at it and began typing something.

I left him to commune from afar with Amber and returned to the table, where Jamie was suggesting Phoenix as a suitable all-purpose name for either a girl or a boy.

He appealed to me for support, but luckily just then the lights dimmed.

"Time for the concert!" Josh exclaimed.

Chapter 29

The choir members began slowly marching in, two by two, all carrying candles—battery-powered candles, I was relieved to see—and softly humming "Silver Bells" in three- or four-part harmony. Once they were all standing on the risers, they wrapped it up, singing the words and receiving thunderous applause.

The rest of the concert featured a mix of what Minerva called "light" Christmas carols—the more secular ones like "It's Beginning to Look a Lot Like Christmas," "The Christmas Song (Chestnuts Roasting on an Open Fire)," and "Rockin' Around the Christmas Tree," along with winter songs—"Jingle Bells," "Winter Wonderland," "Happy Holiday." They also included a few Hanukkah songs—"Hanukkah, Oh Hanukkah" and "Light One Candle"—and a few spirituals with Old Testament themes, like "Down by the Riverside" and "Joshua Fit the Battle of Jericho." Aida's daughter Kayla, one of New Life Baptist's most popular soloists, did a fabulous version of "Blue Christmas." And a surprise hit was the duet of "Go Down Moses" by Ezekiel and Joyce Grossman, Rabbi Grossman's wife.

The choir was in the midst of a novelty number—Alan Sherman's "The Twelve Gifts of Christmas"—when I felt a tap on my shoulder.

"Meg," Delaney said. "Don't hate me, but I'm getting really sleepy. And Rob went off to fetch something—could you—"

"Take you to the cottage? No problem." I stood, went around to the back of her wheelchair, and released the brake.

Farther down the row, I saw Dad leap up and point vigorously to his chest. I shook my head. Then I put both hands together at a slant, laid my head on them, and closed my eyes. He seemed to get the message. He gave me a thumbs-up and sat down again.

Then again, maybe I could have used his help, if only to make our exit. Not only was the ballroom standing room only, there were even a lot of people sitting on the floor, blocking the center aisle. Some of them noticed us and began standing, but—

"This way." Ekaterina had appeared at my side. To my immense relief, she led the way to a door marked STAFF ONLY and then down a service corridor. Although the banquet was long over, there were still quite a lot of Inn employees dashing back and forth. But at the sight of Ekaterina, they all leaped to clear the way and wish us a good night. Before we knew it, we went out through a door at the end and found ourselves back in the long corridor that led back to the Gathering Area.

"Do you need any additional assistance?" she asked.

"I think I can handle it from here," I said. "Unless—do you have the room key?" I asked Delaney.

"Here." She handed it to me.

"Then we're fine. She's just tired," I said, noticing that Ekaterina was studying Delaney with a slightly anxious expression.

"Ah," Ekaterina said, looking relieved. "If you need anything, just call."

She went back into the service corridor. I set the wheelchair in motion, still softly singing "'statue of a lady with a clock where her stomach ought to be,'" from the Sherman song—at least at the start. Then, inside the ballroom, the choir launched into a full-throated rendition of "Deck the Halls."

"I wish I could stay for the rest," Delaney said. "But I'm about to fall asleep sitting up."

And as far as I could tell, she actually did just that on our way back to the cottage. She stirred slightly when we left the main hotel for the brick path to the cottages and the cold air hit us. I hurried as much as I could to reach the doorway of the Washington Cottage.

I found Rob already there.

"What's wrong?" he asked. "Is she—"

"Too tired to sit up," Delaney said, sleepily. "I'm really tired of falling asleep all the time and missing everything."

I refrained from suggesting that she sleep while she could, since the odds were they wouldn't be getting all that much sleep in the next few months. Of course, they'd only have the one baby. I well remembered our first Christmas with Josh and Jamie tag-teaming us—at any given time one would be sleeping while the other demonstrated how well developed their lungs were.

"I really would like to hear the rest of the concert," Delaney went on, "if I could just listen lying down."

"We could invite the choir to come back here for an encore," I said. "But we'd have a hard time fitting all of them in."

"And we don't need to fit them all in here," Rob said. "Dad predicted Delaney might want to crash before the end of the concert, so Kevin and I set something up."

He pulled out his phone, aimed it at a small speaker that sat on one of the bedside tables, and—

"—*the new, ye lads and lasses, Fa la la la la la la la la!*"

We all jumped at how loud the sound was, and Rob quickly

tapped his phone, so the rest of the carol was at a more soothing level.

"Sing we joyous all together! Fa la la la la la la la la!
Heedless of the wind and weather, Fa la la la la la la la la!"

"Lovely," sighed Delaney as the final bars of the song gave way to loud applause. "Turn it down just a little more and they can sing me to sleep."

"I'm going to head back to the concert," I said.

"Thanks, Meg," Rob said.

The applause had died down, and the choir began their next song—"White Christmas." I glanced back before pulling the door closed. Rob had climbed onto the bed next to Delaney and was cradling her against his shoulder. They looked almost like a modern-day nativity scene, except that instead of gazing down at a newborn infant they were both gazing dreamily at Rob's iPhone. I wondered if Kevin was streaming video of the choir along with the audio.

And maybe I should tell Rose Noire to stop worrying that Delaney was being secretive. Maybe what looked secretive to her was just the natural inward focus many pregnant women seemed to feel as their due date approached. The look you'd see in dozens of Renaissance paintings of Mary. Delaney would be fine.

I shut the door.

I was about to head back to the concert when I remembered something. We'd deduced that one of the ways in which Norton's killer could have escaped the Inn unseen was by entering one of the cottages and leaving through its terrace. By now, Horace, Vern, and the chief had probably checked out the feasibility of this. But I was curious. I decided to take a quick look myself.

I opened the sliding glass door to the terrace—carefully, so I wouldn't disturb Rob and Delaney. Although I didn't need to worry—the door moved on its track with an impressive lack of noise. Then I quickly slid it shut again when I realized how cold it was. My coat was back at the coat check behind the front desk. But maybe someone had left one here.

Aha! I found a bulky jacket that I recognized as one of Grandfather's. I put it on, pulled up the hood, and donned the gloves I found in the pockets. Then I slid the door open and stepped out onto the terrace.

The cottages' terraces were lovely places to relax in summer, which I'd often done, either when Grandfather was staying in one or when Ekaterina, taking advantage of a rare time when all three cottages weren't fully booked, held elegant picnics for her friends. I had fond memories of relaxing with a cold beverage in one of the recliners or sitting in a wrought-iron chair around a table that held pizza or fondue or wine and cheese.

The table and chairs and the recliners were under waterproof covers now, and since no one expected the cottage guests to be using the terraces, Enrique and Jiro hadn't shoveled here.

Maybe I was wrong about this being a viable escape route. I'd forgotten that the terrace was surrounded on all sides by a hedge, low enough to peek over, but too high to vault, and thick enough that anyone pushing through it would leave traces.

I made a circuit, starting just to the right of the door, and following the edge of the terrace, peering intently at the hedge for any signs that someone had gone through it. I had no luck until I came to the place where it joined the outside wall of the cottage again. The last bit of shrubbery was noticeably less full and bushy than the others. Maybe it suffered a little, being right next to the wall. And there was a space between it and the wall—not a very wide space, but if you were careful, and held the branches back, you might just manage to slip out.

I tried holding the branches back. Yes, it was just possible for someone to slip past.

And then I noticed something. On the ground, in an area that the dense shrubbery had so far kept clear of snow, was a footprint. Not a complete footprint, but enough that it might be useful.

Had Horace found this?

I pulled out my phone and took a picture of it. Then I opened up my phone's picture stash—I'd taken a photo of the footprint Vern had found when I was trailing after him and Horace, hadn't I?

Yes. There it was. I opened it up and held my phone beside the new footprint. They looked to me like a perfect match. Of course, that didn't mean they came from the same shoe. Correction: same boot—Horace had said, hadn't he, that it was a boot print. Odds were, this was from the same brand. And it would certainly be quite the coincidence if the two seemingly identical footprints found during the investigation of Norton's murder came from two different people wearing the same brand of boot. The chief had already remarked on how much he disliked coincidences when he was investigating a case.

I closed the picture and was about to pocket my phone when something caught my eye. One of the hundred or so photos I'd taken on Friday, when I was trying to capture the atmosphere of the convention. Pictures of speakers. Pictures of the rapt faces of the audience. Pictures of groups of people conversing in the Gathering Area.

This picture showed Amber Smith. She was wearing sleek but practical looking boots.

I had to show this to the chief. And Horace. And—

"I knew you were trouble."

I turned to find Amber standing behind me. She was holding a gun.

Chapter 30

I considered screaming, but the only people likely to hear me were Rob and Delaney. Under ordinary circumstances, Delaney would have been an excellent ally, but there was no way I wanted to endanger her or the baby. Or Rob, for that matter, who would insist on trying to rescue me. I didn't want to orphan my new niece or nephew before they even entered the world. Okay, maybe I was doing Rob an injustice, but even under the best of circumstances he wasn't all that great at dealing with crises. Especially crises involving deadly weapons.

"You found the exit," Amber said. "Go on. Use it."

She gestured with the gun, though she managed to keep the business end pointed right at me.

I looked back and forth between her and the thin place in the hedge. I didn't much like the idea of leaving the hotel and hiking out into the golf course. The increasingly snow-covered golf course.

But at least if I left the patio, I'd be leading Amber away from Delaney and Rob. I could stay here and try to reason with her, get the drop on her—but I'd be distracted, worried every minute that one of them would feel the sudden need for fresh air, or want to play with the snow. Better to get far enough away that I had only myself to worry about.

So I slowly turned and began carefully slipping through the thin spot in the hedge. It was actually pretty easy. I could see what looked like freshly cut edges on some of the branches. She'd probably done a little strategic pruning to create her exit. At least while fumbling with the branches I managed to slip my phone into my pocket. I had no idea what I could possibly do with it, but it was potentially a tool. A weapon.

"Sometime this century," she snapped from behind me.

I stepped out into the snow. It was around three inches deep, and still coming down. Not good—it meant that any tracks we left would start being covered over immediately.

"Keep your hands up," she ordered.

Yeah, she probably didn't want me shoving my hands into my pockets. She wouldn't care if I started getting frostbite. A good thing I'd found Grandfather's gloves.

I wondered if she was planning to shoot me, or if her plan was to hold me at gunpoint until the sub-freezing temperatures got me. The latter would be the smarter move—it might even look as if I'd wandered off for some reason and died by accident. Even Grandfather's jacket would hold off the cold for only so long, and my feet were already starting to feel numb.

I needed to find a way to distract her. Throw her off balance. It was slow going, trudging through the snow. I had no idea how far she planned to make me walk before she did whatever she was planning. I should get her talking. We were far enough from the hotel that she probably wouldn't worry about someone overhearing us.

"So killing Norton wasn't just a spur-of-the-moment thing, was it?" I asked, turning slightly to look over my shoulder. "You had to do a considerable amount of planning. Like bringing the burner phone with you."

She started slightly at the mention of the burner phone but covered it quickly.

"Yeah," she said. "I'm good at planning. I had a couple of plans for bumping off Norton that would have worked just fine if the jerk hadn't complicated things by getting himself thrown out."

"Such as?"

"Oh, so you want to keep me talking to delay the inevitable." She chuckled. "But we've got a little time, and I don't mind telling you. They were good plans, and thanks to his stupidity, I never got to use any of them. You want to know what the best one was?"

I didn't, actually, but I wanted to keep her talking, so I nodded.

"I got here a day early so I'd have plenty of time to learn my way around the hotel," she said. "And I pretended to lock myself out of my room and borrowed a key card from one of the housekeepers to let myself in again. She was stupid, and let me take it with me, so on top of letting myself in I also used a little machine that I just happened to have to make a copy of her key card."

"That you just happened to have," I echoed. "Funny thing, that."

"Does a nifty number on credit cards, too," she said. "I'd have starved without it, these last couple of years. And I've practiced enough that I could do the cloning part really fast, so I just told her that she could stay there with her cart—I only needed her card to open my door and find my own card, and then I'd bring it right back. I even left the room door open and kept talking to her nonstop the whole time, so if she even remembers anything about it, I bet she'll say the card was never out of her sight."

"Pretty clever," I said. And it was, although I had a hard time mustering much enthusiasm.

"So the plan was to fake a migraine," she said. "And get some gullible soul to help me to my room. Then I beg her to give me one of my migraine pills, so I've got a witness to my taking it, and pretend to doze off."

"Pretend?" I asked. "They don't actually knock you out?"

"The real ones do," she said. "Not the actual migraine meds, but the Phenergan they give you for nausea. And I've got some fakes that would fool most doctors, and that's what my Good Samaritan would watch me swallow. Then as soon as she leaves, I sneak down to Norton's room, lie in wait, bump him off, and make tracks. If possible, I use my cloned key card to hide the gun in someone else's room, but if I can't pull that off, I just drop it in the trash can in the little room with the vending and ice machines. And back in my room, I take the real pill, so when they come looking for me, I'm out like a light, and if they get really suspicious, I insist that they draw my blood and test it, and they'll see exactly what I told them I took."

She looked very pleased with herself.

"Weren't you worried that people would be suspicious?" I asked. "Given how very much the scenario you just described resembles the murder you've already been convicted of?"

"That's the genius of it," she said. "If anyone even started to suspect me, I could wail about how someone has tried to frame me, because why would I even think of killing someone in the same way the prosecution claimed I killed my husband? Why would I be that stupid?"

"What were you going to use the burner phone for?" I asked.

"In case I needed to lure Norton to his room," she said.

"And if they searched your room and found the burner phone?" I asked. "Or the fake pills, or the little machine you used to clone the housekeeper's key card?"

"By the time they got around to searching me or my room,

anything suspicious would be long gone," she said, with a smirk. "I figured out a great hiding place for them. So you see—a really great plan. A pity the jerk got himself kicked out before I could pull it off."

"You got him anyway," I said.

"But it was a lot more trouble." She sounded indignant, as if Norton's unintentional sabotage of her original plot to kill him was a moral outrage, and possibly grounds to have his murder declared a justifiable homicide. "You can stop walking now. This is far enough."

Far enough for what, I wondered. I turned to face her.

"How did you pull it off?" I asked.

"I did a good job of regrouping." The self-satisfied tone was back—and she reminded me of someone. I tried to figure out who, in case it was a clue that would come in useful to thwarting her. "I called him—with the burner phone, of course—and told him I could get him back in the conference, but he had to do something for me. And I ordered him to pick me up right outside the hotel's front gate."

"And then you used the housekeeping card key you already had to borrow a maid's cart and uniform," I said. "And someone else's hooded coat. And you trundled the cart out as if going to take care of something to the Madison Cottage, used your card again to let yourself in, left through the terrace, and took off across the golf course toward the gate."

"Yeah." She looked annoyed that I'd figured that out. "And I told him that I had some dirt on your family that would make your grandmother happy to let him back in, but we had to sneak over and surprise you all, or you'd never let us in."

"And he fell for it."

"Of course he did. Nothing made him happier than ruining someone's reputation, and if he couldn't find any real dirt, he'd make it up. I'm sure he was planning to use whatever I told him to get back into the conference, and then broadcast it to the world when he got home." She grinned and nodded. Then she looked at her watch, blew out a breath in a gesture of impatience, and looked back at me.

I suddenly realized what she was waiting for.

"I get it," I said. "You're planning to use the sounds of the fireworks display to cover up the sound of the shot when you kill me."

She smiled at that. How had I never noticed before how sly and nasty her smile was?

I wished I could look at my phone—since I never wore a watch, it was my usual means of telling the time. But did I really want to know how much longer she planned to let me live?

"So we hid his car down by the stream," she went on. "Behind the self-storage place. And we started sneaking across the fields and through the woods like some kind of guerrilla fighters. Which was kind of fun for me, but since he was only wearing a light jacket, I don't think he enjoyed it nearly as much. It was really satisfying, pretending to hear someone coming and telling him to freeze, and listening to his teeth chattering."

She smiled a predatory smile, and I realized who she reminded me of: Lurk, the sleek miniature panther who was the smaller of our two barn cats. When Skulk caught a mouse, he dispatched it quickly and dragged it off into the shrubbery to consume it in peace. Lurk liked to play with his prey. But he was a cat. It was his nature. Amber was enjoying this way too much. She'd enjoyed killing Norton.

"Anyway, he was pretty miserable by the time we got to a good hiding place behind your barn. I told him we'd have to wait there a while, and he was so cold he tried to insist that we just barge in and confront you all. So I shot him."

"Weren't you worried about the noise of the shot?"

"I had a suppressor," she said. "Which, in case you didn't know it—"

"Is the correct term for what the general public calls a silencer," I said. "I know. It doesn't suppress all the noise."

"Yeah, but I figured out there in the middle of nowhere, you probably hear hunters in the woods all the time," she said. "And by the time anyone came out to investigate, I'd be long gone. And that's what happened. I fished out his keys and went back to his car. I drove it back as close as I could to the Inn and abandoned it on a dirt road that didn't seem to get much use. And then I hiked over the golf course to the Madison Cottage and sneaked back in with my housekeeper disguise. I'm kind of bummed that you figured out it was me. I didn't think anyone would pay much attention to a housekeeper coming and going, but even if they did, I was sure they couldn't figure out it was me. Not sure how you did."

"I hadn't really," I said. "I just figured that the other people who had the most reason to dislike Norton all had little or no alibi for the time when he was killed, and would they really be stupid enough to murder someone then? I mean, I wouldn't, if I were them. I'd wait until everyone else had gone to bed and either had no alibi or were alibied by someone the police might assume was willing to cover for them."

"Yeah," she said. "I figure either the redheads or the two nosy little old ladies will end up taking the fall for it. And for you. I'll figure out which one fits better and plant the gun in their room."

I mentally apologized to Lurk. Yes, he played with his prey, but he didn't know any better. He was just carrying out the programming in his tiny apex predator's brain. Amber didn't have that excuse.

And she wasn't an apex predator. Just a sly, nasty, greedy little gold digger.

Just then I saw the first few streaks of light soaring into the sky. The fireworks had begun.

Amber saw it, too. She frowned.

"Where the hell's the noise?" she demanded.

"They're silent fireworks," I said. "Well, not completely silent. Quiet fireworks. Less traumatic for wildlife, pets, and people with PSTD. Most people don't know that the really colorful fireworks don't make a lot of noise, and—"

"Are they all going to be like this?" she asked. "No big rockets or anything?"

"All like this," I said. "And what's more—"

Okay, it was corny, but I faked spotting someone sneaking up behind her. She didn't fall for it.

"Nice try," she said. "Looks like I'll just have to keep you here till you freeze to death. Which is taking way too long. I need you to ditch that jacket."

"They'll figure out you did it, when you show up with frost-bitten toes." Something caught my eye behind her. Something real this time. I tried not to react, but I couldn't help it. "And another thing—"

"Oh, cut out the faking," she said. "I'm not going to fall for it so—"

That was when Ruth leaped up out of the snow, landed on the small of Amber's back, and tried to sink her teeth into the back of her neck, though she probably only got a mouthful of polyester and down. Amber shrieked and fumbled, flailing at her with her free arm and almost—but not quite, dammit—dropping the gun.

But the barrel was pointed away from me, at least for a few seconds, so I charged, bowling Amber over with a flying tackle and getting my hands around the wrist of her gun hand. Ruth let go of the down coat and got a better hold, this time on Amber's other arm.

Amber was thrashing wildly, landing kicks on Ruth or me, whichever she could reach. I might have had trouble holding onto her gun hand without Ruth's help. But I realized she was maneuvering to point the gun at Ruth. I shifted one of my hands from her wrist to the hand—if I couldn't take the gun away from her, at least I could do what I could to keep her from firing. But Ruth, in her efforts to hang onto the left wrist, was gradually being pulled closer and closer to where Amber wanted her—in front of the barrel. Dammit, I couldn't let Amber hurt Ruth! If—

"Drop the gun and put your hands up or I'll shoot."

Amber and I both froze.

It was Ezekiel's voice, but his tone was so cold and hard that I almost didn't recognize it. He had dropped to one knee and was reaching down to press something against the back of Amber's neck. While I couldn't see it, I deduced from Amber's expression that it was a gun. I could see the thoughts crossing her face—the impulse to renew her struggles with me over her gun, followed by angry surrender.

She let go of the gun. I secured my hold on it, then rolled away from her. I stood up and put more distance between us. Ruth let go of Amber's wrist but hovered next to Ezekiel, as if ready to spring again if needed.

"Don't you realize it's illegal for convicted felons to possess guns?" Amber snarled.

"I'm no longer a convicted felon," Ezekiel said, in his ordinary, gentle tone. "And this was never a gun."

He pulled his arm back and, with a flick of his fingers, aimed a tiny beam of light on the snow in front of her face, revealing that his weapon was one of Kevin and Casey's promotional pens with the built-in LED flashlight.

Amber snarled and turned, leaping up toward Ezekiel. He dodged her, falling back into the snow.

"Stop that! And put your hands up!" I considered firing a warning shot, but decided it wasn't safe. Even in this weather there could be someone else out here in the snow.

And just then Ruth lunged at Amber's face, teeth bared. Amber froze again. So did Ruth, only inches from Amber's nose—but she growled softly, as if saying, "I dare you to move a muscle."

"This, on the other hand, *is* a gun," I said. "Probably the one you used to shoot Norton. Try anything like that again and I'll use it."

Amber actually growled at that, causing Ruth to respond in kind.

"Lord, have mercy," Ezekiel said as he awkwardly got to his feet. "I couldn't figure out what was up with Ruth when she suddenly took off like a mad thing. Didn't realize she had such good guard dog instincts. Maybe I should be training her to be a K-9 officer."

Ruth, hearing her name in close proximity to the words "good" and "dog," interpreted this as praise and wagged her tail—but without relaxing her vigilance.

"Meg, you keep Ms. Smith covered with that firearm of hers," Ezekiel said. "While I see if I can figure out how to call nine-one-one on this newfangled gadget Festus got me."

"When you're finished with that, call Grandfather," I said. "Tell him to bring some chicken jerky for Ruth."

"I'll do that," Ezekiel said. "Of course, your mother must have nagged him about dressing properly for the concert—he's all gussied up in a fancy suit instead of those safari clothes he usually wears. He might not have any chicken jerky on him at the moment."

"Then tell him to drop by the restaurant and bring out a roast chicken," I said. "Ruth deserves a T-R-E-A-T."

Chapter 31

"I am astonished to see you here this early," Ekaterina said. "I assumed you would stay in bed to recover from your ordeal. And here you are—in spite of the snow! Which I know is difficult to cope with for you Southerners."

Although Ekaterina had been born in Russia, her family had emigrated when she was very small, so I wasn't entirely sure she remembered all that much about her homeland's legendary winters. But every time it snowed, she made a great show of being undaunted by it, and sympathizing with the native Virginians around her, as if we were beautiful but fragile hothouse flowers.

"It's not so bad," I said. "And I wanted to come and help wrap things up—make sure all the guests who are leaving get off on time, and help Cordelia pack up before the second round of snow hits."

"Yes." She smiled with satisfaction. "The next storm looks as if it might produce a satisfactory amount of precipitation."

Although I was tempted, I didn't ask "satisfactory to whom." Six inches wasn't apt to be satisfactory to very many people in town. Nor did I point out that she was running a luxury hotel,

not a ski resort, and that very few of her guests came to Caerphilly in search of snow.

"I also wanted to catch the church service," I said. Which
wasn't an official part of the conference but had been a hit with
most of the attendees. The Reverend Robyn Smith of Trinity
Episcopal and Father Donnelly of St. Byblig's had conducted an
ecumenical service, with the assistance of Deacon Washington
of the New Life Baptist Church. Not to mention Ezekiel Blaine
reading one of the lessons and thirty members of the New Life
Baptist Choir singing Christmas hymns.

"Very moving," Ekaterina said. "And I also hope to attend the
final panel—it should be most informative and inspirational."

I nodded my agreement. The final panel would actually be
a two-hour-long question-and-answer session, featuring most
of the experts who had spoken during the weekend—Festus,
Horace, Kevin, Chief Burke, Dad, Grandfather, and several rep-
resentatives from the Innocence Project. We'd allowed an hour-
long gap between the end of the church service and the start of
the final panel, so anyone who wanted to could pack up and be
all ready to leave when it ended. And so all of us could enjoy a
generous continental breakfast of gourmet pastries and fresh
fruit. I was nibbling on a croissant and sipping the Diet Coke
that Ekaterina had added to the tea and coffee.

"Have you and Kevin figured out what you're going to do to
improve hotel security?" I asked.

"We are working on it," she said. "As Kevin pointed out, the
Inn is not a penitentiary, and his mission was never to make it
escapeproof. Only burglarproof. We will be discussing the costs
and logistics of adding a few additional cameras and other de-
vices to the system, but in a way that still respects the privacy of
our guests. Are Michael and the boys not coming? I did not see
them at breakfast."

"They're taking advantage of the snow to get in a little cross-country skiing," I said. "Which the boys wouldn't have wanted to do if Kevin hadn't promised to set up a camera and video the final panel for them."

"Excellent," she said. "Now—what is he doing?"

She frowned, and then dashed across the Gathering Area. The door to the lobby was just closing. I wasn't sure what had caught her attention—a feckless staff member? A wayward guest?

Whatever it was, she'd deal with it. I took another bite of croissant, and then another sip of my soda, and sighed with contentment.

"Recovered from your ordeal?"

I turned to find Chief Burke, with a cup of coffee in one hand and a bear claw in the other.

"Mostly recovered," I said. "It would help complete the healing process if you told me that Amber Smith is still in jail and likely to remain so for the indefinite future."

"No question of that," he said. "I rather doubt if any Caerphilly judge would agree to giving her bail. And we'll be sending her back to Virginia Beach in the morning. She was only out on bail, remember—and getting arrested's grounds for revocation."

"Especially getting arrested for another murder," I said.

"Yes." Then his face grew somber. "Such a waste. A beautiful, intelligent young woman who could have done anything with her life."

I nodded. I didn't feel much sympathy for Amber. But yes, I could agree about the waste part. And what about Godfrey Norton? All his curiosity, passion, and boundless energy—what if he'd put it to some good use?

I imagined, for a moment, a happier ending to the conference. What if Norton had actually been swayed by some of the panels? What if he'd seen the light and realized that sometimes the system did fail innocent people? What if, like Ebenezer Scrooge, he'd transformed completely and gone home a better person? Just for a moment I imagined the Gadfly apologizing to the Keepers and the Redheads and setting up a GoFundMe to give Ezekiel a nest egg for starting his new life.

Evidently the chief's mind was running along similar channels.

"'For of all sad words of tongue or pen, the saddest are these: *It might have been!*'" he quoted. "I bet back in high school I could have told you who said that."

"Whittier, I think," I said. "But don't quote me on that. We'll all find out for sure when the boys hit high school. And yes. It's sad."

"Don't let it get you down," he said. "I think a lot of good will come out of this conference. And I take back what I said—this was a good time to hold it. A time when people are thinking about the meaning of the season."

"And when the new year is just around the corner," I added. "And people might be thinking about their resolutions and plans."

"Here's hoping quite a few of them go home fired up to do something meaningful," he said. "And now I'm going to go find your grandmother and see what she wants me to do in this final panel."

"I'm looking forward to it," I said.

He strode off. I spotted Ezekiel, sitting nearby, with Ruth at his feet. I strolled over and wished him a good morning.

"Enjoyed your performance last night," I said to Ezekiel. "And the reading this morning. And I don't even have to say again how I feel about the rescue in between."

"Thank you," he replied. "It was wonderful, not just to be singing again but to be doing it as part of such an excellent choir."

"Minerva Burke is going to be devastated when you leave town," I said. "She's been looking for a bass of your caliber for years."

"And I have no desire to cause unhappiness to such a gracious lady," he said. "So it looks as if I'll have to stay around for a while. Good thing I found me a job."

"Awesome," I said. "Where?"

"Working for Dr. Clarence Rutledge, the town vet," he replied. "His current assistant is going to be leaving sometime this spring, and the doc wants to start training up his replacement."

"That's—wait. Lucas is leaving?" I rather liked Clarence's young assistant.

"Just got himself accepted to law school," Ezekiel said. "At the University of Virginia, no less."

"Go Lucas!" I exclaimed. "I like that he chose my alma mater. And that's not exactly an easy law school to get into—I'll have to drop by and congratulate him."

"He's over the moon," Ezekiel said. "And I expect Clarence will be inviting you to what he's calling Lucas's victory party. Anyway, the plan is for us to swap digs. Lucas has a truck, so he doesn't mind living outside town. He's going to move into the apartment over Festus's garage until it's time for him to head down to Charlottesville for his classes, and I'll take over the room where he's been staying at the veterinary clinic. Which will be handy. Festus suggested that I might try to get a driver's license, but I'm not sure either my eyes or my reflexes are up to it anymore. So it's nice that just about everything I might need will be within walking distance."

"And when you find something that isn't, there are plenty of us who can give you a ride," I said.

"I'll keep that in mind." He chuckled. "I already owe a lot to your family—first Festus and your granddaddy, getting me out of prison, and then your grandmama, inviting me to her conference and helping me find a new life when I wasn't sure it was possible. She keeps telling me not to worry, she's found a charitable organization that's happy to help cases like mine. She won't tell me who, though."

"Isn't there something in the Bible about not boasting about your charity?" I asked.

"There is indeed," he said. "'So when you give to the needy, do not announce it with trumpets, as the hypocrites do in the synagogues and on the streets.' I just hope she passes along my gratitude to whoever's helping me out."

"I'm sure she will." Cordelia was probably thinking of Caerphilly Cares, a social service organization that took on a wide range of worthwhile projects. Unless, of course, she'd succeeded in founding a similar group in Riverton. Or maybe she'd brought Ezekiel's case to the attention of the Ladies' Interfaith Council, which united the women of Caerphilly's churches and temples to carry out good works. Or perhaps the New Life Baptist Church had stepped up to help their newest bass and were using Cordelia as cover to avoid any embarrassment Ezekiel might feel at accepting charity from his new congregation. Or Festus might be doing the same thing.

Or, knowing Caerphilly and its residents, all of the above would pitch in, politely but relentlessly jockeying to be the ones to help Ezekiel. I might never know, and he certainly wouldn't.

"Lucas is an exoneree himself, you know," I said, by way of changing the subject.

"I didn't know that." Ezekiel's face lit up.

"He was framed for a murder, and Festus managed to get his conviction overturned. I have a feeling I know what kind of lawyering Lucas will be doing when he graduates."

"There's plenty of it for him to do," Ezekiel said. "And Festus can't do it alone, though he does try, bless him. And good for young Lucas. Well, if you'll excuse me, I'm going to take Ruth out to the dog park before this big final panel starts."

"I'll see you at the panel," I said.

I spotted Kevin, going out of the door into the lobby. His slouched posture and shambling gait suggested that he wasn't in a particularly festive mood, so I followed him to see if I could cheer him up.

"I gather Ekaterina will be keeping you busy with enhancements to the hotel security," I said.

"Not all that busy," he said. "I think I've convinced her that she wouldn't like it if we turned the Inn into an armed fortress. We'll add a few more cameras to cover the ways the boys found to sneak out, and that should keep her happy."

"You don't exactly look happy yourself," I said.

"Not really."

I wasn't sure he was going to say anything else, so I stood, sipping my soda, nibbling my croissant, and looking expectant.

"I guess we all owe an apology to the Virginia Beach police," he said finally. "They were right about Amber after all."

He still looked a little shaken. I wondered how long Amber would be on Kevin's mind, dammit.

"I'm sorry," I said. "I know you liked her."

"I liked who I thought she was," he said. "Who she was pretending to be. Kind of relieved she showed her true colors before . . . er."

"Before you got too deep into trying to get justice for her," I finished, to spare him having to admit that he might have been interested in her. And I pretended not to notice that he was— quite uncharacteristically—blushing. "How were you supposed to know she'd already gotten justice—and didn't much like it?"

"If the Gadfly were still around, I guess I'd have to apologize to him. He had her pegged."

"Even a broken clock tells the right time twice a day," I said.

Kevin chuckled softly at that.

"Yeah," he said. "And when you come down to it, he's kind of like the boy who cried wolf, isn't he? When you spend all your time arguing that everybody's guilty, no one is going to believe you when you come up with someone who actually is."

"And Norton didn't get everything right," I went on. "Maybe you and Casey were wrong about her being innocent, but you were right about something else."

"Like what?"

"She didn't get a fair trial," I said. "The cops did hide potentially exculpatory evidence. They did focus on her and ignore other equally valid suspects. All the things you covered in your podcast, the things her appellate attorney used to overturn her conviction. They really did happen."

"You know," Kevin said. "That might be a good theme for a podcast. I can think of a couple of other cases like that. Guys who definitely didn't get a fair trial but who I'm pretty sure weren't innocent. A couple of them were really stone-cold killers."

He looked more cheerful. Nothing like coming up with a new podcast idea to lift his spirits. Although I hoped he wouldn't start trying to tell me about all the cases he planned to include. I wanted a moratorium on talking about stone-cold killers until after the holidays.

"And why are we talking about stone-cold killers?" came a voice from behind us. We turned to see Festus joining us. "Can't we find a more cheerful subject? The upcoming holiday celebrations? Our plans for the new year?"

"Good idea," Kevin said. "Now that Ezekiel's free, you need to decide whose case to take on next."

"That's right," I said. "So is it the Keepers or the Redheads or someone else entirely? Have you decided?"

Festus sipped his coffee. I knew a deliberate dramatic pause when I saw one, so I let Kevin be the one to ask, "Well? Have you?"

Chapter 32

"I have." Festus closed his eyes, shook his head, and then opened them again. "I'm going to take both of them."

"Awesome!" Kevin exclaimed.

"Good," I said. "They both sound like deserving cases. But aren't you stretching yourself a little thin?"

"I might be," Festus said. "Then again, thanks to this conference, I seem to have recruited several potentially useful new helpers. In return for my taking on their case, the Keepers, as you call them—Ginny and Janet—are going to help out with some of the research needed for other cases."

"That's great news," Kevin said. "They missed their calling, you know. They should have been private detectives instead of whatever they were."

"A stay-at-home mom and an accountant," Festus said. "I can't wait to see what a forensic accountant can bring to the table."

"And don't minimize the investigative skills a stay-at-home mom has probably developed," I said. "Especially if she's ever had to raise teenage boys."

"She raised three, and they all seem to have turned out well,"

Festus said. "And I'm seriously thinking of having her interview the alleged perpetrators in any future case I'm considering. If she doesn't like them, thanks but no thanks. She's a damned fine judge of character, Ginny is. Apart from Norton, who thought everyone was guilty, she was almost the only person who saw through the Black Widow."

"And you," I pointed out. "After all, you didn't take her case."

"Yeah," Kevin said. "But that wasn't because you thought she was guilty, right? It was because you didn't think she had much of a case?"

"No," Festus said. "She fooled me the way she did everyone else, and I actually thought she had a decent case. I just didn't like the way she was trying to . . . er . . . enlist my sympathy. Even if the Virginia Bar didn't frown on it, I prefer to keep my love life separate from my legal practice."

"Do tell," I said.

"I guess you had a lucky escape," Kevin said.

And from the look on his face, I decided he was well aware that Festus wasn't the only lucky one.

"And Ginny approves of Ellen and Madelaine," Festus added. "And they're going to take her along on a visit to Madelaine's mom after the holiday."

"To check her out?"

"No need, really." Festus laughed. "She's pretty upfront about having killed her husband. And even if she turns out to be no-where near as nice as Ellen and Madelaine, the facts of the case speak for themselves. Maybe she should do time. But there's no way she should be doing life. Ah, there they are now."

I glanced over at the other side of the lobby, where the two redheads were standing, talking to Ekaterina.

Kevin also spotted them, and his face brightened.

"She actually has a pretty interesting case," he said.

Was it just the case? Or had learning the truth about Amber opened his eyes enough that he could notice Madelaine?

"I'm going to have a strategy session with her over brunch in the restaurant," Festus said. "Her and her aunt—want to join us?"

"Sure." Kevin looked eager. Maybe it didn't matter if it was the pretty Madelaine or her case he was interested in. Either way, he'd have something other than Amber to focus on.

"Have fun," I said. "I've got to run—I've still got a few things to finish up for Cordelia." I wasn't sure the invitation included me, and I was sure I'd hear all about the case over the coming months. And it was a good sign if Kevin had sufficiently recovered from his infatuation with Amber to take an interest in the much nicer Madelaine. He didn't need me and Festus both hovering over him.

Besides, I'd just spotted two other attendees that I wanted to say goodbye to—Ginny and Janet. One of these days I'd have an absent-minded moment and call them the Keepers in front of someone other than Kevin. But if they heard about it, I could always explain where the name came from, and maybe they'd be flattered.

They were at the front desk, chatting volubly with Becky, the receptionist. When they saw me, they turned and greeted me with enthusiasm.

"Guess what!" Ginny exclaimed. "We have exciting news!"

"You've found another murder case in which you can be suspects?" I asked.

"Don't get her started on that," Janet said.

"We're going to become detectives!" Ginny crowed.

"From what I can see, you already are," I said.

"Yes, but now we're going to get the training we need to become licensed private investigators."

"*Registered* private investigators," Janet corrected. "Remember what Stanley said—in Virginia agencies are licensed; investigators are registered."

"I assume we're talking about Stanley Denton, our local private investigator?"

"Yes," Ginny said. "He came early for his session yesterday and sat in on our roundtable discussion about the case. And apparently he was impressed with what we've been doing."

"And Ginny happened to mention that if she had a time machine, she'd use it to go back and do whatever it took to become a police officer or a private investigator, because investigating the case was by far the most interesting and rewarding thing she'd ever done in her whole life."

"It is!" Ginny insisted.

"I won't tell your husband and kids you said that," Janet countered. "Anyway, Stanley came up to us afterward and said if we were serious, we didn't need a time machine—we just needed to take training from an approved training school or instructor."

"And he is one!" Ginny was so excited she broke out in a little happy dance, and even more reserved Janet was smiling.

"We start our training as soon as the holidays are over," Janet said. "So you'll probably see us around town a lot for the next few months."

"If you have trouble finding an affordable place to stay, let me know," I said. "We have plenty of spare bedrooms, and we like having company."

"Oh, that's so nice," Ginny said.

"But wouldn't it be an imposition?" Janet asked.

"Not at all," I said. "Things are going to be too quiet around our house when the holiday season's over. In fact, they're too quiet now—normally we'd have a house full of relatives, but my sister-in-law's on bed rest for a high-risk pregnancy, and Dad vetoed any kind of fuss and bother around her."

"Would that be the young redheaded woman in the wheel-chair?" Janet asked. "We saw her at the concert last night."

I nodded.

"Looks as if she's going to have that baby any minute now," Ginny said. "Have they picked a name for her yet?"

"If they have, they haven't told anyone else," I said. "And they don't yet know if it's a girl or a boy. They ordered the doctor not to tell them when they had the sonogram."

"Oh, it's a girl," Ginny said. "You can tell from the way she's carrying. Wide and high."

"That's nothing but an old wives' tale," Janet said. "You can't tell a thing that way."

"I call it folk wisdom," Ginny said. "And it works. When I was pregnant—"

Enrique dashed up.

"Ladies! Your taxi!"

"You're going to miss the final panel?" I asked.

"Unfortunately." Janet held out her hand for me to shake. "We're already cutting it close for our plane. But we'll see you again soon."

"It's been wonderful!" Ginny gave me an impulsive hug, then ran to follow Enrique. "Let us know when your little niece arrives!"

"Niece or nephew," Janet said, as she followed more slowly.

I was about to follow them to the door to wave goodbye when—

"Hey, Meg!"

I turned to see my brother, Rob, pushing Delaney's wheel-chair across the lobby toward the restaurant entrance.

"Afternoon," I said to them both. "You're becoming quite the gadabout," I added to Delaney.

"Seeing the restaurant last night reminded me how much I miss occasionally doing the Inn's Sunday brunch," she said.

"And since we had the wheelchair," Rob said. "And we're here anyway, thanks to Grandfather letting us have his bed in the cottage—"

I decided not to point out that Cordelia was the one who had rented the cottage, as part of her conference setup, and had actually given Grandfather use of the bed he had so graciously passed along to them.

"My mom was so tired when she got in last night that she just went to bed, almost as early as I did," Delaney said. "She's meeting us here for brunch. And remember—we have something to celebrate." Delaney glanced up at Rob. "On three—one, two, three—"

"We found a house!" they shouted in unison.

"Wonderful," I exclaimed. "The one you went to see yesterday, that wasn't even technically on the market yet?"

"Good grief, no," Rob said. "That turned out to be a vintage double-wide, in such bad shape I was afraid to walk inside. The whole thing's going to fall apart the next time we get a bad windstorm."

"You could always bulldoze the wreck and build," I said.

"We thought of that," Delaney said. "But it turns out it's actually across the county line. Not in Caerphilly at all, but in Clay County."

Rob shuddered dramatically at the thought.

"And not the house in Westgate?" I asked.

"Luckily, someone else snapped that up," Rob said. "It was horrible. But then we were telling a few people about it last night after dinner—"

"And I asked why they were running all over the county looking for a house," Iris Rafferty said, coming up beside me. "When they could just buy mine."

"That's where we were last night when Rob called you," Delaney said. "Iris came by, and wanted to show us the house. And we made a deal—we're buying the house and the land, and Iris gets life rights to live in the mother-in-law suite."

"Wonderful!" I said. "But please tell me you're not moving immediately. You have no idea how crazy your life is about to get when the baby arrives."

"It'll take some time," Rob said. "Jeanine's still drawing up the paperwork. There's going to be a lot of it."

"Partly because before I sell, I'm going to get your cousin Festus to draw up that conservation trust thing," Iris said. "The one that makes them promise never to turn it into condos or anything like that."

"Which we're completely in agreement with," Delaney said. "We want the sprout to grow up in the peace and quiet of the countryside."

"And that also gives me time to get some more soundproofing installed between the mother-in-law suite and the main house," Iris said. "Because the sprout's going to do a number on that peace and quiet for a while."

We all laughed at that.

"Rose Noire will be thrilled," I said. "She has been mourning the fact that you were going to move away and not let her help with the baby."

"And believe me, we are going to appreciate the heck out of that help," Delaney said.

"Before long she'll have a well-worn path between the two houses," Iris said.

"And Ben Shiffley can keep on farming there," Rob said. "I bet he was worried about where he'd find farmland that good when you sold the place. But now he doesn't have to worry about anything."

"Oh, he'll have plenty to worry about," Iris said. "You don't know farmers. Rain, untimely frost, insects, plant diseases, equipment maintenance, commodity prices—"

"But not having the land he's farming sold out from under him," I said. "Which makes one great big worry taken care of."

"Want to join us for brunch?" Rob said. "Mother and Dad are coming, and Delaney's mom, and Grandfather and it would be great if you could—"

"I don't think so, Rob," Delaney said.

He glanced at her in surprise.

"Why wouldn't we want Meg to join us for brunch?" he asked. "I know she's got stuff to do for Cordelia but—"

"We'll have to give her a rain check on brunch," Delaney said. "And everyone else, too. Go have them bring the car around."

"Bring the car around?" Rob repeated. "Why—"

"She's going into labor, you nitwit," Iris said. "Go fetch the car so you can take her down to the hospital. Don't worry—Meg and I will look after her."

Rob stood for a few seconds, mouth hanging open in shock. Then he bolted for the front door, shouting for Enrique and frantically searching his pockets for the parking stub.

"I guess it's too late to change my mind about this whole thing," Delaney said.

"Relax, honey," Iris replied. "You'll be just fine."

"I'll notify your obstetrician." I pulled out my phone.

"Meg!" Delaney grabbed my wrist with a convulsive strength that suggested she was in mid-contraction. "You've got to do something for me."

"Of course," I said. "But don't worry. Everything will be just fine. You—"

"Go home as soon as you can and put some seed out for my chickadees," Delaney insisted. "Your dad promised to do it last night, but with all the excitement about that horrible woman, I bet he forgot. And they'll need it in this weather."

"Of course," I said. "Just—"

"Cordelia says they need to eat over a third of their body weight every day," she persisted. "That's a lot of sunflower seeds. And they probably need even more in weather this cold."

"I'll make sure they're fed while you're away," I said. "Don't— Oh good! Look who's here!"

Mother and Dad had just entered the lobby, and Rob was telling them the news. Mother beamed. Dad hurried over to Delaney's side. Mother undertook the job of calming down Rob.

"Call Dr. Waldron!" Dad asked. "And ask her—"

"Just texted her," I said, looking up from my phone. "She's already at the hospital and will meet you all there. Let's have someone other than Rob drive, or Delaney will end up giving birth in a ditch."

"Don't worry," Dad said. "First babies rarely come all that fast. But yes, probably a good idea not to have your brother driving at a time like this. I don't think Enrique can have had time to park our car—your mother and I can run them over." He grabbed the wheelchair's handles and began pushing Delaney toward the main entrance. Iris and I trailed along behind them.

"It never rains but it pours," Iris remarked, as we stood gazing out of the glass wall of the lobby, watching Dad and Rob helping Delaney into the back seat of Dad's car while Enrique stowed the wheelchair in the trunk. Mother was already riding shotgun, looking alert and eager.

"What's wrong now?" Cordelia had arrived in the lobby and strode over to where we stood.

"Nothing's wrong," Iris said. "The baby's coming, that's all. Although I guess it means the celebratory brunch on Rob is out."

"Why don't you and Meg have brunch on me instead?" Cordelia said.

"I won't say no," Iris said.

"Mother will keep us posted on how it's going," I said.

"And we can all revile Rob and Delaney for what they're doing to that poor kid," Iris said, with a chuckle.

"Revile them?" I echoed. "Why? The kid's not even born yet—isn't it a little early for recriminations?"

"But look what they've already done to the poor thing," Iris said. "Giving him or her a birthday this close to Christmas. Mine was a week ago, so I know what a pain it is, especially for a kid."

"Tell me about it," I said. "As a December baby myself, I understand—but it wasn't my choice, giving birth to two December babies. I don't think it was Rob and Delaney's choice, either."

"Today's bad enough," Iris said. "But she could easily be in labor for hours—December 23 would be even worse. Or December 24, or—"

"Never borrow trouble," Cordelia said. "Delaney's very efficient. I'm sure she'll do what she can to have the baby quickly. I just hope the snow doesn't make it difficult for them to get to the hospital."

"Well, if they get stuck in a snowdrift, Dr. Langslow will be with them," Iris said. "It will be okay."

"And they won't get stuck in a snowdrift," I said. "Look!"

Osgood Shiffley, who drove one of Caerphilly's two snowplows, had just pulled into the parking lot, and Enrique had run out to enlist his help in getting Delaney to the hospital. Osgood's snowplow was currently decorated to the hilt, with a life-sized fiberglass Rudolph the reindeer mounted on the hood, his red nose flashing in time to the dozen strands of blinking multicolored holiday lights. As we watched, Osgood finished scraping a clear path for Dad's car. Then he turned around and waited until Dad had pulled in behind him to form a caravan, and they all headed for the exit.

As they set off, Osgood turned on his snowplow's sound system, which was hooked to two loudspeakers on the roof of the cab. Rudolph reared and pawed the air wildly, while a jovial voice boomed out:

"Ho, ho, ho! Merry Christmas! Merry Christmas to all! And to all a good night!"

Acknowledgments

Thanks once again to everyone at St. Martin's/Minotaur, including (but not limited to) Claire Cheek, Hector DeJean, Stephen Erickson, Nicola Ferguson, Meryl Gross, Paul Hochman, Kayla Janas, Andrew Martin, Sarah Melnyk, and especially my editor, Pete Wolverton. And thanks also to the Art Department for another beautiful cover.

More thanks to my agent, Ellen Geiger, and all the folks at the Frances Goldin Literary Agency for taking care of the business side of things so I can concentrate on writing.

For this book I owe a special debt to the dedicated people who create my favorite true crime podcasts. Alas, Virginia Crime Time, Meg's nephew Kevin's podcast, does not (yet) exist in real life, but you could always check out some of the true crime podcasts that helped inspire it—*Buried Bones, Crime Analyst, Cup of Justice, Mind Over Murder, The Murder Sheet, The Philosophy of Crime, Real Crime Profile, True Crime Garage,* and *True Sunlight* . . .

Many thanks to the friends who brainstorm and critique with me, give me good ideas, or help keep me sane while I'm writing: Stuart, Aidan, and Liam Andrews; Deborah Blake, Chris Cowan, Ellen Crosby, Kathy Deligianis, Margery Flax, Suzanne Frisbee, John Gilstrap, Barb

Goffman, Joni Langevoort, David Niemi, Alan Orloff, Dan Stashower, Art Taylor, Robin Templeton, and Dina Willner. And thanks to all the TeaBuds for two decades of friendship.

Above all, thanks to the readers who make all of this possible.

About the Author

Joe Henson, NYC

Donna Andrews has won the Anthony, the Barry, and three Agatha Awards, an RT Book Reviews Award for best first novel, and four Lefty and two Toby Bromberg Awards for funniest mystery. She is a member of the Mystery Writers of America, Sisters in Crime, and Novelists, Inc. Andrews lives in Reston, Virginia. *Rockin' Around the Chickadee* is the thirty-sixth book in the Meg Langslow series.